TANGLED

JAMES W. LEWIS

The Pantheon Collective (TPC)
www.pantheoncollective.com

The Pantheon Collective (TPC)
P.O. Box 799
Santa Cruz, CA 95061

ISBN: 978-0-9965318-2-5 (Paperback)
ISBN: 978-0-9965318-3-2 (Ebook)

Printed in United States of America

Cover: Designed by Damonza
Interior: Designed by Stephanie Casher

Dedicated to my mother, Phyllis Estelle Garrard-Lewis.

You are the reason for the fire that burns within me. I hope you're smiling at your boys through the clouds!

Acknowledgments

It's. Been. Six. Freakin'. Years.

Yes, that was the last time TPC published a novel that I've written, which was *A HARD MAN IS GOOD TO FIND*. Any author will tell you (especially an indie), it's crucial to keep publishing content. Otherwise, people will forget about you and move on to someone else. I admit, coming back to this writing thing, I feel like, "Uh… hi. Remember me?"

You may wonder where I've been. Well, I blame higher education.

After retiring from the Navy, I went from junior college, to my undergrad, all the way to a graduate degree. That meant I switched from writing for pleasure to essays and research papers. Cool thing is, I chose a creative project for my final project in graduate school, which became *EXERCISES FOR OLDER VETERANS WITH PTSD*. Although a book, I still wrote it for academic purposes. Hell, I needed to pass!

But I'm finally done. No more school for me. Time to don the Author James W. Lewis hat again, baby, and get back at it. Next up: *TANGLED*.

Of course, I'd like to thank my Circle of Usual Suspects once again for pushing me—my family and close friends (damn it, ya'll know who you are!). They be like, "When's your next book coming out?" I don't have to hear that anymore… for now.

Thank you to all the indie authors out there still grindin'! You are my biggest inspirations. I love to see creative folk paving their own lane and following their dreams.

Thanks to all my Facebook friends, keeping my creative juices flowing. I swear, I think of new book ideas all the time based solely on your comments!

TANGLED wouldn't be nearly as good without the help of my army of test readers. You kept it all the way real with me, pointing out what worked, what didn't work, plot holes, typos, yada yada. Because I hadn't written a novel in a while, I was concerned about the direction of the book, pacing, characters, and frankly, the subject matter. Part of me thought none of you would accept this book. Luckily, I was wrong. You put me at ease, and I can't tell you how good it felt to read your enthusiastic feedback. I truly appreciate the time you took to make my third effort better. Special shout out to:

Danielle Hill
Jamie G. White
Janet Y. Caldwell, Reviewer
Rebecca Reinertson
Sharon Blount

Can't forget the book clubs, especially Sharon Blount's B.R.A.B (Building Relationships Around Books)! As I've said many times, book clubs are an author's buzz makers, from social media, to word on the street. I look forward to reconnecting with you all!

Thanks to Michelle Chester of EBM Professional Services for copyediting and proofreading *TANGLED*. You gave this book the finishing touches it needed and I'm ecstatic that you enjoyed my crazy story! :-) If you're looking for quality editing, check out her website at: http://www.ebm-services.com.

To my TPC partner and friend, Omar: Thanks again for hyping up *TANGLED*. You have a unique gift of making me feel like I'm on my way to becoming a New York Times bestseller, even from thousands of miles away. I admire your keen business sense mixed with a passionate and youthful exuberance for the written word. You have a talent for critically deconstructing an entire book, and I've yet to meet anyone who's as good at "breaking it down" as you.

Well... except maybe...

My wife, Stephanie Casher-Lewis. The ultimate Homie-Lover-Friend. You are the Michelle to my Barack. I'm always amazed at your capacity to excel at your day job while finding the time to content edit/typeset *TANGLED* and Omar's upcoming book *LEADERBOARD*, outlining and writing your own books, and devoting your energy to special events involving family and friends. You're on some Queen B sh*t. And still, your zest for travelling to exotic places makes our journey together a non-stop adventure. I know I'm not the easiest companion to get along with at times, but never forget DWK loves you! Always! Despite the ups and downs, you constantly remind me of how lucky I am to have you by my side.

If I've forgotten you, I'll try to get ya in the next one! In the meantime, you can always hit me up at james_wil_lew@yahoo.com. And check out our websites at www.jameswlewis.com and www.pantheoncollective.com.

One last request: Once you finish *TANGLED*, please take a moment to rate and review. I'd LOVE to read your feedback. ;-)

Thank you ALL! Hope you enjoy!

Peace and love,

James W. Lewis
The Pantheon Collective (TPC)
07 Nov 2017

CHAPTER 1

YARA

"Omigod, you *again*? First my sister, now you? That's twice this week!"

The number blew up Yara's cell phone, one she knew all too well. "Sorry, not anymore. We are done." Yara placed the phone back in her purse. She stuffed her mouth with trail mix, mumbling, "And, sis, I'll be with you in a bit. I have a show to watch."

Yara turned back to the potential crime scene unfolding before her. Marcus was the star of a one-man Improv, marching up and down the steps that led to her now former apartment.

"Yara! Why the fuck did you do this to me? Why?" He disappeared back up the steps, his third time. "You ruined my life!"

"Stupid man. Just like the rest of his species." Yara shook her head, munching from the bag of trail mix while enjoying the free show. Marcus had a porous brain no bigger than the thimble dick curled up behind the zipper of his Hertz Rent-a-Car khaki pants. Like any other fool with a penis and no forethought, he wore his work clothes and nametag to the party.

Although Yara had rolled up the car windows, she could still hear the bass in Marcus's thumps against the apartment door. Again, he hightailed it back downstairs and stood underneath a window with no curtains, a hand cupped over his eyes, staring, as if Yara would pull a David Copperfield and appear from behind the glass. Little did he know Yara was watching the public meltdown from her driver's seat while parked next to a mega-sized truck that slightly concealed her Kia Optima. With the last of her belongings in the trunk and back seat, Yara was ready to drive off and head back to her old area code for good.

But once she caught Marcus barreling up and down the stairs toward her empty apartment, forward progress paused for a moment. It had been months since she last saw him. How he found her address, she had no idea. It didn't matter; Yara didn't live there anymore. If he had showed up five minutes earlier, though, Yara probably would've become an unwilling participant in his ratchet reality show.

"Yara!" he cried. "You hear me calling you?"

An average idiot could surmise that no one occupied apartment 212 anymore. Since her parking spot was empty, too, that should have told him something. Yara had already moved most of her stuff back to Monte Clara, her home city.

Yara glanced at Philip's picture dangling from the rearview mirror. Her husband stood fearless in his camouflage uniform, holding a rifle with the hard gaze of a warrior accustomed to blood on his hands.

"Looks like I got him, babe," she said. "I'm pretty sure his wife wasn't happy."

"I'm gonna fucking kill you!" Marcus cried, now bawling. "You hear me?" He picked up a rock, then hurled it at Yara's old bedroom window, cracking it.

"Mmmm," she uttered, trying not to explode in laughter.

If she somehow found it in her heart to give a damn, she could muster some sympathy for poor Marcus, considering the pain she apparently caused him.

He deserved it, though. His married ass shouldn't have pursued her in the first place. It's no wonder men make rash decisions from below the belt instead of the heart and head. Marcus obviously used neither heart *nor* head, still trying to act like he wasn't married— when anyone could see the faded circular imprint on his finger. He thought since he wined and dined Yara for close to a month, even lucky enough to come up in her a few times, some kind of love connection had formed. Drunk in love, Marcus even slipped out the L word once, as if a shot of her potent goodies made him more in touch with his emotions. The fool had said, "I think I'm falling in love with you. I can't explain it."

Yara had heard that before. She'd possessed a kind of hypnotic power over grown men as far back as middle school. Yara had put on an Oscar performance for Marcus, but she could never truly reciprocate. The gates to her heart had locked down long ago, reserved for Philip, her high school sweetheart. But Philip was dead.

Right on cue, a black and white rolled up. Two doors swung open at the same time. Yara whispered, "Geez, finally."

"Get on the ground, now!" one of the police officers yelled. With two tasers drawn on him, Marcus regained his senses, then dropped to the ground, arms and legs spread. Yara noticed a few nosy heads staring out the windows, probably enjoying the uncensored reality show, too. One cop still locked a taser on Marcus while the other cuffed his wrists behind his back, a knee on his shoulder blades.

Yara dropped the trail mix bag in the passenger seat and started the car. As she eased forward, Marcus spotted her. Snatches of grass pasted to his forehead and lips, he looked like a clown. She smiled and waved at him while his two new friends buried his face in the dirt.

Driving off toward the main road, the scene now behind her, Yara thought about the weeks ahead. One particular night stood out. "I hope I have this kind of fun at the reunion. I'm sure Marcus won't be the last one."

CHAPTER 2

GERALD

I can't believe that fool got the job over me.

Gerald restrained the titanic urge to cave in someone's skull by clutching his fists. The folks around Fisherman's Wharf weren't at fault; they had no clue about Gerald's inability to climb the corporate ladder. A young woman pushing a baby carriage said something as he passed, probably a "hello," but Gerald kept his eyes forward and mouth shut. Not in the mood. No greeting for her or anyone else near him. Gerald could barely digest the news that an old high school classmate who used to smash his wife was going to be his new boss.

Gerald strolled down the recreation trail and passed the main entrance to the Wharf, where hordes of visitors clogged seafood restaurants and souvenir shops on the pier overlooking the bay. Although October, bicycle riders and joggers still wore shorts and T-shirts, spoiled by the California sun and blissfully ignorant to the sharp seasonal temperature drops wrecking other parts of the country.

The further Gerald walked—hands cuffed behind his back, staring at his footsteps—the more the people around him thinned out. He found a bench near the bay, gazed out into God's creation, and sat down. Easing out a long sigh, he watched seagulls dive-bomb into the water as if on some kamikaze suicide mission for fish and other seafood delicacies. A sea otter perfected the backstroke while wiping its whiskers with the back of his claws, and Gerald smiled for the first time today. He took a quick snapshot of the sea mammal with his phone.

Something about large bodies of water, marine life in their natural state, sailboats... the ocean's tranquil powers instilled a sense of calm, exactly what he needed to turn down the volume on the chatterbox in his head. Chill mode. Finally.

Gerald took a moment to reflect, wondering how his life had become a porta potty filled with a fresh batch of excrement. The death of Geraldine Durston five months ago started it all. As if losing Mama wasn't bad enough, his sole sibling, Quinton, felt binging on whiskey the night before the funeral was more important than seeing Mama laid to rest. Gerald found his fraternal twin brother passed out in his downtown rental office-slash-home immediately after the service, an empty bottle of Jack next to a used condom and fresh vomit on the floor. They hadn't talked since.

Lisa added to the mountain of crap a few weeks after the funeral, cutting him off mid-sentence during an argument when she screamed, "I can't stand you! No wonder you can't get ahead. I bet your dumb ass won't get that promotion, either." This from a woman who had lost her job as a real estate agent and no solid work in at least five months. But she was right about Gerald. Her prediction had come true today.

The downslide between him and Lisa had gone on for a while, but Gerald wasn't sure exactly when it started. He had long suspected Lisa didn't want to do the matrimonial dance anymore—at least not with him. But he still loved his wife, sass and all, and wanted nothing more than to continue the journey with her. A part of him knew their fractured vows had widened into irreparable cracks. Whether out of fear or a sliver of denial, he never addressed their marriage woes. Neither did Lisa.

But Gerald understood the root of it all. Failing to make ends meet as a real estate agent in a slow economy had murdered her self-esteem, sucking Gerald into her tirade of mood swings. And still, Gerald played the dutiful husband, kept his mouth shut, and took her crap like a man.

However, Lisa's Queen Bitch alter ego couldn't drop a load on Gerald as much as Greg Stephens did today. An old, snot-nosed classmate from Monte Clara High, Greg was cool with Gerald on occasion, but not really a friend. Kind of an odd mix back in the day—a wannabe thug, solid basketball player, and self-proclaimed playboy with Ryan Gosling looks and lean frame—yet, an honor roll student and teacher's pet. Those devil-angel qualities cast some kind of teeny-bopper spell on the honeys, including Lisa.

In a jacked up coincidence, Gerald and Greg ended up in the same field of employment after high school and college graduation. Ten years later, Greg pulled a free agent move from a rival company and stole the position Gerald had been eyeing for months. Gerald had even stepped in as interim director after his old boss transferred to a new post. He thought he had the job locked up.

But it didn't work out that way. Gerald lost out and would stay stuck in middle management, supervising slacker employees and handling low-level assignments. Greg, in his new position as regional director—the same position that should have gone to

Gerald—would oversee top-level projects like account portfolios, policy revisions, and budget analysis for all the west coast offices. Big money items. In other words, "Bossman" stuff.

Maybe Lisa knew something he didn't know... like perhaps he wasn't good enough to be a Bossman pulling six figures. Something about him, a personality quirk, maybe, wasn't up to par for the next level. That same social defect had apparently contaminated his relationship with Lisa.

The vibration from his phone tickled Gerald's thigh, reeling him back from the deep probe into his psyche. On autopilot, he jammed a hand into his pocket. Lisa's cries had clobbered his eardrums more than once because he took three rings too long to answer, so he tried to pick up within two rings. He sighed when he saw the name. Since Mama's passing, not a week went by without a call from Aunt Frieda, Mama's 50-going-on-30-year-old younger sister.

He pressed the Answer button. "What's up, Aunt Frieda?"

"Hey, sweetie. How you doin'?"

"I'm cool, I guess."

"You guess? Uh huh." She paused. "What her ass do this time?"

"What 'chu mean?"

"Boy, I don't know why you always try to play your aunt. I can hear it in your voice. You know you can't hide anything from me. Ever since you broke—"

"Mr. Robinson's window when I was nine and tried to lie about it, I know, I know."

"Exactly. So, what did that wife of yours do?"

Here we go. "Aunt Frieda, c'mon, now. How come every time something's bothering me you think it's her?"

"Because it always is!"

"Whatever."

Gerald slouched on the bench, spreading his legs. Frowning, he ran a hand over his midsection. The spare tire under his shirt looked like a pitcher's mound from his La-Z-Boy position, reminding him for the umpteenth time to restart his gym membership.

Aunt Frieda said, "She still ain't working yet, either, huh?"

"No. Well, she has this side hustle where she promotes books and writes reviews for 'em. Still collecting unemployment, but I think that's about to run out."

"Um hum. Side hustle, huh? Probably lazing around the house all day, too."

"No, she's not. Matter of fact, she's keeping busy with planning our upcoming high school reunion."

"Boy, that don't pay the bills! Hasn't it been about six months since she got laid off?"

"Five, actually. I mean, she gets some money here and there." He ran his hand against his scalp. "But… it's a little tight. We're doing all right, though."

"So, basically one income. And y'all renting out a four-bedroom house all because she wanted to. I swear. Boy, why didn't you stay broken up with her after high school?"

He rolled his eyes. *Yeah, yeah.*

"Can't believe y'all got back together…"

I got back with her because I love her!

"…and I'm so happy you two didn't have kids because…"

Well, getting cut took care of that.

"…which is why I told you to leave that bitch a long—"

"Whoa, whoa," Gerald cried, rising up. "That's my wife you're talking about, now. Don't ever call her that again."

"Well, excuse me." She sounded surprised. "About time, nephew. Finally showing some balls. Now, you need to show them to her."

Gerald grunted. A pause followed. He heard a few jumbled words, but couldn't make them out.

Finally, Aunt Frieda said, "Look, you know I can't stand her. I wanted to rip the weave off her nasty ass head that time we fought. But… I shouldn't have called her a bitch, so… I apologize, okay? Forgive me."

"It's cool. Look, my mood has nothing to do with her, all right? I found out I didn't get that promotion I was telling you about last week."

"Oh. I'm sorry to hear that. I know you've been trying for that job for a while. You okay?"

"I'll be all right. Just sitting by the water, you know. Thinkin'."

"I see. How did Quinton react when you told him?"

"See, now you trying to play me. You know good and well I haven't spoken to that fool since Mama's funeral. A funeral he *missed.*"

"Look, nephew," she said after a long sigh, "I know what he did was wrong, but I wish you would forgive him. You're brothers! You know your mama wouldn't like you fighting like this."

"Anyway."

"You guys need to talk and work it out. Promise you'll talk to him."

No. "Yeah. Sure." Gerald had no idea when that would happen. "Just need a little time, but I will."

"Good. And promise you'll visit your aunt soon. I came to see you and Quinton not too long ago, so it's your turn. You know it's only a three-hour drive to Vallejo."

A couple with a small child walked in front of Gerald's view. The man held the child's hand, a boy who looked no older than three. Little man pointed, screaming, "Look, Daddy!"

Gerald stared at the Filipino tripod, saw the sunshine in their faces. The parents were in their late twenties, early thirties, around Gerald and Lisa's age. Peek-a-boo games exploded a giggle outburst from the small boy. His father caught the same bug, nearly buckling over from laughter. The young woman was not immune to the infectious chuckle, clapping at the G-rated show before her. Cutest high-pitched giggle Gerald ever heard. Flipped his frown upside down.

"Boy, did you hear what I said?"

"Huh?" Gerald said, blinking. "Oh, yeah. I'll see you soon, Aunt Frieda."

"You better."

"I will, dang!"

"Good. Silly." She laughed. "Okay, sweetie, gotta run. Don't forget about your brother, now, okay? I love you."

"I won't. Love you, too. Bye, Aunt Frieda."

Gerald slid the phone back into his pocket, still staring at the mini-family... and his possible future. A little boy. *His* boy, a *son*. Same bushy eyebrows, crooked smile, "five"-head. Would probably get lucky and end up with his mother's gray-green eyes. The man picked up the boy, then propped him on his shoulders. Little guy slapped his father's forehead, but the man didn't flinch. Love taps never hurt.

The man and wife kissed, then the tripod strolled away.

They look so happy. Damn. I want that. He and Lisa could make a tripod, too.

He propped a leg over his knee, resting the full-length of his arm on top of the wooden park bench. No doubt, he needed a healthy shot of joy in his life, anything to make him and Lisa happy again. It seemed a child could possibly do the trick. He only had to reconnect the "teste pipes."

I wish my dumb butt didn't get cut while we were apart. I guess I never thought we'd get back together. Never thought I'd want a baby, either. But now I think... I do.

Gerald's eyelids fluttered while he mapped out a new avenue in his head—a road he had no plans of traveling down at all. But now, as he re-examined poor decisions made in the past, he shrugged and thought, *Why not? I love my wife. I know she wanted a child at one point, but I screwed that up. Time to make it right. We're going half on a baby.*

He didn't care that she wasn't working, nor about the promotion he lost. At that moment, what truly mattered waited for him at home.

Gerald stood up, stretched, and then headed toward his car, feeling brand new, his funk overhauled. Smiling at the romantic idea materializing upstairs, he knew a quick stop at Walmart would help rebuild the blocks of a happy home and repair the shattered fragments of his soul. He missed that glow on his wife's face. Cheesy Hallmark cards used to do the trick for Lisa, no matter how she felt at the time. In a two-for-one deal, that smile would also repair his heartache.

Gerald remembered words Mama once said that resonated. Simple, yet powerful: When she's happy, *he's* happy.

CHAPTER 3
LISA

"Gerald! Gerald! Ugh!" Lisa pressed the Power button and flung the cell phone onto a pile of *Traveler* magazines stacked on the bed. "Dumb ass butt-dialing me again!"

Already pissed, Lisa went back to her computer and grabbed the mouse. She stared at the Monte Clara ten-year reunion Facebook page and her mood spiraled downward. Two weeks and still nothing changed. Despite touching base with the entire senior class via social media, only 24 out of 127 graduates from the Class of 2005 had marked "Attending." As the committee's head promotion and publicity chair, the stats disappointed her, and as much as Lisa hated to say the word failure, the numbers spoke for themselves.

Lisa had tried everything she could think of to pump up the numbers. She created a website with reunion information to facilitate ticket sales; spent hours scanning photos from yearbooks to create an online album; and even compiled a playlist of the hottest tunes from 2005, along with trivia questions to trigger the nostalgia factor—all posted on the website. The only thing missing was Quinton's website banner and the Monte Clara YouTube channel. She had hired Gerald's brother for the job, but his punk ass hadn't started yet. With the reunion a few weeks away, she expected the class of 2005 to represent in full force by now.

That didn't happen.

Pictures of her and Gerald appeared on her computer screen. She stared at the screensaver slideshow of throwbacks, most of them from that special day when she declared "I do," and as each picture blurred into a new one, her frustration eased a bit.

She looked like a chocolate queen, classy yet sexy. Wearing a gold tiara atop a bouncy head of curls, her ivory charmeuse gown hugged a figure-eight she had sculpted from months at the gym, securing a matrimonial fantasy with the regal presence of a bridal goddess. Flash forward years later and Lisa could still rock that dress.

A picture of Gerald in a tuxedo killed her smile, as if bliss drained away at the sight of him. Lisa thought she'd found what she always wanted in Gerald—stable, smart, faithful—but some frogs aren't meant to be princes. She'd been all smiles at her wedding, but those beams of joy had withered away over the years, contaminated by the strains and stresses of married life. All that remained were fractured fantasies and a lifestyle nowhere near what she had pictured countless times in her head.

She'd expected the normal progression of events—engagement, marriage, house, kid—in that order. But in their senior year, one of Gerald's little soldiers almost hijacked their future together by impregnating her. Fear of stolen hopes and dreams led to an abortion, but then Gerald killed their four-step plan with a vasectomy shortly after high school—a pretty drastic measure for a 19-year-old kid to literally snip away any chance of offspring. To this day, Lisa didn't know what ran through his mind that led to such a crazy-ass decision.

They had already broken up when he cut the pipes that could create another life. Lisa initiated the break-up shortly after graduation, thinking she had outgrown him, but as she entered her 20's, Gerald had an apartment, car, job, and a few credits shy of a four-year degree—while she lived at home, still stumbling at the Start line. From design school, to makeup and hair, to eventually real estate, it took her a minute to get it right, all the while messing around with man-boys drunk off Mama's breast milk, doing the same dumb high school shit. Gerald had outgrown *her*, barreling down a path that could result in CEO dollar signs. When she found out he still loved her, she weaseled back into his life before another warm body could, becoming the wedded woman she now viewed on the computer screen.

He told her about the vasectomy *after* they became legal, but she stayed with him anyway. By then, her friends and some family members had popped out babies, so she saw firsthand the struggles of raising little ones. Never a big fan of losing her independence, Lisa questioned whether or not she even wanted a child. With no kids in their near future, she figured since Gerald was destined for top dollars, they could travel the world.

Now looking back, Lisa wished they had stayed broken up. At 28 going on 29, Gerald had fallen behind on the track he had blazed years ago, while the down economy muscled Lisa out of the race entirely. Still, if Gerald was the man she thought he was, Lisa wouldn't need to run at all, which is what she wanted from her man all along. He would've owned the whole fuckin' field.

Lisa's upside down smile turned into a scowl. Gerald now stared back at her from the screen. She nodded, tapping the side of the chair. *Yes. It's definitely time. I'm so ready.*

Lisa stood up and glanced out the bedroom window, spotting Gerald's Acura pulling up. Again, Gerald reminded her why it was time to make that move. Parking in the driveway may have been a simple task for other folks, but another epic fail in Lisa's eyes. With Gerald's fickle brain apparently encased in cement, he hogged up the center driveway again, blocking her car parked in the garage.

"Ugh!" She slid back the curtain and cracked the window as Gerald cut the engine. When he stepped out, Lisa cried, "How many times have I told you not to park in the driveway? Park on the street! How the fuck do I get out?"

Spinning around, Gerald dropped his keys. "Oh! Hey, babe, sorry about that." He picked up the keys, still heading for the front door. "How are you—"

"Uh, you need to turn your ass around and back your car out the driveway. Now!"

Gerald froze, his face like that of an angered yet muffled 12-year-old with enough marbles left in his head to know not to snap back at a woman like Lisa. Instead, he returned to his car and did what the woman with the iron fist told him, like a good little whipped boy.

She slammed the window shut. *His ass.*

As she stepped into the kitchen for ice cream, Gerald walked in, a leather case strapped around his shoulder. "Hey, babe. Sorry 'bout that."

You said that already. Idiot. "Um hum." She opened the freezer, her back toward him. *Shoot, no more ice cream.*

"So, how was your day? Making any progress on the reunion? Any new attendees?"

Lisa closed the fridge and faced him, arms crossed. His eyes shifted downward, anywhere but Lisa. Gerald jammed questions together when nervous or trying to avoid something.

"Let's see," she said. "Fine, no, and no."

"Oh. Okay." He turned toward the short hallway. "Um, need to hit up the bathroom."

"Like I really need to know that."

"Right, sorry." He took one step, paused, then turned back to Lisa. "So, um, what do you think about revisiting the baby idea?"

"What? Where the hell did that come from?"

"Well… I had a rough day, so I was sitting by the water, thinking about stuff, and—"

"Let me guess. Rough day because… you didn't get that promotion?"

His lips flipped in and out of his mouth, as if trying to bait and hook the right words from that pea he called a brain.

"No, I didn't," he said, now leaning his back against the hallway wall, head down. "You'll never believe who got it, either."

"Who?"

"Greg Stephens."

She looked around, processing the words. "From high school?"

"Yeah. Came in, did the interview, and stole my spot."

"What, you work for him now?"

He nodded. "Can't get more jacked up than working for a former classmate."

"Um, okay. And then you had an epiphany?" Hands stretched high, staring up, she cried, "This is a good time to have a baby! Yes!"

"Well, not exactly like that," Gerald replied between chuckles. *What a fuckin' idiot! The man I married.*

Sighing, she said, "Gerald, we're already struggling as is and you get this wild hair up your ass to have a baby? Which, you never wanted, by the way."

"I changed my mind."

"I can't believe this. And let's not forget that part of you doesn't work, remember?"

"I know. But I can get the tubes reconnected. I read it's a simple procedure. And... you know... I figured..." he shrugged, "...a child would make us a happier home."

Lisa erupted in laughter. "A happier home?"

"Yeah. I know you've been unhappy. And, I do admit, finding out your ex will be my boss made me—"

"Whoa! Hold up. I told your ass he's not my ex! It was a one-time thing, so... never mind." She grabbed her keys and purse off the kitchen counter. "I need to get away from your ass. You make my head hurt."

"Where are you going?"

Out of the corner of her eye, Lisa noticed Gerald had retrieved a card from his briefcase. She was nowhere near in the mood for a Hallmark moment. She opened the door that led into the garage.

"Babe, look, I'm sorry if—"

Slam!

She climbed into the driver's seat of her Altima and closed the door. As the garage door rose, she saw a father and son riding their bikes together on the street. Apparently, Daddy moments around the neighborhood gave Gerald ideas.

He didn't get the promotion. That meant no extra funds in the household. Still the perpetual nobody—an office lackey. The same role he held for eight years. Gerald didn't have the skills for an upward move; missing the ironclad balls needed for a lateral move to another company. All the while, bills stacked up and Gerald's delusional ass wanted to reattach the sperm juice pipelines, add a third party to the mix, and play Daddy. Backward, shortsighted, and dumb.

Lisa needed to retreat to her happy place. A small grin crept up the sides of her cheeks. *He should be off work, now, too.*

She pulled out of the driveway, the garage door sinking behind her. Headphone in her right ear, Lisa clicked the burner icon on her phone, a password-protected application that allowed creepers to make secret phone calls and text messages. She tapped the one number that brought her a smile nowadays—and much more.

A play-by-play of their secret "rendezscrew" a week before flashed in her head. Lisa was ready to fog up the car windows again, but they couldn't leave the windows cracked this time. She could've sworn workers on the late shift heard them, even though she'd parked her car at the far end of the parking lot well after business hours. Although risky, the thrill of public sexcapades with someone other than her ill-equipped husband made it worth an accidental recording on a security camera.

But she also needed to get the ball rolling. Her plan couldn't stay stuck in fantasy mode anymore; time to make it happen, and the man at the other end of the phone could seal the deal.

The phone rang twice. No response.

Damn it. His ass better answer. I need to get my plan going. Now.

CHAPTER 4

QUINTON

"The hell," Quinton whispered while semi-conscious, squinting at the phone number on his cell phone. "Is that who I think it is?"

"Shit!" Toccara threw the blankets off her and sat upright. "It's 5:37? I'm supposed to be somewhere at six!" She grabbed her silk bra from off the floor. "Can't believe I fell asleep, messin' with yo' ass."

Still a little discombobulated, Quinton placed the cell phone on top of the mini fridge next to his bed, then raised his back against the headboard, the ends of his thick locks grazing the pillow. "We were both out for close to two hours," he said, smacking her right butt cheek. "My sex game's like NyQuil, girl."

"NyQuil. Okay." She stood and slid see-through panties up chocolate thighs. Quinton watched her ease the silk lining around ass cheeks as plump as two ripe super-sized peaches. Big Daddy awoke underneath the stained sheets, literally pumping up for round two.

He cuffed Big Daddy's sack. "Sure you can't stay a little while longer?"

"Psst, no!" She slid into a tank top, flipped her hair out. "I'm meeting up with my boyfriend. You know this was a one-time thing, anyway."

"Right." He let go of the package. "We did agree on that."

"Yeah, we did. But…" She pulled up her jeans, then stepped into the small bathroom. "I'm not gon' lie, you put it on me."

"Yes, I did. And since I put in work on that ass, I'm thinkin' you got the better end of the deal."

She poked her head out of the bathroom. "How you figure?"

"Because. You one hundred and fifty dollars short on the pictures, but end up with back-to-back orgasms. So you came out on top, really. That ain't fair." He placed both hands behind his head. "Shoulda let you suck my dick and called it a day."

She said, "Whateva. I did what we agreed on. It was your idea. Besides, you got yours, too."

Quinton heard the water faucet. He sat up on the edge of the bed, rolling his neck around. "Damn it," he said, turning his foot inward. A used condom had stuck between his toes, its content smeared against the ball of his foot. As baby said, he got his, too.

"You and your small ass bathroom. I can't believe you live in a downtown office space. They probably sold mortgage loans or sumn' before you moved in here, huh?"

He dropped the condom in a small trashcan, then rubbed his foot against the rug. Grabbing a pair of shorts, he said, "No, it was actually a gym and massage studio. They used to do massages for couples in this room."

"Why not get a regular apartment?"

"Because I don't want one. I like my two-second commute to the job. I do my business and it's the perfect location. Plus, got my Foreman grill and toaster." He tapped his fridge. "Little freezer-fridge, bed, bathroom. Shoot, all I need. I even took a few glamour shots on this bed."

Tocarra stepped out of the bathroom, transformed back to the fully clothed model wannabe, all traces of her X-rated crimes removed. "Anyway, you gonna have the pictures ready tomorrow, right?"

"I told you, yeah. Just need to do a little editing before I upload to Dropbox. You set up an account like I told you?"

"Not yet."

"Well, you need to do that."

"I will." While slipping into her boots, she gazed at the walls. "How many females you get up in here, anyway?"

"What, the 'no cash, so give me ass' ones?"

She smacked her tongue. "Yes, that."

Quinton took a quick sweep of the women staring back at him from all corners, each dolled up to dime piece perfection. From fresh-faced newbies to veteran rap video vixens, they all decorated the walls in various semi-nude poses. Most of them ended up in his favorite position—spread out on his king-sized memory foam, feet toward the ceiling.

"Well, you can see. Bunch of young, broke females with a twisted dream of being the next Amber Rose. But as you know, I'm a fair man. Not enough cash? No problem; we work out a deal. You still get your headshots; I get shots of head."

"Your corny ass. You ain't nothin' but a loose dick with a camera."

"What that make you? Broke ho with a loose vagina?"

She smacked her tongue. "Anyway. Bye."

"Peace." He grabbed a pack of Marlboros and lighter from his pants pockets. "Nice doin' business with you. Say what's up to your man for me."

"Forget you." She disappeared.

Smiling, Quinton lay his head back on the pillow. "That was wrong."

He stared at the new ceiling fan installed the day before and took a long puff, then blew the cancer cloud out. Alone again. The solitude, Quinton's steady companion, had created a stubborn gap in his soul that a parade of beautiful women couldn't fill. His life seemed to mimic the fast whir of the fan blades—spinning in the same circle with no true direction.

Most men would pay top dollar to be in his shoes—a talented graphic designer, photographer, and "pipe layer" of Monte Clara's finest. But he always ended up in the same place—riding solo, staring at the walls or ceiling, an empty shell of himself. Mama's passing yanked out a big chunk of him, never to fully heal again. His twin, Gerald, shutting him out ripped another piece. Pussy, booze, and photography helped fill the holes, but like an aspirin for a migraine, the temporary fix didn't come close to curing his heartache.

Though he tried, he couldn't make Gerald understand the pain he felt when his number one lady died, which is why Quinton chose to drown his sorrows in a bottle of whiskey the night before the funeral. Rather be hungover and half-conscious than see Mama's final resting place in a cold, steel casket.

These days, thoughts of Mama led him straight to the bottle, so he pulled back from the psychological abyss before he fell back in. "Aw'ight, stop it, Q," he said, rising from the bed. "Let's get it goin'. Got things to do." It's always better to stay productive than wallow.

After a few more puffs, he put out his cigarette, then checked his email. Yet another message from his sister-in-law, Lisa, bitching about the ten-year high school reunion website appeared in his inbox.

He shook his head. "Told her stupid ass she don't need a website for a damn high school reunion. Just Facebook!"

She didn't want to listen. Things had to be her way. Gerald knew that all too well. But a deal's a deal. She had already paid half upfront for him to create a banner and YouTube channel, hopefully to boost interest in the reunion.

A new text popped up on the small screen of his phone, the same number that had called earlier. The short message asked him to meet at Seaside Park. He stared at the number. It came from *her*.

"'Need your help,' huh?" he said, reading the message. He texted back, **Good to hear from you again. When do you want to meet?**

CHAPTER 5

YARA

"Looks like that's the last of it," Ladan said, surveying the trunk. With the help of a young man who was kind enough to lift the heaviest items, they finally finished moving the last of Yara's boxes into a small storage unit. Ladan handed the young man a fifty-dollar bill and headed toward the driver door.

"Appreciate it, Ma," he said, stuffing the bill in his back pocket.

He directed his laser-beam focus back on Yara. She wore shorts, her smooth stems on public display, the curve in her rump enough to make him stumble once or twice while carrying her things. With that hungry-like-the-wolf look in his eyes, Yara knew he was scrambling to drop the perfect game on her. But like Marcus, she toyed with him, flashing a flirty smile and twisting her hair with a finger. He looked barely legal, and at that age, hormones are like Chinese fireworks. Yara didn't even know his name.

"So, where y'all from?" he asked Yara. "Y'all look Arabian or sumn'."

Yara laughed. "Our father is from Somalia, and mother from Egypt, but my sister and I were born here."

"Oh, damn, fo' real? Egypt? The pyramids and shit, huh?"

"Yeah. The pyramids." *Wow.*

"No wonder you look all exotic. So what 'chall 'bout to do?"

Opening the driver door, Ladan said, "We have to—"

"What do you have in mind?" Yara cut in, ignoring the evil eye from her sister.

"I don't know." He leaned forward, trying to get up close and personal. "Maybe hit up a place to eat. I can call up one of my boys. We can all roll together. So what's up?"

"Boy, how old are you?" Yara asked.

He shrugged. "Twenty. But, I'm sayin', though, you look my age. What, you 'bout—"

"Too old for you," Ladan interrupted. "Thanks for your help, but we have to go." Gesturing toward the car, she motioned for her sister to cease, desist, and stop messing around.

Yara opened the passenger door. "Well, damn, baby," he said. "Can I get your phone number or—"

"I'm not your baby!" Yara cried, shoving his chest. The weight of her thrust pushed the door against the hinges. "Call me that again and I'll—"

"Yara!" Ladan yelled, hightailing around the back of the car toward her sister.

The young man backpedaled, bottom jaw hung low, as if stuck. He kept his distance, hands up. "The hell wrong with you? Why you flippin' on me like that? Crazy bitch."

"Fuck you!" Yara yelled, her cry louder than her initial outburst. A projectile of spit flew into the air.

"Okay, that's enough." Ladan grabbed Yara's arm, pushing her into the passenger seat. Ladan mumbled something and handed the kid more money. He turned around and walked off. As Ladan made her way back to the driver seat, Yara asked, "What did you say to him?"

No response. Seatbelt strapped on, Ladan turned her head and backed up out of the parking spot. Placing the car in drive, she gunned the accelerator, speeding out of the gate.

"Hello?" Yara said. "Why are you driving so fa—"

Ladan swerved toward the curb and slammed on the brakes. Yara's head jerked, her shoulder bumping the door window.

"What the hell's wrong with you?" Yara cried, grabbing her shoulder.

"What the hell's wrong with *you*?" Ladan shot back, slamming her hands on the steering wheel. "Why did you spit on that boy?"

"I didn't spit on him!"

Ladan stared at Yara, like someone had pressed the Pause button on her face. After a few seconds, Ladan snapped out of it. "So, you're going to sit there and tell me you didn't spit at him? I saw you! You went bat shit, pushed him—"

"What? I did not push him!" Yara turned away, a finger pressed against her cheek. "Oh, wait. Okay, yes, I did." She laughed. "You see how stupid he looked, too? You gotta admit it was kinda funny."

Ladan again stared. Exhaling a long breath, she said, "Look, sis, we agreed if you're going to live with me, you have to stay on your meds, remember? *All* your meds."

Yara rolled her eyes. "Here we go again," she said, crossing her arms.

"Yes, here we go *a-gain*. I know you're not taking them. These damn mood swings—up one minute, down the next. Geez. Then what you just did to that boy… You're lucky I was able to calm him down with another twenty dollars." She glanced up the street. "I didn't know what he was going to do."

"It was your idea to ask him to move my stuff."

"Because it was heavy! I didn't expect his help to involve flying saliva."

"He shouldn't have called me 'baby'. You know I don't like that."

"No, I didn't know that."

"Well, I don't."

They cease-fired for a moment, gazing out into the street. Ladan's fingers tapped against the steering wheel, making a rhythmic tone like the thumps on a tin drum.

Yara glanced at the time. "Can we go, please?"

As if still trapped by her thoughts, it took Ladan a few seconds to make a move, but she eventually eased back into the street. This time, she stuck to the 25-mph speed limit.

Approaching a stop sign, Ladan said, "I worry about my baby sister sometimes."

"You have three years on me, so I'm not that much of a baby. And stop worrying. I'm fine."

"You're *not* fine." Ladan looked left, turned right. "I know you're not sleeping well and you refuse to talk to your psychiatrist since you moved here. She called me yesterday and said she's been trying to call you. She still wants to have sessions. If you want, she said she will SKYPE—"

"I don't need to talk to her anymore."

"Why not? It's not like you have to pay for it. The VA covers it."

"I told you I'm fine."

Ladan sighed. "Yeah, right. You don't even remember spitting at that boy. I don't think you're fit to go to your high school reunion, either."

"I'm a grown woman. I will go wherever I please. And look, once I get a job I'll find a new place, all right? This is just temporary."

"Well, the money you got from that military life insurance after Philip died seems to…oh."

Yara didn't say a word. She rested the back of her head against the seat, staring outside the passenger window. Cars, people, structures—they all zipped by, blurred by the figment of a dead man, triggered from the mere mention of his name, like a dark cloud had settled around her. Tears bubbled at the corner of each eye.

"I'm sorry, Yara," Ladan said, placing a hand on her sister's lap. "That sounded insensitive. I didn't mean it."

"Don't worry about it." She wiped each cheek with the back of her hand. "It's not your fault he died."

"Still, I… I'm sorry. And I'm so damn pissed about what he did before he passed."

"I don't want to talk about it."

"Okay, okay."

Ready to drop the subject, Yara turned up the radio volume. Rihanna echoed her high-pitched screech through the speakers. They didn't speak again until Ladan pulled into the parking spot in front of her townhouse a few minutes later.

"Okay," Ladan said, "gotta get back to work. What are you going to do?"

"Probably keep updating my resume. Password to your computer is Mom's middle name, right?"

"Yes."

"Okay."

They hugged. "For the record," Ladan said, "I like you living with me. You don't have to rush to move."

"Thank you, big sis." Yara winked with a smile. "And thanks for helping me with the rest of my stuff. Sorry for what I did earlier. I'm trying to do better."

"I know you are, and I'm sorry, too. Oh, feel free to stop by the hospital for a visit. I don't think I'll be that busy tonight."

"Okay."

Ladan put the gear in reverse. "See you later. Love ya."

"Love you, too."

Yara watched her sister drive off, back to Monte Clara County Hospital to finish her twelve-hour shift nursing cardiac patients.

"Damn, finally," Yara said, hurrying toward her car parked in a guest spot. She snatched the keys out of her purse. "About time I got her nosy butt off my back."

She checked the texts on her cell phone. Five new messages littered the virtual message board, all from the same number. They came in while she, Ladan, and Mr. No-Name were moving her stuff. One of the messages included a hotel address and room number.

"He's a little anxious, huh, babe?" Yara said to the picture of Philip staring back at her. She started the car. "I'm on my way. Horny toad."

It took her less than ten minutes to drive to the Beachside Hotel & Spa, the premiere five-star getaway of Monte Clara. Overlooking the bay, the scenic view inspired love songs for musicians of all genres and was one of the best romantic spots for honeymooners. Apparently, he wanted to make a big impression.

Yara wasn't impressed. At all.

As Yara had done with Marcus, she wrote a check next to his name in her notepad. She had added Oliver McCluster weeks before, along with three other "honorary" alumni. Each entry had a date and location next to the name, as well as the letters "BB"—except for Oliver. No "BB" for Oliver until the deed was done.

Oliver's moment for a one-on-one with Yara had finally arrived. According to his last message, he left work early and lied to his wife and kids to spend a few late afternoon hours with her. But that didn't surprise Yara; it's not like a little thing called marriage stopped anyone from sampling the goods of someone else. Two-legged hounds rarely turned down a fresh shot at pussy, so she knew his "BB" status would change in the next hour or so, confirming that all male cognition originated somewhere around the testicles.

She pulled out her red lipstick. In the rearview mirror, a woman with dark shadows under her eyes stared back, but still harnessed a vixen beauty that made thirsty, married men creep, including a few dogs that finally had a chance to capture a moment they never had in high school. Like Oliver.

On the third floor, Yara found Oliver's room and knocked on the door. She somehow concocted a smile when he opened it.

"Hi," she said.

The look in his eyes took a short trip from legs to breasts, before landing back on her face. "Hello to you."

He was nothing special. Short, probably no more than an inch taller than her 5'5" frame. Average build, pitted scars across his pink-peach cheeks. Stubbles of hair around his chin, eyes a bit beady. Far from GQ, but not really a "Shrek," either.

Before he contacted her on Facebook and revealed his adolescent crush, she hadn't known he existed. She probably passed him in the school hallways a thousand times, but since he didn't match her physical standard back then, Yara had no memory of Oliver, even though they graduated in the same class. After she and Philip became an item, all the other boys at school became invisible.

Now, she had only one short-term standard, a single agenda—to attract married men. Looks didn't matter anymore. Oliver was a nobody back then, and a nobody now, a number. But based on his wedding ring and the Facebook pictures of his family, he more than qualified. The high school reunion Facebook page had provided her with access to lots of easy prey. Once she clicked Attending, the floodgates opened and married dogs like Oliver ran through, hoping for a shot at Yara. His lucky day had finally come.

"Wow," he said. "Still so beautiful. I can't believe you're here. Please, come in."

"Thank you," she said, walking in. *You're next.*

CHAPTER 6

GERALD

"Damn, 7:55."

Gerald still had five minutes to kill before his morning appearance at work, so after shutting down the engine, he leaned back, stared into the parking lot, and allowed his mind to wander. As if on repeat, thoughts of Lisa took root yet again.

That seemed to be Gerald's new theme the past few days—drag himself to work stone-faced and mentally battered, while obsessing over ways to make his wife smile again. A cold front had enveloped their unhappy home with no signs of lifting. So much dead space between him and Lisa, gaps everywhere, including the bedroom. No sex for months. He couldn't remember the last time.

But despite Lisa's frigid demeanor, Gerald didn't poke and prod for a remedy. Women needed time alone sometimes; he learned that as a child. Being unemployed was clearly eating at Lisa's pride and self-esteem, while elevating mental stress. Through no fault of her own, she would sometimes rain her frustrations on Gerald. All he could do was be the supportive husband Lisa deserved.

Grabbing his cell phone, he browsed the thread of texts between him and Lisa, going back three months. The last text ordered, **Get some paper towels**. Short and heartless, like most of the texts from her, far from lovey-dovey. At least five of his texts ended with a "love you," but no such salutation from her. By phone, as in person, Gerald held doormat status in his marriage.

But despite the obvious signs, Gerald refused to give up last-ditch chivalry efforts. Like a good husband, he stayed committed to his wife and marriage, believing if he tried hard enough, they could go nowhere but up.

Most of the time, his efforts crashed and burned. Lisa never acknowledged the card he placed on her keyboard a few days ago. She had darted out the house when Gerald proposed the idea of a baby. Like with most of his attempts at romance or a little conversation, he'd managed to jack it up. "A" for effort, "C-" for execution. Still, he knew his heart was in the right place.

"A text won't hurt," he said with a little smile, tapping the digital keyboard on his phone. "Just to let my baby know how I feel. Still." He hit Send, then noticed the time.

Damn.

His smile flat-lined. If he didn't separate himself from the car seat, he would be late for work. His ex-classmate and new boss, Greg Stephens, was back from his training orientation at the company's headquarters in Los Angeles. That meant their first face-to-face since Greg stole his position was imminent. As much as Gerald hated the idea of working for Greg, he reminded himself to keep their eventual run-in as professional as humanly possible and earn his paycheck, money the Durston household needed.

The moment he stepped into the elevator, he knew he couldn't fake it. As the claustrophobic metal box ascended to the 4th floor, his mood plunged, falling into a black hole of dread.

"Good morning, Gerald."

Alicia always greeted Gerald with a kilowatt smile, but Gerald was nowhere near trying to go there with her.

"Hey," he replied, walking past the front desk, face forward. Barely looked at his mini-crush Nia, his pet nickname for her since she favored Nia Long, circa *Boyz n the Hood* era.

Gerald glanced at the door to what should have been his corner office. He knew the office layout well. Leather seat. L-shaped mahogany desk. Office window facing Monte Clara Bay. And most importantly, a damn door that he could open and close whenever he pleased. Bossman space. Upgraded real estate. Way better than the makeshift "office" he occupied—an open cubicle half the size with a slit for a door. It looked no different than everybody else in Cubiville, just a little more square footage.

Gerald walked toward the kitchen. Before stepping inside, he stopped by the fountain for a sip. As the cool water stream touched his lips, he heard two of his subordinates, Bethany and Christine—A.K.A. the Office Gossip Twins—babbling loud enough that anyone within twenty feet could hear Christine was all on Greg's nut sack.

"The new regional director is hot!" That was Christine.

"Yes, he is. Can you believe he's only 28? A baby!"

"Yes, and he went to my high school. Of course, he graduated twelve years after me."

"Really? That's all right. You know you like robbin' the cradle." They laughed.

Blood pressure rising, Gerald wiped his lips and walked in. All ass-kissing on the new director ceased with a simple "morning" from both of them. Special lip puckering wasn't reserved for office managers, at least not for Gerald.

"Mornin'," Gerald replied, his voice barely above a whisper. He grabbed the coffee pot and poured a caffeinated dose in a cup. The heat seared through the Styrofoam, a steady burn growing against his hand, but he didn't care. He was already boiling inside.

"Hey, Gerald," Bethany said. "You went to Monte Clara High. Do you know the new director? I think you two are the same age."

"Yeah, we graduated together," Gerald replied, stirring sugar in the cup, his back toward them.

"Really?" Bethany said.

"Yes, really."

Gerald turned, saw two women in heat. Panties probably soaked at the mere thought of a single status.

"Soooo, does he—"

"Yes, he's married." Gerald killed that wet dream.

Bethany froze, mouth on stuck mode with a donut hole in the middle, as if thrown off by Gerald's response. "Oh, okay. I wasn't going to ask that, but thank you for letting me know."

"You're welcome."

No one else said a word. The ladies grabbed their breakfasts and coffees, then headed toward their desks.

As they left, Alicia popped in. "Gerald, Mr. Stephens would like to see you."

Mr. Stephens. Yeah. Sure. "Oh, he's here, now, huh?"

"Yes, just got in."

"All right. I'll be there in a minute."

Summoned by the new Bossman. At that moment, Gerald fully acknowledged his status as second fiddle. An errand boy, really, to be whipped around whenever "Mr. Stephens" felt like it. He returned to his cubicle, glanced at the picture of him and Lisa next to the oversized Mac monitor. Powering on the computer, he sipped his coffee then sat down. At that moment, he decided checking his calendar and browsing the email inbox held priority status over Greg.

While reading his third email, he heard, "Gerald?"

"Yes, Alicia, I'm coming," he said, still facing his computer. "Thanks."

As he stood up, cup in hand, coffee dripped on his white button-down shirt. "Damn," he said, looking down at a brown wet spot. "Figures."

After a quick dab with a napkin, Gerald donned his fake invisible facemask and dragged himself to "Mr. Stephen's" office. Door cracked, he still knocked.

"Come on in, Gerald."

Gerald stepped in. "Hey, you wanted to see me?"

Greg greeted him with a handshake and a smile that seemed to test the strength of his cheek muscles. "Gerald Durston. How are you?"

"Greg Stephens. Good to see you again. Welcome to Coastal Insurance."

"Thanks."

Not much had changed with Greg. Dirty blond hair, basketball player lean. Thin eyebrows shaped like the wings of an eagle, the same color as his hair. Still had the pretty surfer boy looks, a certified panty dropper.

Gerald said, "Still look the same."

"You, too," Greg replied, "except you're a little pudgy around the middle with a stain on your shirt, I see." He slapped Gerald's belly. "Same old Gerald, though. Must be from the wife's good home cooking, huh?"

Can't believe this fool tapped my stomach. "Yup," he lied. "She loves to do it up."

"I bet. Have a seat."

They sat down, with Gerald in a hard wooden seat and a flat cushion; Greg in the plush chair behind the desk. Greg crossed a foot over his knee, leaned back, and asked, "How is she, anyway? You two were an item in high school."

"She's good," he lied again.

"Cool, cool. You know Lisa and I had a little thing going on for a minute, right?"

A rush of heat burned inside Gerald's chest. "I know about that."

"I mean, it was nothing." Greg shrugged. "Just a small little thing, no biggie. Teenage stuff. Besides, it was before you two got together. At least, I hope so." He laughed.

Gerald pressed his hands flat against his thighs, suffocating the urge to ball them up into fists. "So, how's Aanya?"

"Aanya? Oh, she's fine. Married four years, man, about as long as you, I think. Working on that baby, you know. You guys trying to have kids, too?"

He swallowed. That question hit a sore sport. "Yeah, eventually. Maybe in the near future."

"Cool, cool. Going to the reunion?"

"Yeah. You?"

"Most definitely. Hell, I'm curious to find out who's been posting those crazy videos and old pictures of our graduating class."

Gerald frowned. "Videos?"

"Yeah, you haven't seen them? Somebody in a mask speaking in different dialects. Pretty funny. You gotta see for yourself. It's linked on the reunion Facebook page."

"I'll be sure to check them out."

"Good, good." Greg paused. He leaned forward and said, "So, you've been here about seven, eight years, right?"

"Right."

"And you applied for this position, too?"

Gerald swallowed another glob of saliva. Somehow, Greg made Gerald his personalized keyboard, pressing all the right buttons for the desired output. But Gerald didn't show what he felt inside; he maintained the same level of chill. Whether he applied for the position or not, that business didn't apply to Greg's nosy ass.

"Yes, I did," Gerald replied. "I was doing a lot of the work until they hired you."

"I heard. Well, guess the right man got the job."

Gerald's heart rate rose, but his staunch ability to uphold self-control decreased. A minimal amount of words would keep him steady, so he said, "Guess so."

A phone buzzed on the desk. "Hold on a sec."

As Greg checked the phone, Gerald scanned the office and noted Greg had marked his territory. Saw a nice picture of pretty Aanya on the desk, a leather case that resembled Gerald's, a stack of documents beside the keyboard. Small remnants, but all Greg's.

He texted whomever back. Gerald could tell Greg wanted to break out in a fit of laughter from whatever he saw on the phone, but didn't.

"Sorry about that," Greg said, holding a goofy grin. "Just… an old friend."

"It's cool."

"So, anyway, you already know the whole tradition here for new employees, correct?"

Gerald nodded. "Of course."

"Good. You can go ahead and let everyone know where to be this Friday, then."

"Okay."

"In the meantime, I'll be in and out of the office this week, meetings and such. Director stuff. Then we can have more of a formal meeting."

This fool is testing my limits. "That'll work."

"Okay." Greg stood up. "Good to see you again, buddy. Glad we could catch up. We'll talk again soon." He extended his hand.

Gerald itched to karate-chop the smug look off Greg's face. He remembered Greg as a smart ass in high school, but over the years, Greg had apparently graduated from smart ass to straight up asshole. It seemed once Greg took over the new role of regional director, all the million or so asshole molecules bubbled to the surface. But Gerald promised himself to stay professional, so he held eye contact, grabbed Greg's hand, and shook it like a man.

"Oh, before you head out." Greg opened his desk drawer and handed Gerald a thin metal name plate. "You mind putting this on the door for me?"

Gerald stared at it a moment, processing the title: Greg Stephens, Regional Director.

"You can slide it through the placeholder. Thanks, buddy."

"Sure." *Bastard.*

Gerald did what Bossman told him, like a good whipped boy. A title that had become his namesake at home, and now, at his job, it seemed.

"And, oh, Gerald?"

Gerald stuck his head back in the door. "What's up?"

"Next time I ask for you, that means straight to my office, not back to your fuckin' cubicle. Got it? Good." Greg smiled. "Now that you know where we stand, you can close the door. Thank you."

Greg had flipped on him with the swift velocity of a Bruce Lee-round house kick. Gerald capped the steam building up and willed himself with all the strength he could muster to keep cool so he didn't end up on the news, strapped in handcuffs.

Gerald somehow cracked a smile, too. He said, "My mistake," then closed the door.

Although his heart was like a fist steady-pounding a hollow surface, he suppressed the thunder. Not his style to erupt pent-up anger, especially in public. Still, he needed a moment away from it all, so he escaped into the bathroom.

He placed his hands on the sink and stared into the mirror. The stain on his shirt faded a little, but still noticeable. Lines indented his forehead as he stared. Eyes turning red, he begged for answers to the same damn questions: *Why the hell am I not getting my life the way I want? And how much more can I take before I snap?*

Gerald pulled out his cell phone and checked the messages. He re-read the text he sent to Lisa earlier, but still no response. As usual.

CHAPTER 7

QUINTON

"Damn," Quinton said. He rested his hand on the car door handle, but didn't want to exit yet. The view before him required a step-back.

A flood of memories rushed to the forefront when he saw Aanya sitting cross-legged on the park bench, black shorts hiked up her thighs. Smooth legs the color of cinnamon, the same legs he once had wrapped around his waist.

She was watching her cell phone through dark shades, her sandy-brown hair slipping off bare shoulders, caressing her right arm. Quinton longed to burn one, but Aanya couldn't stand cigarettes, so he stayed smoke-free for over twenty-four hours, a personal record. A week had gone by since Aanya sent the text message asking to see him and finally, their schedules fell in sync for a private one-on-one, a moment he had salivated over for years—them alone without her sorry ass husband, Greg Stephens, in the mix. Taking a deep breath, he shook off his boyish nerves. After a quick check in the rearview mirror, Quinton the Man left the car.

As he stepped onto freshly cut grass that looked straight out of a golf course, he said, "Hello, pretty lady."

Aanya raised her head and stood up. With a smile that could stop any man, she said, "Hey, you."

They hugged. *Damn, she smells good, as always.* "Every time I see you it's like time stands still," Quinton said.

"Well, you're not looking bad yourself." She placed her shades on the bench as they sat down, revealing her heart-shaped face. "We last saw each other when Greg and I ran into you at Walmart, huh?"

Hearing Greg's name stung a bit, reminding Quinton she already had a number one in her life. But he kept his composure, playing along with the chit-chat.

"Damn," he said, "that was a year ago. The same time you hired me to design your business cards. I think you were heading back to India to visit your parents, too."

"Yes, I was," she said, nodding. "Good memory."

"Photographic." He winked.

She snapped her fingers. "Of course."

"Yup. So, uh, are you still working at that massage therapy place?"

"Yes. Doing some on the side, too. Business is picking up."

"Good, good." Quinton leaned back, placing an elbow on the bench, staring. "I... wow."

"What?"

"It's just really good to see you again. I was trippin' off how long it's been since we first met. I think I'd just turned fourteen, fifteen?"

Aanya's shoulders slumped. "Yes. Right after we learned about 9/11."

"That's right. You were crying in the hallway, saw me walking by, and just hugged me. Never said two words to you before like *ever*; didn't know your name—nothing. We got to know each other pretty well after that, though."

"I still don't know why I just pounced on you." She looked away, probably channeling her 14-year-old self, reliving the memory. "God, I was very emotional, you know? That day was so horrible. I guess I needed someone to hold me. Seriously, what did you think when I grabbed you like that?"

Quinton smiled. "I was thinking, 'Who is this fine ass girl all up on me?'"

"Yeah, right!"

"Naw, for real. I remember you smelled so good, too. I'm glad you hugged me and not Robert Poncheko. He was right behind me."

She cocked her head sideways. "I don't remember seeing him. I only saw you."

Quinton grinned. "You only saw my handsome face, huh?"

Aanya rolled her eyes. "What I mean is, I—"

"I know what you mean, pretty lady," Quinton said, winking at her. "I saw you, too. That little encounter turned into the best year of high school for me."

"Really? Me, too. We were quite the freshman couple, huh? Hey, remember the talent contest at the dance?"

"You mean the contest we should've won? Oh, yeah. We did that song *Dilemma*." Quinton laughed. "Man, to this day, that end of the school year dance was the best fun I ever had! I rocked the Nelly look, too, boy. Had the white band-aid, headband, big ass St. Louis T-shirt—er' thing."

"You sure did, Quinny Binny!"

"Oh, shit, Quinny Binny!" Quinton cried, slapping his hands together. "I haven't heard that in a minute!"

"Well, you were my Quinny Binny!"

"Ha, Quinny Binny," Quinton said, repeating the pet name he hadn't heard in years, but still touched the same special corner of his heart. He stared out into the dark-green grass, rewinding the latter part of 2001, through mid-2002. A flood of fresh memories rekindled a slice of the serenity he always felt with her. He remembered the teenybopper times—their "peach-fuzz" love—like a manifestation of a cheesy Justin Bieber song. Pool parties, hours of Xbox, going on their first "date night" to watch the original Spiderman. But it all changed when Quinton snuck into her bedroom window on a school night, graduating from a bubblegum affair to grown folks' business... at least, for about a minute.

"What 'cha thinking about? You over there smiling."

Quinton didn't want to talk about the night he lost his virginity to her, so he shrugged and said, "I was just thinking I was your Quinny Binny, and you were my first... everything."

"Oh." She nodded, swiping a strand of hair that had crossed over her left eye. "I see."

Aanya breathed a deep sigh. She also looked out into the grass, cohabiting the same space of reflection. Quinton wondered if her flurry of happy memories carried a stubborn sting of regret, as his did.

"Quinton?"

"Yeah?"

"Why did we break up again?"

Quinton didn't answer right away. Careful with his words, he said, "I think we kinda drifted apart the summer before we turned sophomores. I definitely wasn't mature enough to know what we had. Besides, the shelf life of a couple at that age is short."

"Hmmm. I guess, you're right. We were way too young."

"Yeah," Quinton replied, nodding. As he glanced at the bench, he caught Aanya's French-cut nails—and the shiny rock on her left finger. It flickered a spot of light, but seemed to yell at Quinton, reminding him that no matter how many times he stepped into the past with Aanya, shared history didn't change the present. He could also make a strong argument about being her "first everything," but none of that mattered anymore. He simply opened the doors for someone else, a punk named Greg.

Facing the hard truth, he closed off memory lane and kept it casual. "Sooo... are you going to the reunion? I didn't see your name on the list."

"I signed up a few days ago. Looks like it's going to be fun." As if a mini-bomb exploded in her head, Aanya's eyes lit up. She cried, "Omigod! Have you seen those crazy YouTube videos? I was just watching them."

"What videos?"

"Someone's been posting them on the reunion page."

"Oh, yeah." Quinton nodded. "I saw one of them on my newsfeed but didn't click on it. Someone dressed up in the mascot uniform, right?"

"Yeah, another one was posted this morning. The first two were just talking about the reunion and stuff." She edged closer with her wide-screen smartphone, closing the space between them. "But look at this one."

It took a second to tilt his head toward the phone because of another Aanya-induced "pause" moment. Her lips were a taste-test away, and he fantasized about pressing his lips against hers. Instead, he peeped out the video.

To his surprise, Quinton cracked up. Someone wearing a mask of the Monte Clara High mascot had appeared on the screen—a pointy-headed devil with a blue face and yellow hair, its blue horns with tips as sharp as its ears and bearded triangular chin. Dark slits concealed the mystery person's eyes. Blue Devil said:

"Heeeey, Monte Clara High, class of 2005! It's your favorite Blue Devil mascot again! So, what do you think? You like my new autotuned voice? I know, I know, I sound like a bad mix of T-Pain and Future, which I like to call 'Torture,' for short." The screen flipped to a still picture of a young man standing in front of a locker, wearing white shorts and flipped sunglasses to match. "Now look at this guy. What the hell was Paul Murphy thinking when he wore this to school? For real, Paul? Are those 70s NBA shorts, or a new underwear line for boys from the Sears catalog? Oh, and why do his glasses look like the shutter blinds in my grandmother's house?"

Quinton slapped his knee, buckling over from laughter. Aanya hollered with him. She said, "Hilarious, right?"

"Yeah! Who is that?"

She shrugged. "I have no idea!"

The mystery person didn't let up: "Okay, guys, listen. Let's start a new rule, shall we? If your shorts don't cover at least 90 percent of your raggedy thighs, give them to your little brother. Or donate them to Goodwill. Look, unless they're swim trunks or underwear, they are *not* allowed, okay? It's a matter of public decency here, folks. Nobody wants to see that."

Quinton and Aanya lost themselves in hysterics, carrying on like high school teenagers. Blue Devil roasted three other poor souls, including an 11th grade picture of Zoe Flannigan who he dubbed "Chloe Kargrassian" because of her reputation for blazing cannabis on school grounds after class. After dissecting everything from her smoking habits to her shirt with the *Usual Suspects* movie poster on front, Blue Devil finally showed mercy and said:

"Okay, Monte Clara High alumni, class of 2005, that's it for now. But much more to come soon! If you want to find out who I am, bring your ugly mugs to the reunion! Check Facebook for details. Until next time!"

The video faded out with the song "My Humps" by the Black Eyed Peas. Quinton cried, "Damn, funny as hell! I've never seen any of those pictures before, either."

"I know, huh? Pretty crazy. The other videos use different voices, but the same mask, so you can't tell who the hell it is. I'm dying to know." She lifted her head, then squinted her eyes while gazing at Quinton, as if trying to peel back layers of a secret.

Quinton matched the frown lines in her forehead. "What?"

"Is it you?"

"What, no!" he said, laughing. "Hell no."

"Uh huh. You sure?"

"Yeeees. Whoever it is, they obviously don't want to be found out. At least not yet, anyway. Can't tell if it's a man or woman with that big ass coat and mask."

Aanya chuckled, then sighed. She closed several web pages on her phone, one of them the reunion website. Quinton caught a glimpse of the banner he had finally uploaded that morning before Aanya placed the phone in her purse.

Now stone-faced, she said, "Quinton, I need your help with something."

"Oh." Quinton sensed an end to the small talk. "Is that why you wanted to meet?"

"Yes."

He crossed his arms. "What do you need?"

"I… I want you to follow my husband."

Quinton's head dipped a bit. "Come again?"

"I want you to follow Greg. I think he's cheating."

"Oookay." Quinton dropped the foot off his knee, allowing her request to marinate for a second. He searched her face and saw a woman staring back, no expression. *She's dead serious.*

"Why do you think he's cheating?" Quinton asked.

She broke eye contact and looked down, as if ashamed. "The classic signs. Always trying to hide his phone, comes home late, the smell of perfume on his clothes. Little sneaky stuff. He's always had a super high sex drive, especially when I'm ovulating; I just can't keep up! But he doesn't touch me like a husband should anymore, you know? I'm just… a sex toy."

Quinton wished he could've muted "high sex drive" and "sex toy." He knew it made no sense to harbor jealousy, stupid even, but he could barely stomach a highlight reel of Greg inside of her. Still, Quinton smelled opportunity. "Yeah," he said, "I bet your alarm bells are loud as hell."

"They are. So, what do you think?"

"Um, I think I wasn't ready for this. Why me?"

"Well, you have the right camera equipment, especially for close-up snapshots, right?"

"Yeah."

"And you don't do the nine-to-five. At least that's what you said when I last saw you. I figured you have flexible time."

He nodded. "True, true."

"Plus, I trust you."

He smiled. "Thank you. I'm sorry you're going through this, but I can't say I'm surprised. I never understood why you married that dude. He was the biggest ho in high school. He even messed around with Lisa Townes, my brother's now wife. Remember her?"

"Of course, but I didn't know they hooked up. How is your twin, by the way?"

Her question threw Quinton off balance a bit. "Um, he's good. We're not really talking right now. Had a falling out. He'll be at the reunion, though."

"I see. I hope you guys can patch things up. He was always so nice to me. I had so much fun when we all took that photography class together."

"Yeah, that was cool. So, anyway, we way off track. Back to the man ho, I mean, your husband. What—"

"Hold on, wait!" She laughed. "You have a lot of nerve calling somebody a ho! What about you, Mr. Hot Shot photographer? I've seen some of your pictures around town, local magazines and stuff. I bet you're having your fun now, huh?"

"Naw, naw," he said, waving his hands. "I never mix business with pleasure. Nope."

"Um hum."

"For real!"

"Sure. Whatever."

"Aw, man, that's messed up. You don't even believe a brotha."

Aanya play-punched his arm. "I'm just messing with you."

"I hope so. But, for real, if I find anything, what are you gonna do?"

"Well…" Aanya's voice trailed off. The reality of it all seemed to seep in for her. She said, "I never really thought about it, but… I don't see how my marriage will survive. I guess I'll cross that bridge when I get there."

"That bridge, huh?" Quinton repeated. She nodded, a slight curve at the edge of her lips. So beautiful, more so now as a woman. Natural. Not like the fake make-up splattered chicken heads littering his walls, trying to fit a classless magazine standard not much different than a porn star. How he wished to absorb the fragrance of Aanya again, let her fingers run through his locks from underneath him. He always imagined the music he and Aanya made in his dreams as a soulful melody. "You know what?"

"What?"

He held her hand. "If things don't go the way you want, I'll be on the other side of that bridge. I'm here for you, okay?"

"Thank you, Quinton. I think I needed to hear that. You could always make me smile. And laugh, too."

"You're welcome. And I'm going to bust his ass. Believe that. A so-called man should never treat his lady like a has-been."

After what seemed like minutes, a flustered Aanya blinked a few times before she said, "Um… Greg works at Coastal Insurance now. He'll probably—"

"Wait, what?" He released Aanya's hand. "My brother works there!"

"Really?" Aanya said, head tilted. "I didn't know that. Greg is the new regional director."

"What?" Quinton almost fell off the bench. "I think Gerald was going for that job."

"Seriously? Greg is going to be Gerald's boss? That's awkward."

"Tell me about it."

"Wow, I—oh." She reached into her purse. "Before I forget. Here's a keyless remote to his car."

Quinton glanced at it, frowning. "Why are you giving me this?"

She shrugged. "I don't know. To look for anything he may leave behind, I guess. Or maybe you can bug it or something."

"Bug it? Wow, girl, you want me to go all in, huh?"

She nodded. "Yes. I wouldn't be surprised if he's doing nasty things in his car, too."

Quinton slipped the remote into his pocket. "And you trust me not to plant fake evidence? Or go joy riding?"

"You'd better not." They laughed.

Quinton scooted back, his posture upright and business-like. *All right, Greg done fucked up. Messing around with Aanya's heart and my brother's money? I got that ass.*

"When can you start?" Aanya asked.

"I'll get on him as soon as I leave here. What do you expect his work schedule to be today?"

CHAPTER 8

LISA

"Aw, sheeick. Fluct."

Greg garbled his words through clenched teeth, mumbling in his trademark fuck language. The moment Lisa wrapped her mouth around it—an eight-inch tree trunk of hard flesh—that suave slick tongue of his broke down.

Though Greg still rocked a gold wedding band, another woman savored his rock, its spit-shine courtesy of Lisa's expert "lube" job. No wonder he kept coming back to Lisa. And coming back *in* her.

Lisa cocked her head, a hard stare facing upward. With the driver's seat leaned back, she could only see the bottom of Greg's chin, nostrils, and mouth partly open, but when Lisa hit that right spot, his torso and head jerked forward. Greg's eyes were closed, lips quivering, as if each lip struggled to touch each other. There it was—Greg's rare ugly fuck face. Based on what he said about the weak head game he sometimes received at home, Lisa figured she was the only one capable of bringing out that twisted look, at least better than Aanya, his charity case of a wife.

The tip of her tongue crept down a large worm of a vein that protruded his tight skin, little curly blond hairs tickling her cheek. While her hand controlled the "joystick," licking his two "nutty buddies" and teeth nibbling the shaft, Greg stabbed the fingers of one hand into the seat cushions, pushing the other hand against the back of Lisa's head, having a fit.

"Awww. Waabaa! Ffffff!"

She could tell the peak was close, his will all but abandoned, it seemed. At near-climax, Lisa had the power and control in her hands—literally. Desperate to get her plan underway, she thought about messing with his emotions by pulling back and making demands. Men would do anything for a big bang nut.

A growl escaped Greg's lips. She set aside the crazy thought of stopping pre-eruption. A plan of this magnitude required Greg clear-headed, relaxed, and satisfied, so she kept slurping on the rock like it was a peach-flavored popsicle.

Greg banged the tinted window with a fist, let out a few choppy huffs, and a gush of baby cream splattered his beige button-down shirt. "Awww, d-damn!" he said, twitching. When his little geyser stopped, he left a gooey wet spot the size of a small pancake under the pocket of his shirt. Lisa smiled as he tried to compose himself amid the tremors, proud of the job she had done.

"Better now?"

After a deep breath, Greg flattened the shirt, surveying the damage. "All over myself. It looks like I'm leaking breast milk. I thought you were going to… you know."

"You thought wrong, lover."

"That's so cold." He unbuttoned his shirt and stuffed it in a gym bag on the backseat. Pulling out a similar shirt and a washcloth, he said, "Good thing I always come prepared. I keep a change of clothes with me at all times."

"I see," Lisa said, admiring the view of pecs and biceps. "Oh, by the way, you 'come prepared' with my help."

"Got a point there." Greg cleaned himself off as best as he could, then pulled his underwear and pants up. "Wooo! Just what I needed after my official first day on the job."

She wiped her lips with the back of her hand. Grabbing a handy wipe and compact mirror from her purse, she said, "That's my way of congratulating you."

"Appreciate that."

As Lisa checked her face, Greg raised the seat upright and said, "You always gave the best head, Lockjaw. I remember—"

"Boy, you know I don't like that name!" She slapped his arm. "Stop calling me that. Ugh! Same old dumb shit from high school."

Greg laughed. "You know I'm joking."

"Tsk! Whatever." Lisa put the mirror away and glanced outside. Greg had moved the car to the remote end of the parking lot, and except for a few people in the distance coming from or going to their own cars, the coast was clear.

"When you texted me this morning I was meeting with your hubby," Greg said, buttoning his pants.

"Really? How'd it go?"

"Fine. I know he hates that I got the job over him, but honestly, I don't give a shit."

"I know you don't."

Greg looked at his watch. "You know he'll be leaving soon, right? He was finishing up a report for me when I left."

"Yes. And I don't care."

"I guess not."

Lisa looked at the ten-story corporate structure in the distance. While Gerald punched the clock, Lisa had "munched the cock," as Greg would say—this time just yards away from where Gerald received his paychecks. A bold first for her, but she liked it that way. It added to the thrill.

"I'm just so tired of him," Lisa said. "I don't want to do this anymore. I don't." She pulled out her phone from her purse. "Look at this text."

Greg read the message. "What's wrong with it? It says he's thinking about you and loves you."

"Ugh. I didn't even respond. He's so pathetic."

"What, pathetic because he *loves* you?"

"No. I mean… He's… I don't know… really annoying. The way he eats and snores all loud, farts. Ugh! Everything about him. He's getting so fat, too."

Greg chuckled. "I noticed that."

"His presence alone disgusts me. He annoys me when he's not around, too. That fool butt-dials at least once a day."

Greg laughed. "You know, I always wondered why you were with him. I mean, he was thinner back then, but…" He shrugged. "You just seemed out of his league."

She sighed. "I was. And I still am."

"Yeah. He's always been sort of an awkward type, unlike his twin brother."

"Exactly. And can you believe he got a vasectomy after high school without telling me? I didn't find out until after we got married."

Greg's jaw dropped. "Seriously?"

"Yes! What man does that? Then he tells me the other day, 'I'm ready to have a baby, now, so I'm gonna get it reversed.' Can you believe that?"

"Wow. That's crazy."

"Ugh, he gets on my nerves! And do you know—"

"Slow down, geez," Greg said, a hand up. "You sound like you hate him."

Lisa processed the word "hate."

"Yes," she said, nodding. "I think a part of me does. He's not a real man. He damn sure hasn't given me the life I deserve."

"What kind of life is that?"

"You know, the kind with a man who knows how to treat his wife." She turned to him, dropping her voice. "A life where my husband can afford to surprise me with trips to the Bahamas."

Greg said, "Oh, like I did with Aanya last year, huh?"

"Something like that."

"I see you're all over my Facebook page. Or hers."

"Well, it is how we reconnected."

"Right about that, Lock… Lisa. But, look, I'm not made of money, even with this new position."

Lisa rolled her eyes. "Huumph. You're still better than the man I got."

"Lisa, if you're so unhappy with Gerald, divorce him."

"Why don't you divorce Aanya since you're here with me? You know I rock the mic better than her."

"Okay, first off, don't ever say her name like that again. Second, you knew the rules before we started this little thing. I'm not leaving her, all right? It's not my fault you're catching feelings for me. You know what they say—stay in your lane, side piece. Got it?"

Lisa clamped her teeth together to stifle a smart-ass clap back. She knew where she stood, but didn't care. Greg was nothing more than a means to an end, the middleman for a much bigger prize.

"I made a mistake saying that, so... I'm sorry, okay?" Lisa said. "I know what I got myself into. I admit, I wouldn't mind having what she has, but I know my place."

"Good," Greg said. "Now, I need to go. I have plans with *my wife*, so until next time." He pointed to the door.

"But..."

He grunted. "Bitch, what?"

Lisa cut her eyes at Greg. Again, she bit her tongue. She couldn't cuss him out, yet. She needed him.

Instead, she brushed off "bitch" and replied, "Look, I need your help. You still keep in contact with that cousin of yours? The one that got locked up for carjacking?"

Greg's face shuddered in a way that only a question out of left field could do. "How do you know about that? That was like fifteen years ago."

She snickered with a side eye. "C'mon, now. Everybody knows you were with him when he pistol-whipped that guy and stole his car."

"Hey, all that matters is nobody could prove it."

"Whatever. You're just lucky he didn't tell on you. What, he was like seventeen and you fourteen?"

"Yeah... I mean... anyway. What the hell you bring up Patrick for?"

"Because I want him to do a job for me."

"Job?" He frowned. "What kind of job?"

"I need him to take care of a problem of mine."

"Problem?"

Cell phone in hand, Lisa swiped through pictures in the photo gallery until she landed on a solo wedding snapshot of Gerald decked out in his tuxedo, hands in his pockets and cheesing for the camera. Index finger still touching the small screen, Lisa didn't say a word as she stared at Greg, cocking her thumb back.

"Are you serious?"

"Yes, I am," Lisa said, her face deadpan.

Greg studied her. "And why the hell would Patrick and I want anything to do with this job?"

Lisa handed him a life insurance policy. "I can give you five hundred thousand reasons. You help me out, and I'll split the payout with you, fifty-fifty."

Greg ran a hand through his hair. "Man, two hundred fifty g's to split between me and Patrick, huh?"

Lisa nodded. "You want to get paid or what?"

Although his sex drive was off the charts, Lisa knew that nothing made Greg more hard and high-rise erect than a payday with lots of zeros. She could almost see the dollar signs flying around his head.

"Yeah," he said, tapping the driver door. From the looks of him, all starry-eyed, Greg had taken a quick mental getaway off to somewhere, probably already spending his six-figure payout.

Got him. Patrick on the other hand...

"So, do you think he'll do it?" Lisa asked. "I heard he got out a few months ago and went back to Oakland."

"He did." Greg paused, as if struck by an epiphany. "Wait a minute. All this dirt we've been doing, you were just buttering me up for this," he threw up air quotes, "'job?'"

Lisa looked away, watching a car drive up a small embankment and exit the premises. It made a quick right toward a strip mall. "It wasn't just about that, baby. But yes, I figured you would want in on it."

"I see. You could divorce and walk away, you know."

Lisa turned back to Greg. "Or I could become a widow and walk away with five hundred thousand dollars."

The tapping against the door turned into a fist pound on Greg's knee. "Damn, Lisa. Didn't know you were so cold-hearted."

She smiled. "Me either. I guess years with a dull, broke, sorry-ass husband made me this way."

"Uh, if you say so."

"I do. Now, one more time: Do you think Patrick will do it or not?"

With a slow nod, Greg said, "Yeah. I do. My cousin is a straight-up gangsta, always looking for the big payday."

"Good." Lisa smiled. "I swear, you still have a little thug in you, Mr. Prom King. You always liked hanging out with the bad boys. I remember how you used to brag about Patrick in the cafeteria. 'My cuz beat up this, my cuz stole that.'"

"Yeah." He let out a nervous chuckle. "This job could maybe make things right between us. Patrick feels like I owe him because he didn't snitch on me. We've never really been the same since."

"Well, if he can do this, we'll *all* be happy. You may have to give him a bigger chunk of your half, though."

Greg shifted toward her, his back against the driver door, holding an intense stare. "Lisa," he said, stone-faced. "This is some serious business. Are you sure?"

She mimicked his move, but leaned toward him, her face inches from his lips. "I'll put it to you this way: I'll make sure to cry at his funeral." Sealed with a wink and kiss.

Greg pulled back, his eyes like probes analyzing every wrinkle, every facial tick. But Lisa gave him no morsel of doubt.

"So, are we on?"

"Yeah, but now I have to find a new freakin' office manager."

She laughed. "You'll find one."

"I'm sure I will. Anyway, I'll contact Patrick. But I'm gonna need a down payment."

She pulled an envelope from her purse. "I knew you would say that. I have five thousand dollars, so I can give you fifteen hundred and him thirty-five hundred."

"That's it?" Greg replied, eyebrows furrowed. "And why does he get two grand more than me?"

"Are you pulling the trigger?"

Greg had nothing to retort. "All right. You have a point."

"I know I do. And I'd like to meet the man who's going to make me a widow, so you'll get the money then. I want to make sure we're all on the same page. Sound like a plan?"

He took a second, then said, "Yeah. I'll contact him and let you know through the burner."

"Good. Thanks, baby." She stuffed the envelope back in her purse, then pulled out a pair of sunglasses.

"When do you want this to happen, by the way?"

Pushing the door open, she said, "Reunion night."

CHAPTER 9

QUINTON

"Get. The. Fuck. Outta. Here."

She stepped out of Greg's car wearing dark shades, but with the high-powered zoom of his Canon camera, Quinton spotted the strawberry-shaped birthmark on his sister-in-law's neck. Positive ID. "For real, what the hell is she… Ain't this a bitch?"

As he clicked away, freeze-framing the apparent aftermath of creeping, it didn't take long for him to confirm Aanya's suspicions. But he never imagined his brother's wife would be tangled up in it. Quinton knew Greg tapped it before, so it made sense they completed the remix version ten years later. But within view of Gerald's job, messing around on the low while Gerald slaved at a desk to take care of his unemployed selfish bitch of a wife?

"Oh, hell naw," he said, still clicking. "Man, she got some nerve."

He had arrived a little after five, when he expected most workers already hightailed out, as Aanya described. Quinton parked at a nearby strip mall, which provided him with the perfect aerial-like view of the half-empty car lot because of the mall's inclined position. Through his camera lens, he stumbled on Greg's Rover next to a silver Altima, the only two cars parked in a secluded corner near a dumpster. He couldn't see what was going on inside because of the tinted windows, but Quinton documented every second of Lisa exiting Greg's Rover, her looking around, and then getting into her car. With her reputation for porno-level blowjobs in high school, even given the nickname "Lockjaw," it didn't take a rocket scientist to figure out what went down.

Lisa sped up the hilly road that ran alongside the strip mall. Quinton dipped behind the steering wheel as she slowed to a Stop sign. His demon sister-in-law was tapping the wheel, bobbing to whatever was playing on the radio. She drove off, heading down the back roads that led to his brother's house.

"I oughta run her over," Quinton said, flaring up to exact street justice in his brother's honor. "Bet she—damn!"

The camera juggled between his hands and banged the steering wheel, but Quinton kept it from hitting the floor. Blinded by his rage toward Lisa, he had missed Greg pulling out of the parking lot. Like he had ants in his pants, Quinton placed the camera in the passenger seat and re-strapped his seat belt. Engine revved up, he backed out of his spot and hit the strip mall exit. A small dip between the lot and road rattled the car, causing the camera to bounce off the seat onto the floor mat.

Unfazed, Quinton zeroed in on Greg, his focus sharp as a laser. Greg turned right on the main street that led to Highway 1.

"You ain't gettin' away, punk."

Quinton covered the quarter-of-a-mile distance between his car and Greg's in seconds, mimicking the route of his new nemesis, the drumbeat rhythm of his heart rising at the same pace as the odometer. On one hand, playing undercover cop electrified him, the power he felt, knowing a target couldn't see him but he could see their every move—like when he was a kid playing hide-and-seek from his friends and brother. But on the other hand, Lisa had lit a fireball of anger that made his forearm muscles twitch. That bold bitch apparently got pipe from the man that would write Gerald's checks.

And yet, as Quinton approached the highway on-ramp that Greg had hit a moment earlier, a giddy sense of joy also bubbled in him. Within minutes of parking near the crime scene, he already had evidence against Aanya's husband—the same evidence that Quinton hoped would send Greg packing.

But he had dirt on Lisa, too. A two-for-one deal, since he knew his brother could do better. Quinton never understood how Lisa had him suckling on the same pussy juice for damn near half his life.

Quinton stayed in the right lane about three cars behind, while Greg rode the middle, their speed teetering on 75 miles-per-hour. He mulled over the next course of action—tell Gerald, confront Lisa, text Aanya—*who* and *what*? Glancing at the phone in the passenger seat, he thought about texting Lisa to out her ass.

But he shook off the what-to-do's, at least for now. Quinton knew the playa's handbook well, and a franchise playa like Greg wasn't heading home. Not yet. Too early. Greg would slip up again before the end of the day, and Quinton would use footage of some other stray broad to incriminate him.

Greg exited on Carmel Road and entered a residential area, with mostly one-story houses. A typical suburban neighborhood, the kind where a ball would bounce in front of a driver with a kid running behind it. Or where lonely housewives and single moms creep with married men, while little Timmy goofed around in a classroom.

Greg passed a cul-de-sac on the left side of the street, slowed, then parked in front of a small blue house on the right. Quinton hooked a left on the cul-de-sac and parked behind a truck. He pointed his camera at the front door of the mystery house. Operation Private Eye recommenced.

A grin crept up the corner of Quinton's cheek. He had Greg's bitch ass in the cross hairs of his lens. With the precision and cool demeanor of an assassin, Quinton snapped away. If his camera had been a rifle, he could've splattered half of Greg's brain against the windshield.

"For real, I should've been a hitman."

The front door opened. A woman with shoulder-length, black hair stepped onto the porch, wearing a tank top and short shorts that Quinton first thought were panties. She looked like a bombshell version of a much younger Connie Chung, and had the same kind of physical traits that qualified for Quinton's wall of fame.

"Got 'em again," he said, snapping shots of a hug and kiss before they disappeared inside.

Greg had taken the label "dog" to new heights. Quinton had smashed multiple women in the same day before, but Quinton's instinct told him Greg had pulled his unprotected dick out of Lisa's mouth twenty minutes earlier, and was now rollin' up on some other piece of ass—all before coming home to wifey, Aanya. Lowdown super ho scandalous shit.

In his stream of text messages, Aanya's last text said: Just wanted to let you know it was wonderful to see you again. I've been thinking about you ever since. Thank you for taking this on.

Easiest gig I ever had, Quinton thought. As he predicted, Greg's afternoon booty call detour came shortly after hooking up with Lisa. He typed a message bound to spark a major life change: **Hey, we need to talk soon. Got dirt already.**

While digging up dirt on Greg, he didn't know his sister-in-law would come up soiled, too. He clicked on his contact for Gerald. They hadn't spoken in so long—not a voice message, a text, a damn Facebook comment. Quinton stopped the cold war between them with a phone call. No answer, though, only Gerald's voicemail.

"Hey, bro. It's been a while. We need to meet up and squash this. Gotta talk to you about something urgent, too."

CHAPTER 10

GERALD

"Must be kinda cool to work for a guy you went to school with, huh?"

Gerald felt a tick against his cheek. If not low enough already, Gossip Twin Bethany shoved his ego down another notch. He grabbed a plastic fork that he wanted to jab into something other than salami and cheese and nibbled his bottom lip before he said, "Yeah. It's just… peachy."

Gerald loaded up his plate with sourdough bread, macaroni salad, and fruit. As he walked back to his seat at the conference table, he surveyed his staff. Typical chatter among them. Blabbing about nothing with their mouths full, from last night's episode of *Grey's Anatomy* to a run in somebody's panty hose. They had no idea of the smoke polluting Gerald from the inside, a gaseous cesspool swirling and growing closer to detonation. He'd rather roam the streets of Times Square naked in ten-degree weather than wait with thirsty co-workers for job cockblocker Greg Stephens to make his grand entrance.

They didn't have to wait long. As Gerald leaned over to place his food on the table, Greg walked in with his boss, Managing Director Carla Tibbins. The two were laughing and smiling like bosom buddies. Every nerve in Gerald's body exploded at the mere sight of Greg's smug ass.

"Hello everyone, and happy Friday. I'd like to formally introduce—"

"Gerald, watch it!" Cheryl, his co-worker, cried.

Damn! So caught up in seeing Greg chumming with the woman that backstabbed him, Gerald knocked over his cup of apple juice, spilling it onto the oak table. If not for Cheryl's quick reflex, a liberal dose would've stained her shirtsleeve.

All heads turned to Gerald. Greg broke a few seconds of awkward silence when he said, "Just like in high school, hey, Gerald?"

Laughter filled the room. Gerald tried to join in on the fun with a few chuckles, even at his own expense. Slightly embarrassed with no snappy comeback, he replied, "Yup, still a klutz. Just like in high school."

Gerald used Cheryl's napkins to wipe up the mess while his co-workers stared at the clumsiest man in the department. Cheryl shot him a glare that could slice a man's face off.

He whispered, "Sorry, Cheryl."

"Just get me another napkin, please."

He slid his napkin to her. Cheryl took it without looking back.

"Anyway," Carla said, "if you haven't figured it out, Greg and Gerald went to high school together. You graduated at the same time, too, right?"

"That's correct, Carla," Greg said, cheesing so hard Gerald thought he heard Greg's jawbone crack. Such a master of masks, putting his best face forward for his audience.

"Greg comes to us from Western Financial," Carla said, "and we're lucky to have him as our new regional director." She placed a hand on his back, which Gerald found odd. "I'll let Greg introduce himself to you all."

"Thank you, Carla. I'll make it quick since I know we're all eating here." He rubbed his belly. "I could use a plate or two myself."

Gossip Twins Bethany and Christine cracked a few giggles, all for a comment not meant for comedic relief. But charm dripped off Greg like some kind of mutant swag superpower, and the ladies seemed to lick it up.

"It's especially an honor for me to assume the duties from William Paulson, a man I've greatly admired from afar." He nodded toward Gerald. "And thank you for holding it down after William left, Gerald. You did an excellent job."

Oh, why'd you have to go there? Punk move from someone who clearly won, especially in front of coworkers. But despite the underhanded backslap disguised as a compliment, Gerald kept it cool. He gave Greg a thumbs up while stuffing more macaroni salad into his mouth.

Greg's voice morphed into slow-mo garbled noise, stripped away of anything intelligible. Although zoned out, Gerald watched how Greg moved, his hand gestures, the eye contact. Dressed in a semi-casual blazer and jeans, Greg commanded center stage with an apparent Toastmaster skill of speech. Judging by the famished looks of each female staffer, including Carla, Gerald imagined they would have to wring out their soaked panties at some point.

Gerald reemerged from his spaced-out departure when Greg said, "So I appreciate your time and thank you for having me. I'll be meeting with each of you soon."

In keeping with department tradition once a new employee finished a spiel, most of Gerald's coworkers clapped, although a half-hearted effort on Gerald's part. Greg grabbed a plate and mingled with his new staff, while Carla retreated to her office. Plate in hand, Bossman sat between the Gossip twins, directly across from Gerald.

Great. Now I have to face this fool.

Gerald finished his macaroni salad and was about to excuse himself when Christine asked, "So, what was Gerald like in high school? Was he always so... I don't know..." She looked at Gerald, then back to Greg and said, "Stuffy?"

Greg fist-covered his mouth to stifle laughter while Gerald frowned, his lips parted like he wanted to break his no-cuss word rule, only for her.

Greg swallowed, then said, "Stuffy as in, what? Uptight?"

She giggled. "Yes."

Gerald eased his chair back and stood up. "I like how you two are talking about me like I'm not here."

"Oh, it's all good, buddy. She just asked a question." Greg turned back to Christine. "Actually, this guy was pretty laid back, quiet. Honor roll student, too, so I don't know what happened."

Gerald shook his head. *Did he just say, 'I don't know what happened?'*

Greg said, "And he was dating a nice-looking girl named Lisa Townes, who's now his wife, believe it or not. Hell, even *I* had a little crush on her."

"Oh, I've seen her," Bethany said. "She is pretty. Lovely eyes. I was a little surprised Gerald pulled her."

"Me, too," Greg said.

Gerald stuffed his used Styrofoam in a corner trash can with a fist. "Yeah, we both married up," he said, slapping his hands together to remove leftover crumbs.

"We're lucky guys."

"Hmmph. Yes, we are."

That sleazy look… something about how the corners of Greg's mouth crept up and eyebrows dipped in the middle of his forehead, as if sending reminders that he'd tasted Lisa long before Gerald put a ring on it. Or maybe Gerald simply couldn't shake the video reel of them smacking belly buttons. Whatever the case, the stench of Greg's cologne and arrogance gripped Gerald's throat, suffocating him. Gerald had to get away from that fool and everyone else.

"Excuse me, you guys," Gerald said.

He stepped out of the conference room, escaping the thick humiliation of professional failure manifested into one Greg Stephens. Whether real or imagined, the whispers behind his back grew loud, and they all asked the same damn question: *"How could a man work as interim director for weeks, but lose the permanent position to someone else?"*

The answer would have to come from the woman who betrayed him, Greg's number one nutsack rider, Carla. Gerald headed to her office to demand answers, something he knew he should've done a long time ago. He knocked on the door, which was cracked open.

"Yes?"

He poked his head in. "Hey, Carla. Got a minute?"

"Sure," she said, her fingers still tapping the keyboard. "Have a seat."

Gerald kept the door cracked, then sat in one of the two leather seats across from her—a small upgrade from Greg's wooden interrogation chair, but still nothing like a throne with a "gangsta lean" adjustment for propping feet on a desk. He glanced at the assortment of framed pictures decorating Carla's L-shaped desk—a USC-bound teenage son, twin pre-teen daughters, and her husband being named Attorney of the Year by the California Bar Association. They looked like a Fresh Prince of Bel Air-styled family.

Carla faced him, fingers interlocked. "What's on your mind?"

Gerald took in a deep breath. "Well, I'll just come out with it. I'd like to know why I wasn't selected for the regional director position. I was doing a lot of the work when William left."

"I know. And you did a good job."

"I thought I did, too, so I'm somewhat at a loss. I've been here eight years. *Eight* years. I know the work, the company, the, uh, people, right?"

"I agree."

"Been office manager for nearly six."

"That's true."

"Then this new guy comes in, doesn't know a lick. But he gets the job that I was doing while it was vacant."

"Look, I understand you're upset, but here's the deal." Carla eased back in the chair and crossed her legs. "During your last performance evaluation, William and I discussed with you some areas that needed improvement."

"Yes, but—"

"We also couldn't overlook the fact that Greg has more managerial experience."

"What are you saying? I have plenty of experience. And I was doing a lot of William's work after he transferred. You…" Gerald collected himself before the wrong words forced him into the unemployment line. "Did William give his input before he left?"

"Yes. And he felt you still weren't quite ready."

"Oh," Gerald replied, dropping his head. "I see."

Puncture wound, right to the gut, flattening and deflating the few scraps of pride Gerald had left. True, he had a few episodes of conflict with William, the usual chain of command disagreements, but he never thought William would kick the ladder from under his feet as a parting gift. *Wow*.

"Gerald, it may help to look over your last performance evaluation again."

"Sure. Well, I guess that's that." He stood up and held his head high; yet, struggled to hold together his battered ego. "Thank you for your time."

He closed the door behind him. As Gerald had done when he left Greg's office, he stood still for a moment to compose himself, his spirit dumped, weakened, and drained. He walked past the conference room, saw the gang still having a ball without him.

At his cubicle, Gerald pulled open the bottom drawer of the file cabinet next to his desk. He kept his performance evaluations in a manila folder and grabbed the most recent.

"Hmmm."

Gerald re-read the remarks on the first page. Not the greatest evaluation, but above average, at least. Under most bulleted categories, it had boxes checked for "Exceeds Expectations" and "Outstanding." However, under the bullets "Problem Solving" and

"Cooperativeness - Working with People," Gerald only "Meets Expectations." His ex-boss William Paulson thought Gerald had an okay working relationship with his co-workers and subordinates, but lacked leadership skills. Apparently, not very proactive, either, especially when it came to anticipating problems and suggesting solutions. As a result, William thought Gerald couldn't handle the next step. But Greg could.

Gerald placed the form back in the manila folder and kicked the drawer shut. *I might have to find another job.*

Ten minutes before the close of business at five, Bethany placed a report in Gerald's inbox. "Here you go," she had said, all chipper and oblivious, as if proud she finished a project—although he had told her he needed time to look it over before submission. At least thirty minutes.

Gerald had no plans to stay past five, nor did he feel like dealing with Bethany, so he shut down his computer, grabbed his bag, and dipped out. Gerald couldn't remember the last time he left before five, but he made an exception today. Before he gave the workday a big "F you," he managed to utter a dry "see you tomorrow" to Alicia, but nothing more to anyone else.

Before driving off, he checked the messages in his phone. Nothing from Lisa, but a few days ago, his brother Quinton left a voicemail that Gerald hadn't heard, yet. He promised Aunt Frieda he would try to mend the cracks between him and his twin, but not today. He wasn't in the mood to talk to anyone, including his wife. At least, not now. He even terminated the radio because of the commercials. Too much babble, all noise. With limited mental capacity to deal with people, he set a course for the Wharf to indulge in a main dish of peace.

On Crystal Drive, surrounded by four and five-star hotels that lined the Monte Clara shoreline, he stopped at a red light. Two young girls with backward baseball caps and skateboards rolled across the street. Then he saw her.

Damn!

She rocked heels and a short skirt like a boss. Muscles in her thighs flexed as she sashayed toward the other side of the street, her heels clicking against the pavement. Dark golden skin, tufts of long jet-black hair bobbing against her back.

Fine.

He'd never seen a woman work a downtown street like a catwalk. When she came into better view, Gerald squinted. She looked like an exotic mix between the model Iman and Nicole What's-Her-Name, lead singer of The Pussycat Dolls from back in the day, but with a little more melanin.

"Wait a minute," he said, now watching the hem of the skirt bounce against her backside. "Is that Yara? Yara Bassili?"

As a teenager, he had crushed on Yara harder than Quinton crushed on Aanya. Philip was the luckiest dude in Monte Clara to land her. Unfortunately, Gerald heard Philip passed while on deployment in Afghanistan.

"I need to find out if that's—"

Beep, beep.

The truck behind him yanked Gerald's head out of the clouds. Green light.

He drove on, but fate wasn't in his favor. Scanning both sides of the street, he couldn't find one open meter. When he looked in the rearview, he couldn't find her, either. Gone.

"Damn!" he cried.

Gerald saw a man get into a car about half-a-mile in front of him, parked next to a meter. As luck would have it, the meter was within a few steps of Gerald's favorite bench by the water. He sped up to mark his territory, then slowed to a stop, right blinker flashing. The car pulled out and circled into the opposite lane.

As he parked, Gerald's mood revived and brightened.

"If that was Yara, she must be in town for the reunion," he said, cutting off the engine. He'd been so wrapped up in marriage and work woes, Gerald had no idea who was attending the reunion, although he knew the numbers had increased.

Before stepping out, he checked the Facebook reunion page and noticed Yara had marked "Attending," too.

"Nice," he said, big smile strapped.

He went to her page, checking out the pictures and comments she'd posted. Flawless beauty. Lost in her photo albums, another ten minutes flew by.

He paid the meter for an hour's worth of solo time. Stepping onto the grass, he saw "his" bench empty. "Good. Got my bench to my damn self."

As Gerald walked toward his bench, the salty breeze brushed against his skin. Embracing the solitude, Yara latched onto his thoughts. High school fantasies that he'd long suppressed resurfaced and flooded his mind, as Yara's ghostly presence guided him to a state of tranquility.

Then the light bulb lit up. *Wow*.

He realized something: Thoughts of Lisa sparked emotional disarray, usually a mash of stress and anxiety. Then he would try to repair his own turmoil by initiating moments of love with her, most of the time with fail.

But a woman from his past, one he barely knew beyond a name and hadn't seen in years, somehow became a weapon of serenity. Gerald didn't know if she alone or the possibility of her made the thousand tingles fire up in his gut.

Whatever the case, part of him wanted to find out.

CHAPTER 11
LISA

For the first time in a long time, the thought of Gerald made Lisa smile. But as a *dead* man.

She would be his widow, bestowed with half a million dollars from a life insurance payout. Freedom to do whatever and whomever she wanted without consequence. She watched herself in the mirror while brushing her hair, a sunshine glow rapt in her face.

Gerald poked his head in the bathroom. "All right, babe, gotta pay the bills. I freakin' hate Mondays… What are you smiling about?"

"Huh? Oh, um, just thinking about the reunion," she lied. "Attending RSVPs are up to sixty-two on Facebook."

"Sixty-three. I just checked. Have all those people paid?"

"I think so. I'll find out at the meeting today."

"Wow, good job pumping up the numbers."

"I'm not done yet. My goal is to reach eighty by the end of the week."

"I wouldn't be surprised. Those YouTube videos have really helped out, too, I bet."

"Yes, they have." She yanked pieces of hair from the brush and dropped the strands in a nearby trashcan.

"Soooooo…" Gerald said, leaning against the doorway. "Who's behind the mask in the videos? The reunion page is blowing up.

People wanna know. Shoot, *I* wanna know!"

"It's a secret."

"That's messed up. Well, whoever it is they're hilarious."

"I know, right? Oh, I forgot to ask over the weekend. How was your favorite bench?"

Gerald cocked his head sideways. "How did you know that?"

"You butt-dialed me again last Friday. Something about 'my favorite bench is open,' I think."

"Oops." Gerald bumped his head against the wall in cadence with "dumb, dumb, dumb."

"Boy, you bet not ever commit a crime because you will always get caught."

"Ouch."

"Exactly."

"Okay, well, I'll see you later. Have a good time at your reunion meeting."

Before he headed out, Lisa asked, "Are you feeling better?"

"About what? Oh…" Gerald sighed. "Yeah, I'm good. I had all weekend to make peace with it. Decided to keep doing my job until I find a better one. Speaking of that, there's an opening at my company for an admin assistant. I can send the link."

Lisa turned to him, forehead wrinkled from a hard frown. "What? You okay with me working at the same place as my ex-boyfriend, as you say?" she asked, a hand on her waist. "I thought you didn't like him."

"I don't. He's a jerk. But I know you're having a hard time with good job leads, so I figured I'd be on the lookout. I just want you to be happy. Plus, I trust you."

Trust. Lisa wanted to keel over from laughter. "Well, thank you."

"You're welcome."

Fool, I stopped looking for full-time work a month ago. What's the point? I won't need to work after I cash that insurance check.

Gerald turned to walk away, but stopped. "By the way, I'm sorry about bringing up the baby thing." His back to Lisa, Gerald dropped his head, as if trying to assemble the right words. "I can't apologize enough about the vasectomy. I just went into panic mode, I guess."

"Gerald, stop apologizing. As I told you before, I'm not even sure I want a baby, yet. I just didn't like not knowing about your vasectomy until after we got married, you know?"

Now facing her, Gerald replied, "I know."

"But, listen, if you really want to try for a baby, we can discuss getting your thingy working again when we're truly ready, okay? Have a serious discussion about it." *Yeah, right. You won't be around long enough for that.*

"My thingy, huh?" He laughed.

"Yes. Thingy."

"Okay. I'd like that."

Lisa grabbed a Q-Tip from a cup and noticed Gerald staring. "Boy, why are you staring at me?"

"I don't know. There's something different about you, and I like it. I could stare at you forever. I just hope I get that chance."

The Q-Tip dangled in Lisa's fingers, then fell on the bathroom rug. Gerald had a way of saying the sweetest things at the most random moments, making Lisa drop her guard a bit. But as she bent down to pick up the Q-Tip, she refortified the cold shell around her heart to shut him down. His penchant for spontaneous chivalry and cornball romance had played out.

"You know it's 7:43, right?" She threw the Q-Tip in the trash and grabbed another one. "You're going to be late."

"Right," Gerald replied, looking like a balloon with its air let out. He turned away and picked up his leather case. "Okay. Um, well, I'll see you later."

"Okay. Have a good day at work."

"Yeah. Thanks."

Part of Lisa felt pity for Gerald. His valiant efforts showed her how much he loved her, but every time he tried to get close he slammed into Lisa's brick walls. The dutiful husband, trying to measure up to the standard of a real man, but coming up short. On his best day, he could never be like Greg.

But since Gerald's days were numbered, it didn't hurt to resurrect some semblance of a good wife. Lisa had no doubts that Greg would make the plan work with his cousin. Money always talks; six figures screams. Until then, Lisa decided to bend a little and have a heart. Maybe even cook more and give it up on occasion.

When she heard the front door close, Lisa retrieved her tennis shoes from the closet, prepping to go about her business like any other day. Soliciting a hit on her husband felt natural, about as normal as asking a handyman to fix a leaky faucet. She had treaded into uncharted territory, a dark place where the most malevolent piece of her soul had been given free reign. And now that she unleashed her inner evil, she couldn't wait to get her plan underway.

She grabbed her car keys off the kitchen table. Even if she tried, the new alter ego Lisa had created and welcomed so freely couldn't find one ounce of guilt. It took a special kind of woman to lie about the possibility of a child to a man she planned to murder.

"I guess I'm like one of those women in a Lifetime movie," Lisa said with a laugh. "One cold bitch."

Bellows of laughter clashed against Lisa's eardrums the moment she opened the glass door to Starbucks. The IBRC—Itty Bitty Reunion Committee, as they called themselves—was all there. Craig, Marla, Deb, Mark, and now, Lisa.

The group had huddled up on a couch around Mark, who was holding a tablet. Various drinks littered the small, wooden table in front of them, from water to cafe lattes. None of them seemed to notice the numerous pairs of eyes that cut at them.

"There she is," Marla said, a stay-at-home mom and one-woman pep rally.

Mark patted the cushion of a chair next to the couch. "Hey, Lisa. Glad you could make it. Have a seat."

Lisa sat down, setting her purse between her feet. "If I didn't know better, I would think you guys were getting hammered over here. What's everybody laughing at?"

"Your mystery man," Craig said.

"Or woman," Deb said.

Mark unpaused the video on the tablet. In the clip, a young man stood in front of a classroom chalkboard in a classic Hip Hop stance reminiscent of the ancient 80s, wearing red skin-tight jeans, a psychedelic T-shirt with bright colors, and a fedora hat.

Lisa remembered him from school, widely known through Monte Clara High social media channels as the "father of the modern-day skinny-jeans movement." Andre something.

Mark turned up the volume. In the background, a falsetto voice with a British accent said, "This guy looks like a pack of highlighters. If P. Diddy and Kanye West had a baby, you'd get Andre McGwire." They all hollered, including Lisa.

"He does look like that, though!" Mark cried, wiping a tear from his cheek. "That's what makes it so damn funny!"

"Kanye Diddy," Marla said. "Or K. Diddy, maybe?"

Deb blurted out, "Kanyiddy?"

More outbursts of laughter. In hysterics, Craig leaned back and kicked the table. The cups threatened to tip over, but quick hands from Marla and Lisa stopped them, preventing a puddle.

"Oh!" Craig grabbed his plastic container of ice water. Others followed suit. "Sorry about that. That was close."

Marla turned to Lisa. "This is all your fault."

"What are you talking about?" Lisa asked.

"We've spent the last fifteen minutes laughing at these videos. And you won't even tell us who it is." She wagged a finger at Lisa. "That's *you* in the videos, isn't it?"

Lisa paused, mainly for theatrical effect. After about five seconds of suspense, she said, "Like I told you guys before, I'm not revealing my secrets. Too bad, so sorry. Like the Blue Devil says at the end of each video, if you want to know who he or she is, you have to come to the reunion."

"Ugh!" Marla grunted. "You are so evil!"

Lisa smiled. *Bitch, you have no idea.*

"I think these videos are brilliant," Mark said. "They've gotten people talking and excited about the reunion."

"Exactly," Lisa consigned. "From a marketing standpoint, it's genius."

"All right, all right." Marla looked at her phone. "Sorry, but we need to move on. I have to be somewhere in thirty minutes."

"Yeah, she's right, me, too," Craig said, retrieving a tablet from the bag near his feet. "Let's get this underway."

The group had met three times, and in each meet up, Lisa was impressed with committee leader Craig and his grandiose approach to event planning. Lisa had never even heard of a reunion committee, much less one as formalized as the IBRC. But in Craig's view, former classmates were parting with hard-earned money for reunion tickets, gas, and in some cases, flights and hotels—all to mingle with old friends, acquaintances, and former lovers for a few hours. That kind of night didn't come around often, so Craig convinced committee members that the evening should be epic and memorable, a party talked about for years.

"First off," Craig said, "I just want to say great job to Lisa for coming up with the video idea. Very creative." They all clapped.

"Thank you," Lisa said.

"I can't believe your husband, Gerald, got clowned in one of those videos, too," Mark said.

Lisa shrugged. "Hey, no one's off limits, so beware. You may even see me on there."

Mark said, "That's cold."

"*Very* cold," Craig said. "But I like it. The videos definitely have an impact. I was looking over the Facebook page analytics and participation has jumped 600 percent. Average attendance of previous 10-year reunions at this school has hovered around 37 percent, and we've far surpassed that number."

"And Yara Bassili will be there." Deb winked at Craig.

"Oh, stop it," Craig said, brushing her off. "That was just a high school crush."

"Yeah, right," Mark said. "You and everyone else. Say, how'd you get that data, anyway?"

"C'mon, he's a statistician at a marketing firm," Marla said. "He knows where to look."

"Right about that," Craig replied. "Also, did you know our class has one of the highest number of high school-sweetheart marriages? In at least the last thirty years. Lisa and I are included in that stat."

Not for long, Lisa thought.

Craig continued, "If you take a look at the Facebook comments, you can see that people are really engaged. Attendance payments have quadrupled in the last two weeks. I know some folks who weren't coming until those videos started, so we want to keep that momentum going."

Lisa asked, "How, exactly?"

"With money," Mark said. "Something simple, like a Guess the Identity contest. Before you got here, Lisa, we had the idea of some type of raffle where the attendees can guess the identity of the person in the video to win two hundred and fifty dollars."

"Money always motivates people into action," Deb said. "We have the cash for it, since we're nearing 80 attendees who have already paid. That's 80 out of 127 graduates."

"Really?" Lisa said, wide-eyed. "I thought it was like sixty-something?"

"That's just Facebook, my dear," Craig said. "Since our last meeting we had several people pay Deb directly who don't do social media."

"But, somehow, they saw the videos," Deb said, laughing. "I'm telling you, this video thing has gone viral... at least among our senior class."

"And we need to capitalize on it," Marla said. "So, what do you think about the raffle idea?"

"I like it," Lisa said. "Who's the Blue Devil? Let's do it."

"Nice," Craig said, pressing against his tablet. "So, Lisa, just keep doing what you're doing with those videos and please inform the mystery mascot about the contest. I just hope I don't see any pictures of me featured."

"My contact and I have emailed a few times," Lisa said, "but I have no control over what he or she chooses to post. I'm waiting to see what's next just like everybody else."

"Really? Okay, as long as you can make sure this mystery person shows his or her face at the reunion, then the contest is a go. Lisa, once you confirm, work with Deb about promoting the contest on social media and such." Craig checked his watch. "So that's covered. Let's move on."

The spotlight on the videos dimmed when the order of business shifted to logistics, mainly about catering services and who to hire as deejay. Lisa kept up the charade, but she was preoccupied by the devil on her shoulder. Her alter ego itched for a reply from Greg about the "kill deal."

"Lisa!" Deb said, snapping her fingers in Lisa's face. "Damn, where did you go? Your purse just buzzed."

Lisa restrained her alter ego from yanking clumps of hair out of Deb's scalp; nobody snapped fingers in her face without a verbal whiplash or backhand slap. But when she grabbed the phone and saw an alert from the burner icon, Deb and everyone else became an afterthought.

Lisa stood up. "I have to take this. Be right back."

As she stepped outside, the burner buzzing stopped. "Shoot," she said, scrambling toward the parking lot. This type of conversation wasn't meant for the public. In the safety of her car, her alter ego could let loose.

She was about to call Greg back when a burner text message froze her: Tried to call to tell you it's on. He can meet up this weekend. Get that down payment ready.

CHAPTER 12

YARA

"You feel so damn good!" Their cheeks touched, rubbing Oliver's potholed chin and sweat against Yara's face. "Rachel has nothing on you, baby."

Yara rolled her eyes as she moved her head away, but didn't say a word. In contrast, Oliver couldn't keep quiet; the "NaNa" wouldn't let him. The asshole actually laughed a little the moment he blurted out that nonsense about his wife. He had the nerve to say her name while inside another woman, as if comparing Yara's goods to his spouse of six years—and mother of his children—would somehow translate to a compliment.

Yara felt her stomach turn. She swallowed a glob of saliva that had built up inside her mouth.

"Awww!" Oliver cried, clenching his teeth. Yara saw veins pushing against his neck like small snakes trying to bore through tight fabric. He then raised himself onto his knees, gripping her inner thighs and digging stubby fingers into her flesh. Dr. Long Stroke liked her spread eagle while watching it dip inside and out before the grand finale. Yara knew that "screwtine" from their first time together.

Yara pressed her hands against the headboard, breasts bouncing from her chest to chin. He had kicked into another gear, and judging from the grunts and gritted teeth, he would pop any minute.

As she suspected, Oliver's curses became more rapid and garbled, matching the fury in his thrusts. He seemed to go into a full body arrest before he collapsed on Yara's chest.

Yara swallowed a larger glob of spit.

"Wooo!" he said, heaving in waves of air. "I wish—"

"Get off me." Yara pressed her hands against his shoulders.

Lifting his head, Oliver said, "Oh, sorry, I was just—"

"Get off me!" she cried, shoving him with so much force he almost catapulted into the lamp on the nightstand.

Yara hopped out of bed and sprinted toward the bathroom, nearly stumbling when her knees knocked against each other. She reached the door and slammed it behind her. With acid erupting inside her throat, Yara dropped to her knees, lifted the lid, and grabbed clumps of hair before her stomach contents flooded the toilet.

"You okay in there?"

It took her a few seconds to respond. "I-I'm okay," she said, hauling in breaths. "Just give me a second."

Her gut contracted, and a second ripple spewed into the toilet, but not as much. She hadn't been this sick in a while. The meds usually kept the nausea under control, but she didn't have any in her system.

"You need me to get help?" His voice sounded like a whimper.

"No, I said I'm fine," she yelled, flushing the toilet.

Yara took in a deep breath, then used the sink counter to help her stand. Still a little dizzy, she wiped away sweat beads from her forehead and moist spots around her lips with a washcloth. Leaning over the sink, she turned to each side, spot-checking her face, hair, and breasts in the mirror. No physical evidence of spillage anywhere, just a rancid aftertaste.

Yara heard the television, which brought some relief, since it kept Oliver occupied and out of her business. Her bearings now back, she eased into the middle of the bathroom and stood still, staring at herself in the mirror. Standing alone and naked in her most vulnerable state, she saw a shadow of the woman she once was. A carbon-copy Yara, abused and broken, trying so hard to heal on its own, but still scathed, scabbed, and scarred from personal tragedies that killed her previous life.

So much had changed in the past three years. Before Philip died, Yara blossomed, ready for any and all challenges with her soulmate riding by her side. She loved the adventure that came with being the wife of a career military man, as well as the stability it provided. But most of all, she loved her husband. Philip in uniform was sexier than the best-looking Hollywood bachelor, and she wanted nothing more than to "be all she could be" for her handsome marine.

While Philip was deployed, they became a formidable team—him holding it down during tours in Afghanistan and parts of Europe, and her in San Diego, sending him weekly care packages while keeping the household afloat. After finishing his time in southern California, they moved north where Philip was assigned to the VA hospital in Palo Alto for a short stint. Yara loved this shore-based assignment the most because it meant no deployments for at least two years. Yara actually got to live under the same roof as her husband for an extended period of time.

Like other married couples in their mid-to-late 20's, they had laid a map for new chapters—kids, house, travel. Philip wanted to make all of Yara's dreams come true; he knew how lucky he was to snag the hottest girl ever to come out of Monte Clara High. He made it his mission to make her smile every day, as dedicated to her as he was to the Core.

But life has a cruel way of pulling a 180 and fucking things up, often in ways you never expect. The strain of one tragedy can stretch the human brain to its breakable threshold; Yara had endured three in a row, each one involving Philip. The collective impact then clamped down hard on Yara, paving a self-destructive roadmap that ended up with her naked, spilling half her guts in a hotel bathroom after baiting another married man.

Yara hated what she saw. The old Yara was long gone, a figment.

"Hey, you've been in there a long time. You okay?"

"Yes," Yara said, snapping back to the present. She lied and said, "I'm much better. I'll be out in a second."

After washing her hands, Yara wet a washcloth and wiped the gooey mess between her legs. While removing Oliver's nasty remnants, she noticed a small bottle of mouthwash poking between an unzipped traveler's kit. She swished a few times, and spat it out.

After one last once-over, Yara wrapped a towel around her naked self, then cut the lights. As she stepped out, she saw Oliver lying under the sheets. He muted the TV and said, "Geez, I never made a woman puke after sex. I don't know if that's a good or bad thing."

Really? She walked to the opposite side of the bed. "Well, it's not a good thing."

"I suppose. There's a bottle of water on the nightstand, if you want it."

"Thanks. Do you have any gum?"

"Uh, yeah." Oliver grabbed his pants, digging into the pockets. A piece of gum hit her pillow. "Thanks."

Staring, Oliver said, "I fantasized about seeing you naked so many times."

"Now you have, and more." Yara dropped the towel and stood, sliding the panties up her legs. She blessed Oliver with one last view of her backside before covering it up for good.

"Are you leaving? I was hoping for another round."

Yara bent down for her bra. "Sorry. I have things to do."

"Dammit. Well, do you feel any better?"

"Yes." She strapped on the bra, her back still turned to him. "I already said I did."

"That's good. You're not pregnant, are you?"

What in the world? She turned with the most intense WTF look she could muster. "I can't believe you asked me that. If I was, how could it be yours, ya dummy? We first hooked up like two weeks ago."

"Yeah, duh. Sorry I forgot condoms again."

Yeah, right. "I didn't remember to bring any, either. It's not like I do this a lot, anyway."

"Me, neither, even with my wife." He laughed.

Yara grabbed her shirt. "That shows how much you listen. I told you I can't have kids."

Oliver closed his eyes and uttered something under his breath. "Damn it. You did say that. I'm sorry to hear about your condition."

"It's okay." She sighed. "I deal with it."

Yara donned her shirt and flipped out her hair. She knocked back a few gulps of water while the "cat" had Oliver's tongue, and for the first time, he quit flapping his gums for at least a minute. But as they watched CNN in silence, Yara knew it wouldn't be long before stupid made its comeback.

Sure enough, the brain in his dick took over. He said, "So, when can we do this again?"

Never. "I don't know. Probably not until after the reunion."

"Okay. I tell ya, it's going to be weird seeing you there while I'm with the wife." Oliver propped his head up in his hand. "And I might be a little jealous if you bring someone else."

Yara sat on the side of the bed. "Ha, that's your problem. And like I told you before, as long as you don't say anything, I won't."

"My lips are sealed."

"Then you have nothing to worry about."

"Good. Although I'll be with someone else, I still hope to see you there. And find out who's behind those videos! Have you seen them? Whoever it is made fun of an old picture of me I didn't know existed."

Yara laughed for the first time since she entered his hotel room. She had seen the photo in the video, the makings of a viral meme. A sixteen or seventeen-year-old Oliver, the lone spectator in the picture, sat on the bottom bleachers in the gymnasium, watching girls on the varsity volleyball team in practice. He wore throwback "nerd" glasses. The person behind the mask said Oliver looked like a "creepy Bill Gates stalker."

"Yes, I saw it," she said. She grabbed her purse and stood to leave.

"Hey, before you go, can I ask you something?"

"What?"

Oliver edged toward her side of the bed. "Why did you agree to meet me? I mean, you didn't even know I existed in high school. I don't get it."

The gazillion dollar question. Only the "new" Yara could answer it. She took in a breath, exhaled, then said, "I admit, I was a little vulnerable when you first IM'd me. But I liked how you wined and dined me, even making me laugh."

"Hell, you made me laugh, too. Who knew someone so hot was also funny?"

"Right. Then the more we talked, the more our conversation got… you know…"

"Got a little freaky deaky."

Freaky deaky? Really? "Um, yeah. Freaky deaky. You'd also mentioned the dull sex with your wife, and I was going through a bit of a dry spell, so hey? Why not do each other a favor? Especially since we already know each other. Somewhat."

"Oh, okay. I think I understand. When you say vulnerable, you mean because of Philip?"

Sliding into her flip-flops, she replied. "You can say that."

"Man, I wanted to be Philip so bad back then."

Yara cut her eyes at him. "What did you say?"

"I mean, I would wish it was me instead of him as your boyfriend."

"Let me tell you something, no one can take the place of Philip, all right?" She jabbed a finger at him.

Oliver showed his hands. "Wait, whoa, I didn't mean anything by that. I was just saying—"

"I don't want you to ever say his name again! Bastard!" Yara wrapped her purse around her shoulder and jetted toward the door.

"Yara! I-I… hold on! Why are you getting mad? Let's calm down."

She swung the door open, refusing to look back. "Shut up!"

Storming down the hallway toward the elevator, she passed an old dirty ass geezer gawking at her. Just another prick reject of male vermin, a grandpa version of Oliver—probably cheating on grandma with a stupid skank half his age.

But as she stood alone at the elevator doors restraining tears, Yara knew she had sunk to the same low level as one of those skanks, no matter how hard she tried to justify her pain.

In the car, Yara tightened her grip around the steering wheel, muffling a seismic ripple that fired throughout her body. A thunderous scream erupted out of her, spurred by a colossal meltdown, the fabric of her soul ripping apart. A virus of hate that Yara had suppressed for so long nipped away at the invisible shield that kept her even-keeled. Rage now consumed her.

The cause of Yara's heartache looked down at her from the rearview mirror. "You see?" she cried to Philip's picture, tears streaming. "You're making me do this! This is all your fault!"

Yara slammed her head against the headrest, strands of hair sticking to her wet cheeks. She closed her eyes and let the tears rain down, cleansing the shame and the stubborn stink of male infestation. Taking deep breaths, her heart rate finally slowed, then the rage inside her dissipated, back to the steady ache that started when she learned Philip had done the unthinkable, shortly before he passed.

Yara had no idea how long she sat in the dark, but her storm subsided, so she grabbed the notebook in the passenger seat. Next to Oliver's name, she wrote the letters "BB." With the men before Oliver, she felt a twisted pleasure upon writing those letters, as if exorcising her demons. But not now. Not anymore.

She knew she had to stop her one-way path of destruction for good before it was too late.

Yara dialed a number she hadn't used in a while. The person on the other end picked up after two rings. "Dr. Kazarian? Yes, hi, it's Yara Bassili… yes, you, too… I know, long time… sorry I called your cell phone so late, but, um, you'd mentioned something about SKYPE for another session… yes, I think I need to start back up… tomorrow morning at nine… that will work for me. Thank you so much."

<hr />

"So, how was it?" Ladan asked, a hand on Yara's thigh.

Yara folded her knees up on the couch. "It was good. In some strange way, I missed her."

"Probably because she helps you stay level-headed."

Yara glanced out the living room window. Another beautiful day, sunny, no clouds. After her SKYPE session with Dr. Kazarian, Yara's mood mirrored the weather outside.

"I agree that she helps keep me focused," Yara said, playing with a strand of hair. "She suggested I start writing poetry again."

"Omigod, that's good!" Ladan cried, her response a little over-the-top. "Writing has always been therapeutic for you, sis."

"That's true. I've gotten away from what grounds me."

"I don't need to know what led you to speak to your therapist again. I'm just glad you're getting the help you need. I'm so proud of you." They hugged.

Yara said, "Thanks, sis."

"What about the med…" Ladan raised a hand. "Wait, I'll stop right there. You're taking the right steps, so I'll stop being Mom and Dad."

Yara stood and stretched her arms high above her head. "I'll be fine. Just trust me."

"I do. You want to go to the mall with me? I need to get a few things."

"Okay."

Ladan stood up. "I'm sure you have a lot of material for your poems."

"That was quick!" Yara pushed her sister with a playful nudge. "You're already being nosy!"

"Who, me?"

"Yes, you. Anyway." Yara picked up her tennis shoes. "I think this weekend I'm going to find a nice, quiet spot near the water and let it all flow out through the pen. The ocean has always been a source of inspiration for me."

"You know what, sis? That sounds like a great idea."

CHAPTER 13
QUINTON

"Damn, still nothing from her, yet? What the hell?"

Three texts from Quinton to Aanya, but not a word from her. Quinton thought she would break a finger trying to return his phone call, especially since she had hired him to find out the truth about her bitch-ass husband Greg in the first place. But either she hadn't gotten his messages, or had changed her mind. Quinton hoped that once Aanya kicked Greg to the curb, he would slide into Greg's spot and fill up that fresh hole in her heart. Instead, she ghosted him.

At least he'd gotten his money up front. But deep down, Quinton knew he would give it all back for the chance to comfort Aanya.

Frustrated, Quinton tossed his phone in the passenger seat. He eased to a stop in front of his brother's house, then cut the engine. Surveying his brother's lawn, Quinton didn't see brown spots, but a healthy dark-green and nice low-cut trim.

"Hmmm, much better," he said. The last time Quinton stopped by the house, spring had made its debut, but the grass was dying a slow patchy death. Quinton and Gerald had tag-teamed on a front yard rescue mission with the help of fertilizer, water, and a Tupac Hip Hop station on Pandora. That afternoon, they worked in the yard under eighty-degree heat, pulling up weeds, bumping

Tupac, being brothers. Quinton missed the little things, and as he unfastened his seatbelt, he hoped Gerald did, too.

Gerald walked down the porch steps onto the grass. Quinton noticed his brother's rounder frame and almost clowned Gerald for his new jelly rolls. But judging by a stone-faced Gerald, Quinton chose not to go there.

Quinton angled around the front of his car and stepped onto the curb. "What's up, bro? Long time, no see."

Gerald stopped at the edge of the grass, the width of the sidewalk separating them. "Yeah. It has been a long time. Since… let me see… oh, yeah, when I found you drunk and passed out the day of Ma's funeral."

Quinton rolled his eyes. *Here we go.* "C'mon, man. Why do we keep coming back to this?"

"Why? You know why. She was our mother. And you weren't there!"

"You think I don't know that? Damn, bro, how many times do I have to tell you? I just couldn't do it. Ma's death really messed me up."

"And you think it was easy for me? You didn't even come to the hospital. *I* was the one who visited every day. *I* was the one breaking my bank account for what Medicare wouldn't pay for. *I* was the one who covered for you when she would ask, 'Where's your brother?' All me."

"I know, I know. I regret all of it." Quinton took in a breath. "At least I paid you back. For real, I called a few times when she was in the hospital, didn't I?"

"What, and you think that makes up for not being there?"

Quinton ran a hand over his face. "No. I don't."

"I mean, it's bad enough Aunt Frieda and I were the only ones at the hospital when she passed. But you couldn't even make the funeral?"

Quinton looked away to avoid eye contact. Although he had deluded himself into thinking his brother would let it all go without a verbal assault, Gerald had a bomb on his chest and he wanted to set it off. Quinton steeled himself up and tried to take the blame like a man, refusing to go toe-to-toe with his only sibling.

"Look, bro, I'm sorry, all right?" Quinton said. "I couldn't see Ma like that."

"Like what, Q?"

"You know, all sickly and thin. She was always superwoman to me. I didn't want to see her as anything other than that."

"That's weak, man. No excuse. You should've been there, like I was."

"I know." Quinton looked around. "Why are we outside discussing personal business? Look, can we start over? That's what Ma would want. And you know that's what Aunt Frieda wants, too. She be calling me every week. I want the same thing, though."

Gerald cocked his head sideways. "And what's that exactly?"

"For you to forgive me. For us to be brothers again."

"Uh huh." Gerald nodded, still holding a frontline military stance. "That's hard to forgive, man. I think Ma was a little heartbroken before she passed, wondering about you. You didn't see her face the last few days like I had to."

Tears bubbled in the corners of Quinton's eyes, but they refused to fall. "I have to live with that regret for the rest of my life."

"As you should. And really, how do we start over?"

"I don't know, bro," Quinton replied, throwing has hands up. "How about we catch up like normal brothers do when they haven't seen each other in a while? Shoot, how's the job? How's Greg Stephens treating you?"

Gerald's forehead crumpled. "How did you know about that?"

"Well, let's just say I've been talking to his wife."

"What?" Gerald cried, clearly in shock. "Aanya? I knew you had a crush on her and all, but c'mon!"

"Quiet, man," Quinton said, dropping his voice to a whisper. "It's not like that."

Gerald shook his head. "Yeah, whatever. Trying to get at Greg's wife. You will never change."

"Man, look, she hired... wait, what 'chu mean by that?"

"You know what I mean," Gerald said, his eyes ice cold. "Getting laid was always the priority for you. That's probably why you couldn't visit your dying mother, huh? Too busy messing around with those chickenheads."

Quinton felt his temperature break the threshold of calm. "You need to chill, all right?"

"Chill? Forget you."

Quinton couldn't remember the last time Gerald let a cuss word slip out his mouth, if ever. But it still sounded as cold as "fuck you."

The gloves came off.

"Oh, it's like that?" Quinton said, stepping to his twin, ready for a trip to the ground if Gerald got froggy. "Uh huh. I see now."

Gerald crossed his arms. "See what?"

"You. Chest all out, tryna flex. You big and bad with me, but you got it wrong, bro. How come you can't break bad with Lisa? She's been whipping that ass for years and you don't say nothin'." Quinton snapped his fingers. "Oh, right. She got your whole fuckin' nutsack on lockdown."

In true Gerald fashion when the heat turned up, he backed away and turned around. "Bye, Quinton."

"Just walk away, huh?" Quinton said, raising his voice. "Why am I not surprised? I was gonna tell you sumn' you need to know, too, but forget it. I'll let you find out on your own."

Gerald reached the porch. "Fine with me."

"Yeah, okay. We'll see. I hope you calm your ass down by the reunion. You *are* still going, right?"

Gerald answered by closing the front door.

Still staring at the porch, Quinton said, "I guess I'll see you there. Punk ass."

When Quinton turned to leave, he saw Lisa's car coming down the street. Perfect timing.

Lisa stopped beside Quinton's car. "Heeey," she said, her window sliding down. "What are you doing here?"

"Visiting my brother," he snapped, opening his car door. "What do you think?"

"Oh. Okay. Just a little surprised. Haven't seen you in a while."

"Yeah."

As he sat down, the door still open, he turned and gazed at her. She looked stuck. Confused, maybe, as if she didn't know how to marry the words from her mouth to the words in her brain. But in those few seconds of pause, Quinton also endured an inward struggle, each half of his conscience at odds: *I can bust her ass right now. Fake ho. But why did my brother disrespect me like that? Bringing Mama into this?*

"Anyway," he said. "Gotta go. See you later." He closed the door.

Lisa said "bye" before she pulled into the driveway. The garage door crept upward.

Quinton grabbed a cigarette from the pack in the cup holder. "Oh well," he said, driving off. "Gerald didn't want to hear anything about his THOT of a wife, so he'll just have to find out on his own."

CHAPTER 14

GERALD

"Is that bacon?"

Gerald raised up on his elbows. The unmistakable aroma of bacon made his nostrils flex and sniff like a Doberman Pincher on the hot trail of a runaway bank robber.

"Hold on," he said, ripping the comforter off him. "It's coming from my kitchen? What the…"

Lisa hadn't whipped up a breakfast meal in at least a year, let alone one that yanked him out of the Sandman's domain on a Saturday morning. He stood up with a smile, stretched until his bones crackled and popped, then stepped out of the bedroom. The closer he got to the kitchen, the more the cloud enveloped him. So good he thought he was floating.

"Wow," he said, pausing in the doorway. Lisa wore a tank top and short-shorts, a welcome visual shift from baggy flannel pajamas that screamed, "Don't touch me!"

A growth spurt swelled underneath his boxers. "Uh, good morning."

Lisa turned with a smile, another shock. "Good morning to you."

A quick scan of the kitchen counter revealed two plates with scrambled eggs and pancakes. Two glasses of orange juice stood between them.

Right on cue, Lisa cut off the stove. She placed three strips of bacon on one plate, and two on the other.

"Here you go," she said, handing him the plate with three strips. "Enjoy."

"Thank you." He kissed her cheek. When Gerald turned, Lisa tapped his elbow.

She said, "Hey, don't forget your juice."

"Right." He grabbed the glass and sat at the kitchen table where an assortment of breakfast condiments had been laid out. He grabbed the bottle of syrup. "This is a nice surprise. Is it my birthday?"

"No, silly," she said. "Just cooking for my husband."

"Uh huh." Buttermilk pancakes melted in his mouth, pausing all desire for dialogue. A small dab of syrup smeared his bottom lip. "Um, um, um."

Now sitting across from him, Lisa chuckled and said, "I don't have to ask if you like it."

Mouth jam-packed with a medley of bite-sized orgasms on a plate, Gerald's eyelids drooped until they closed. He gave Lisa a thumbs up.

"How long have you been up?" he asked.

"A couple of hours," she said, digging into her eggs. "A certain someone kept me up with his snoring again."

"My bad."

"I'm used to it."

"Maybe I should get one of those sleep stu—"

"Are you going to tell me what you and Quinton talked about or not?"

Gerald swallowed, the fork stuck in his mouth. The euphoria from spending quality time with his wife over a home-cooked meal wilted away at the mention of his brother's name. *Why did she bring him up, killing the mood?*

"Lisa, I still don't want to talk about it," he said.

"Please." She stroked his hand. "You've been moody ever since you saw him."

The caress of her fingers cooled a burn within him. It felt good to be noticed. Finally. He took in a breath, exhaled it out.

"Okay, okay. He was trying to apologize." Gerald leaned back against the chair, crossed his arms. "Man, it's been five months since the funeral, but I'm still so mad at him. Just don't know if I'll ever forgive what he did." He bit off a piece of bacon. "Maybe I'm overreacting. What do you think?"

"Um hum, maybe." Lisa took a sip of juice, her gaze piercing through him. "Is that all you two talked about? He seemed pretty fired up when he left."

"I laid into him pretty hard," Gerald said between chews. "Got on him about not being at the hospital, missing the funeral, you know." Gerald paused. "Then I kinda said eff you."

"What?" she said, wide-eyed. "You said that?"

"Well, *forget* you, really."

Lisa laughed.

Gerald said, "What? Why are you laughing?"

"Um, nothing. Just shocked you said that to him. That's like cussing for you."

"I know. I was pretty mad."

"Apparently."

They ate in silence, the clickity-clack of their forks against each plate the only sound. Despite her wifely gesture, the awkward social disconnect between them remained. Initiating a simple one-on-one with Lisa still seemed like hard work. Despite their many years together, Gerald had been walking on eggshells around Lisa for so long, he simply forgot how to talk to his wife.

Still, Gerald knew something provoked her to not only wake up before him on a Saturday, but to take it way back to the honeymoon days, when she would concoct a variety of dishes like a curious chemist in a lab. He wanted to believe the change of heart was sincere, but what triggered it? The doting wife routine had come out of left field.

They finished eating around the same time. With his questions about her motives inching their way toward the tip of his tongue, Lisa pushed her chair back and stood. She grabbed his plate.

"Finished?" she asked.

"Yeah. Thanks."

Gerald followed her into the kitchen, checking out the way her booty muscles flexed underneath her shorts. The spurt between his legs turned into a bulge in seconds. He might have forgotten how to converse with his wife, but he had no problem responding to what her body had to say.

Yet, he couldn't ignore the pricks of curiosity. "I told you what I said to Quinton. Are you going to tell me what this is about? Don't take this the wrong way, but I'm not used to you being so nice to me. At least, not lately."

Lisa wet the dishes, then ran a soapy sponge over them. "Let's just call it a new beginning for both of us. Can we leave it at that?"

Gerald rubbed his chin, staring. "A new beginning?"

"Yes."

"Okay. That sounds good." *I guess.* He stood up, the bulge pushing against the cotton material of his boxers—armed, packed, and ready.

Coming up behind her, he pressed his manhood against her backside. "Can this new beginning include a little... you know. Since we were talking about babies and all."

Lisa looked down at his boxers, made a "humph" sound, then resumed dishwashing. "Still on my question mark," she said, an alias Gerald invented for that time of the month. "Sorry."

"Well, you know you could... never mind." Gerald didn't press it. She hadn't done "that" in years.

Figures, but question mark? It didn't add up. Gerald had been with her so long he knew Lisa's cycle as good, if not better, than her. Her menstrual evidence always revealed itself in the bathroom trashcans. According to his calculations, Aunt Flow should've left the premises three days ago.

In other words, bull.

But he kept his cool, didn't call her out. *Whatever.*

She added, "But I'll be done soon."

"Yeah, okay." The bulge deflating, he headed toward the bedroom. "Thanks for breakfast."

"You're welcome. Hey, what are you doing today?"

"Probably hit up the gym," he replied, rubbing his pooch belly. "Need to get back into it. What about you?"

"Meeting up with someone to talk over last minute stuff for the reunion. Then I'm going to Target to pick up a few things."

"More reunion crap, huh? I thought you already met with your committee?"

"Okay, first of all, it's not crap," she snapped. "We want to make it a special event, so we're going all out. It's hard work putting this thing together."

"My bad," he said, hands up. "Shouldn't have said crap. Sorry."

Wiping her hand on a towel, she said, "What time are you leaving?"

"In a few. Gonna pack a change of clothes, then I'm out. Why, you need something?"

"Nope. Just wondering. Don't let me keep you."

⁂

"Damn, stole my spot."

After finishing his workout at the Monte Clara Wellness Center, Gerald decided to head down to the water to decompress at his favorite meditation spot. But as he walked up, he noticed someone had claimed his favorite bench. Obviously, that person didn't have a clue about the bench's rightful owner.

He glanced up and down the shoreline, then spotted an empty bench about a hundred yards away, perched on the rocky embankment, but no shade. Not ideal, but it would have to do.

As he detoured to his substitute chill spot, Gerald stole a glance at the bench thief. A jet-black ponytail stretched down to a narrow waist, and although he couldn't see her face, he suspected eye-candy material. Her long, slender legs looked velvety smooth, manicured toes painted purple. *Nice.*

He noticed a notepad in her lap. She was gazing across the water, mumbling. The pen in her right hand wiggled, as if trying to connect the ink with whatever was floating around upstairs.

Gerald stopped and did a double-take. *Hold up.* "Yara?"

She turned toward him, revealing the face that spurned a thousand wet dreams. *The* Yara Bassili, unanimously voted "Best Looking" in their senior class popularity poll. Her smile alone could level any man, and she'd left a long trail of shattered hearts and teenage hard-on's in her wake. As Prince once said, "She's the reason why God made a girl." He never imagined Yara in the flesh, sitting on his bench. Alone.

Squinting, she said, "Oh my God. Gerald, right?"

Wow, she remembers me. "Right. Gerald Durston. I had a twin brother named Quinton... *have* a twin brother... I mean... he's still alive and all."

Yara chuckled. "That's a good thing." She stood up and stretched out her arms. "How are you?"

Gerald bent down to give her a hug, not expecting body contact beyond a handshake. For years, he thirsted for her embrace. He wanted to sink into Yara until they became locked into a tight bear hug, merging her scent into his skin forever. Instead, Gerald suppressed his jumpy nerves and kept their hug cool and casual— like associates.

As they broke apart, he said, "I'm good. How have you been?"

"I'm hanging in there." She pointed at his left hand. "I see you're married, now."

"Yeah. To Lisa Townes."

"Oh, I remember her."

"Yup, that's my wife." His voice trailed. "I'm, uh, sorry to hear about Philip."

Yara looked down. "Thank you. It's been tough."

"I bet." *I know she doesn't want to talk about this. Switch it up, man.* "So… you're here for the reunion? I heard you were living in like Oakland or something."

"Yes, I'm going to the reunion," Yara said, nodding. "I moved back here, actually. I'm staying with my sister. You?"

Moved back, huh? "Well, I've never left Monte Clara, and I'll definitely be at the reunion."

"Good. Should be fun."

"Yeah." Gerald glanced at the notepad on the bench. "Sooo… what brought you to this spot?"

Yara smiled. "I love being by the water. So peaceful."

"I agree." Gerald took in a deep dose of salty air. "Just came from the gym to appreciate God's glory, too. Hey, what 'cha doing with that notepad? Working on the next great American poem?"

"Oh, my!" Yara cried, arms folded. "You remember?"

"Of course! In English class, you recited a few lines in front of everybody. I even remember some of it."

She gasped. "No, you don't!"

"I do. It was something like…" He cleared his throat, closed his eyes, then said, *"I feel your wind caressing my face, and I stand alone in your breeze… I close my eyes… losing time and space, I am a wave in the deep blue sea… we drown in a deep embrace… and together, forever… we are—"*

"Free," Yara said. "Together, forever, we are… free. I cannot believe you remember that. I actually wrote that poem when I was twelve. I'm like, literally speechless right now."

Gerald couldn't recall the entire poem, but the words he did remember were seared in his memory forever. Yara's voice was like an angelic whisper in class that day; those three lines haunted him so much that Gerald would pretend Yara had written them for him.

But Gerald couldn't share that tidbit without looking creepy.

He shrugged. "Well, you know, it was that powerful. You're really talented."

His compliment hung in the air. A gentle breeze brushed small strands of hair against Yara's cheek, and for a few seconds, she appeared to manifest the words from the poem: Yara had lost time and space. Gerald cherished the moment he had rendered Yara Bassili speechless.

"Gerald, would you like to sit down with me? I'd love to hear how things are going."

"Of course," Gerald replied, the flutters in his gut turning into a tsunami. He took a seat. "I have to confess, I kinda consider this my bench."

"What, really?"

"Yup. Let me show you." Gerald pulled out his phone and clicked on a picture of an otter. "I took this pic not too long ago. You can tell it's from this bench. See?"

Yara cuffed a hand over the phone. "Yes, I see. I'm sorry. I had no idea I was sitting on your bench." Her tone was serious, but eyes smiling. "I can find another one over—"

"No, no! I don't mind sharing. We can share."

"Ha, ha. Okay, I'll stay. So, Mr. Durston, what is it about this particular spot that you like?"

Placing his arm on the back of the bench, he crossed a foot over his knee, watching the waves crash against the rocks. "I don't know. It's just perfect. Just the right shade, not too much foot traffic, a cool breeze. And of course, all this ocean, it just… centers me. The perfect place to escape from all my problems."

Yara nodded. "That's something. Those are the exact same reasons I was drawn to this spot." She turned to him. "Would you like to talk about those problems you're escaping?"

Gerald sighed. "Well…"

He unloaded the weight off his chest named Greg Stephens, the so-called "playa from da Himalayas," as Yara recalled. While relaying the biggest upset of his professional career, laughter somehow erupted in spurts between them, and Gerald bore witness to rare beauty juxtaposed with comedic flare. Gerald had no idea Yara could break hearts and burst bellies at the same time.

"If it makes you feel any better, you're not the only one having issues with work," Yara said. "After Philip died, I…" She stopped and glanced at the grass, avoiding his eyes. "I'll just say I can't work yet."

"I understand. My mom died recently and I shut down." He placed a hand on his chest. "Wasn't in the mood for anybody. Hell, I didn't want to get out of bed for a while. It's a pain in your heart that never truly goes away."

"I'm sorry to hear that, Gerald. I didn't know."

"It's okay." Gerald watched a seagull ascend into the blue sky, wings flapping with a melodic sway toward the clouds. "I know she's watching over me and Quinton, so I'm at peace."

Yara nodded. "I'm sure she is, watching over her twinzees."

He smiled. As Gerald's comfort deepened, their verbal prose blossomed with an organic flow. Conversation shifted to the reunion, as they gossiped about former classmates and the mysterious Facebook videos.

Gerald glanced at his watch. "Man! We've been sitting here an hour. Getting a little hungry."

"Really, an hour?" Yara checked her phone. "Dang, you're right. I'm a little hungry myself, actually."

"Would you like to walk to the Wharf with me? Get something to eat, maybe?"

"Sure," Yara said. She placed the notepad in her purse.

Yes! "Great."

Gerald played it cool, but was doing imaginary backflips because lunch meant more time with her. As they stood up, he patted his belly and said, "Need to watch this girlish figure, though. I'm growing boobs. I'm like a friggin' C-cup now."

Yara threw her head back cracking up, the ponytail swaying against her torso. "I'll lend you some of my sister's bras. Mine are probably too big." She winked.

"Thanks."

They stopped by Yara's Optima and Gerald placed a few quarters in the meter—a gentleman move Gerald knew Yara would appreciate. He then muted the ringer on his phone and locked it. No more random butt-dials, especially to Lisa.

Strolling toward the Wharf, they shared an easy rapport, a crucial element missing from Gerald's marriage for some time. Even made his childhood mega-crush smile and laugh a few more times. As a teen, he had dreamed of walks with Yara so many times that he lost count. Fate saw fit to make his dreams a reality today.

For the first time, the strain that often weighed him down lifted. The ills in his life—mostly from people close to him—didn't matter. Knowing he may never be able to relive his fantasy again, even a taste of it, he focused on the short time he had with the woman at the center of it all.

As they navigated through the midday crowds on the Wharf, Gerald caught a few laser-like stares on Yara, which pumped up his chest with pride. The Wharf boasted several four- and five-star seafood restaurants, and Yara picked Gilbert's Bar & Grill, the perfect chill spot for waterfront dining. The hostess led them outside to an enclosed patio and seated them near the bar.

Gerald pulled Yara's chair. "Oh, thank you."

"You're welcome," Gerald replied, wondering if his smile looked as cheesy as it felt. As he sat down, he said, "Let me know if you want a drink. I hear their vodka smoothies are the bomb diggity."

"Bomb diggity? Really? I haven't heard anyone say that since I was… ten, maybe?"

"Yeah, I'm pretty good at bringing the 90s back every now and then."

They shared another laugh, one of many. From recounting the days of long gone, to a string of Gerald's corny jokes, they seemed to ride the same wavelength, no static. Gerald settled into his newfound comfort in the presence of a female, the kind that only happens when two people hit it off. He hadn't felt that fire in a while. No antsy nerves, no constant need to purge his tongue for fear he would say the wrong thing. Just Gerald and his dream woman sitting across from each other at a small, wooden table.

Made him smile for no reason.

As Yara studied her menu, Gerald studied her. Her face seemed thinner, and he could tell she had lost a little weight, probably from the stress of losing a husband and everything else going on in her life. But she still looked like an Egyptian goddess who once graced the pyramids.

After placing their orders, Yara excused herself. As she snaked around other tables with the grace of a gazelle, Gerald watched her familiar milkshake hip sway that brought all the boys to the yard back in high school, her thick ponytail like a black snake against the middle of her back. Just a few hours ago, he had a similar posterior view of Lisa at breakfast, but Yara... that woman made him zone out everything in his periphery, forming a tunnel only on her. His wife didn't have that kind of draw power.

Damn. Lisa.

The moment Yara left his view, that "on-edge" state returned. Like he had an immediate urge to look over his shoulder, and he knew exactly why. A tinge of guilt forced him face-first into an obvious truth: He and Yara weren't just catching up; all signs pointed to a date.

He sighed. *Aw, hell.*

Gerald's giddy smile vanished. Lisa wouldn't approve of him spending all day with a beautiful woman, even if they graduated together. What wife would?

He pulled out his phone. A quick text would let Lisa know his whereabouts—and with whom. He prided himself on being a good, honest husband at all times, even when Lisa wasn't looking.

Pressing the digital keyboard, he caught a glimpse of Yara walking back his way. Tufts of hair now free, black strands caressed her cheeks and ran over her breasts, the ends stopping around her abdomen. An extra dab of makeup, but not much. When she met his gaze, her plump lips lifted into a smile that made Gerald freeze his finger against the small phone screen, bottom lip slack.

He put the phone away. Lisa didn't need to know a damn thing.

Shoot, he thought. *We're just having lunch. How many lunches has she had with her little reunion group? It's no big thing.*

"Hey, you," she said, sitting back down.

"Hey, yourself. Wow. You look… wow. Just like in high school."

"Thank you. I just wanted to freshen up a bit." She turned toward the water; Gerald did the same. A postcard view of Mission Point Lighthouse stood in the distance as kayakers shared ocean space with stand-up paddle boarders.

After a moment of reflecting, Yara said, "I really love the view here."

"Me, too," he said, heart thumping. "But I gotta admit, the best view is across this table from me." Eyes bulging, Gerald wished he could yank back his words. Somehow his comfort had morphed into a cocky Mac Daddy alter-ego, trying to take center stage. "I-I'm sorry," he said, flustered. "I can't believe I said that!"

Yara cocked her head, then burst out laughing. "You are so adorable! It's okay. Thank you, sweetie."

"Geez Louise," Gerald said, covering his face with a hand. "Man, Lisa would cut my lips off if she heard me right now."

"From what I remember about her and the little you told me, she'd cut off more than that."

"Ha, that's right, but you know what? Who cares?" He rolled his eyes and said, "Screw it," under his breath. "I may as well tell you."

"Tell me what?"

Gerald scooted the chair closer to the table. With nerves no longer twisting his tongue, he said, "I, uh, had a monster crush on you. Shoot, Lisa knew."

Yara smiled. "Really?"

"Big time. All through high school." *And now.*

"Awwww. I don't know what to say. You're so sweet."

He shrugged. "Yeah, well, I was—what the hell?"

Yara frowned. "What?"

"Look." Gerald pointed at the TV above the bar. "She said Marcus Obohu. We graduated with that guy!"

Yara faced the TV. A picture of a man with his arms wrapped around a heavyset woman flashed on the screen. A newscaster reported a possible domestic dispute gone wrong in an Oakland apartment.

"Police say thirty-year-old Kyla Livingston-Obohu shot her husband, twenty-eight-year-old Marcus Obohu, in the couple's apartment during an argument. Mr. Obohu is a Hertz Rent-a-Car manager from east Oakland. He was pronounced dead at the scene…"

"Wow, she killed him?" Gerald said, wide-eyed. "This is crazy."

"At this point, authorities do not have a motive for the shooting, but neighbors reported cries for help from a male voice before hearing four gunshots. Mrs. Obohu is in custody. The investigation is ongoing…"

"Four freakin' gunshots? Man!" Gerald shook his head. "Sad. I think they have a kid, too. I wonder what happened."

"Only Kyla knows," Yara replied. "Shame. But I wouldn't be surprised if she caught him cheating."

CHAPTER 15

YARA

Looks like Marcus got what he deserved. Dumb ass. Bye, boy.

Gerald, still staring at the TV, said, "That's a really extreme reaction to cheating. She must be messed up in the head."

What? A jolt ripped through Yara, paralyzing her. Forehead tightening, she gripped the butter knife so hard that knuckles popped. If the glare emitting from her eyes was a laser, everyone on deck would've been cleaning splattered pieces of Gerald's skull and brain off their dinnerware. So typical of a man to blame the woman for his crimes and misdeeds. Marcus, the douchebag player wannabe, got what he deserved.

Yara felt that familiar twitch that often followed a stupid comment from a man. Public decorum fading, she was a few seconds away from unleashing her explosive psychosis on yet another clueless fool. But as Gerald engrossed himself in a news report that only touched on half of the story, Yara closed her eyes, inhaled a touch of air, then exhaled it all out—like Dr. Kazarian taught her.

"Man, that's so crazy," Gerald said, turning back to Yara, just as she reopened her eyes. He grabbed a piece of bread, oblivious to the wrath she suppressed.

"It is," she said, glancing around the room. "What the hell happened to our waiter? I could use a drink."

"I could use one, too, especially after hearing that. I'll be right back."

Gerald headed to the bar, granting Yara some time to regroup. Still taking in deep breaths, she honed in on the sound of waves crashing against the rocks underneath the deck. A blanket of calm soon returned, and when Gerald came back with the drinks, she reconnected to his eyes—the tender entryway into his bruised soul.

The moment she saw Gerald at the bench, she sensed a kind heart. He didn't come off as another sleazebag with a polluted, one-track mind like the stupid men post-Philip. Sure, he flirted a little, but he was harmless, and his awkward, somewhat clumsy approach added an adorable puppy-dog quality. Despite his ill-informed comment about Marcus' wife being "messed up in the head," Yara enjoyed his company. She didn't think that kind of connection with a man could ever be possible again.

Their food arrived. With one bite of her chicken sandwich, Yara's eyes rolled back, and a long *mmmm* sound hummed from her throat. Gerald did the same thing.

They wiped their plates clean. After inhaling their vodka smoothies, they ordered another round. Glass in hand, Yara carried on with their private party, conversing about this, smiling about that, laughing about everything—engaged in the sweetest taboo of sharing liquid sin with a married man.

But Gerald was different. A good man, even if his wife couldn't see it. Unlike the others, Yara truly liked Gerald, and had no desire to trap him. A special spot grew sweeter for only him, and the more vodka coursed through her veins, the more the guards came down. Gerald tapped on locked chambers of her heart that only her sister and late husband knew about. Her instinct was to trust him, but with Gerald inching his way toward her center, Yara knew she had to reel herself in before she crossed a line.

Gerald saved them when he looked at his watch and said, "Okay, this is getting out of hand, Yara. We've been here for three hours. I think we'd better get back before your meter runs out. I hope we can walk straight. You okay?"

"Yes, I'm fine. I'm not that tipsy anymore. I actually forgot about the meter, though. Good call."

"No problem. Shoot, I'm sure Lisa is setting up the lynch mob right about now."

"Has she called or texted?"

"Good question." He checked his phone. "Nope. Looks like I'll live to see another day." They laughed.

Gerald hailed the waiter for the bill. Yara offered to pay for her share, but Gerald insisted on taking care of it. After Gerald reminded Yara that he had invited her to lunch, she relented to a man she had deemed a true gentleman.

As they walked back to their cars, a chilly breeze whisked over them, causing hair to brush across Yara's eyes and cheek. She tucked strands behind her ear and hugged herself for warmth.

"Getting cold?" Gerald asked.

"Yes, a little."

He took off his hoodie and handed it to her. "Here. You can wear this until we get to your car."

"Thank you, Gerald." She wrapped it around her shoulders like a cape, but kept her arms free. "You really are a gentleman. It's a shame your wife doesn't appreciate that."

"Yeah," he said with a long sigh, hands cuffed behind his back while watching his shoes against the pavement, a pose that reminded Yara of a sad little boy. "She seems to be making more of an effort lately, but we'll see how long that lasts."

"I know you two are having problems, but maybe you should give her a chance. See how it goes?"

He shrugged. "Maybe."

For the first time, they walked together without saying a word. A mesh of clouds loomed on the horizon, like a field of cotton balls hanging in the sky. Fall weather was finally making its debut, and Gerald's mood had darkened along with the sky. Yara sensed a melancholy aura, even through the laughter, as if all the pressures in his life weighed on his shoulders and he struggled to lighten the load. Yara could relate; she carried a massive load of her own, still trying to break free, but anchored down by past burdens that refused to untangle. They were kindred spirits in that way, and somehow being around Gerald made her feel less alone in the world.

In minutes, they reached Yara's car. "Okay, good," Gerald said, stepping off the curb and checking her windshield. "No ticket."

Yara glanced at the meter. "I got really lucky. Only two minutes left."

"Wow. Time really flew by, huh?"

She stepped off the curb. "Yes. Great company."

He stared for a moment with a soft smile, then nodded. "I agree."

Standing in front of her car, about five seconds of awkward silence squeaked by before Yara said, "Oh, here's your hoodie." She handed it to him.

"Damn, I would've forgotten," Gerald said, draping it over his shoulder. "Thanks." He looked at his watch, then pushed his hands into his pockets. "Okay, well, I had a really great time, Yara."

"Me, too. I haven't laughed that much in a long time. See you at the reunion?"

"Yup, at the reunion. Oh! Unless..." He pulled a hand out of his pocket and handed Yara what looked like a coupon. It said *Free One-Day Pass* from the gym.

"Are you trying to tell me something, Gerald?"

"No, no. Guy at the front desk gave me that for a guest. You said earlier you needed to get back in the gym. I'm going to work out again tomorrow around three. So... you know... if you're not doing anything, I hope to see you there."

She suppressed a chuckle. Cute that he mentioned the exact time.

"Okay, thank you. Maybe I'll take you up on that."

"Good, good," he replied with a head-nod that looked more like a bobble.

As if the rest of his body were stuck in mud, Yara could tell Gerald was having some type of inner tug-of-war, probably wondering if he should hug her or not. *I'll help him out.* "Okay, see you later," she said, leaning forward, arms open wide. Gerald stepped into her embrace, her cheek and hair pressed against his neck. "Say hi to Lisa for me."

They broke away. "Suuuure. I'll do that," he replied, eyes rolling. A dash of sarcasm. Yara liked that.

She pressed the car remote. Injected with another shot of chivalry, Gerald trotted in front of her and opened the door.

"Aw, you didn't have to do that," she said, walking around him.

"Not a problem. Have a good day, Yara."

"You, too, Gerald."

She waved at him while sliding the key into the ignition. He waved back, looked both ways, then darted across the street. Yara paused for a moment. The way he ran, like parts of his legs were made of cement, but arms flailing like the world's slowest Olympic track runner, exposed a man with little flair for athletics. Made her laugh a bit. Yara couldn't recall Gerald gracing any yearbook page in a sports uniform. Etched with a grin, she watched him and his almost running-gallop until he turned a corner that led to his car.

"Something about him," she said, putting the car in drive.

As she eased into traffic, the picture of Philip dangling from the rearview mirror caught her eye. When she glanced at her dead husband, she didn't see eyes of a dedicated soldier; she saw disapproval. A look of anger, contempt. At *her*.

But she didn't give a shit.

"I know you're jealous," she said, slowing down at a red light. "I didn't know I could feel anymore. It's like how you and I used to be, huh?"

As Gerald played around in her head, she realized he couldn't have been more different than Mr. All-American Boy Philip. From looks and body to overall swag, Gerald fell a little short on all counts. Yet, their G-rated "sorta-date" fluttered butterflies in her gut, the same way they fluttered for Philip as a teenager. When Gerald recited that poem she wrote at twelve years old, he cracked open a vulnerable side of her that had long been off limits for vermin disguised as men.

The clock inched toward six o'clock. Yara's sister would be taking her version of lunch soon, so Yara decided to head to the hospital and surprise her. Twenty minutes later, Yara sat in the hospital cafeteria. As she waited for her sister, she watched a young woman lead a small group of older adults in Tai Chi in the courtyard.

Ladan set her tray down and glanced out the window, also watching the Tai Chi group. "I need to get my butt into some type of exercise routine," she said with a sigh. "Maybe do what they're doing."

Yara nodded. "Me, too," she said, thinking about the free pass in her car's cup holder. "I might start tomorrow."

"Only eating a salad?" Ladan asked.

"Yeah, I had a late lunch. At the Wharf."

"Right. How was it? Get any writing done?"

"I did," Yara said, watching an older woman sway her arms slow and graceful as a feather. "I had a good time."

"What are you smiling about?"

Yara frowned. "I'm not smiling."

"Yes, you are. Did you meet a guy down there? And don't tell me no because I'm sure you did. You're always keeping the juicy stuff to yourself."

She rolled her eyes. "I did, but he was a classmate. We graduated together. You probably won't remember him. Gerald Durston. He'll be at the reunion."

"Nope, don't remember him. So, how'd it go?"

Yara recapped her day with Gerald, starting with his poem recital and ending with the funny way he ran across the street to his car. As a side note, she also mentioned his marital status.

"Stay clear of those married guys," Ladan said.

"I don't mess around with married guys," Yara lied. "It just felt good to connect with a man on a deeper level again, even if it was strictly platonic. We laughed a lot."

"Ooookay," Ladan said with a playful side eye. "This is really good, though. I can tell you're in a better place, more relaxed. Maybe we're turning a corner here."

Yara may have turned a corner, but the road ahead was still unclear. She couldn't predict the outcome of her therapy sessions, or if her future somehow involved Gerald, but for the first time, she felt she had options. Yara knew one thing for certain—she wasn't looking back anymore. The road in her rearview led to a dead end, literally, at the grave of Marcus Obohu. Yet, she felt no guilt.

Yara dug a fork in her salad, smiling. "I think you're right, sis."

CHAPTER 16

QUINTON

"There he goes. Bitch."

Quinton watched Greg stroll toward the mall entrance looking like any other Joe Schmoe. Not a worry in the world, it seemed, and no clue that his marriage was about to implode.

When Greg disappeared inside, Quinton made his move. He stepped out of his car in stealth mode and headed toward Greg's ho mobile, parked in a row across from Quinton. He used the keyless remote that Aanya lent him, as he glanced at the mall entrance to make sure Greg was out of sight. Opening the driver door, he then clipped the device under Greg's seat.

He had already emailed Aanya the photographic evidence of Greg's scandalous punk ass, and had no idea why she wasn't returning his texts or phone calls. Quinton figured she needed more proof, like recorded audio of Greg smashing another female.

Back in his own car, Quinton didn't know how long Greg would mess around in the mall, so he pulled up Netflix on his phone. He didn't give a shit if Greg stayed for hours; if Aanya needed a solid case against Greg, Quinton would wait in the parking lot for as long as he needed. Plus, something about playing private investigator released an adrenaline rush.

About forty-five minutes passed before he noticed Greg walking back to his car. "Damn," he said, sitting up. While scrambling for his earpiece, he saw Aanya. "Wait, what the hell is she doing here?"

He watched the sensual grace of Aanya's feminine stride, her figure accentuated in tight yoga pants and a tank top. Quinton's faraway gaze on her turned into a heated glare on Greg as he watched him play around on his cell phone while walking several feet in front of Aanya. Punk didn't even open the door for her.

Through the earpiece, he could hear Aanya utter a few words and some rustling, including the clicking of a seat belt. Although he couldn't make out what she said at first, the audio came through with HD quality.

"Oh my God, babe, she had us doing burpees with those blue ball thingies," Quinton heard Aanya say, happy to hear her voice again. She sounded as clear as if he was sitting in the back seat. "What do you call them?"

Based on the casual tone in her voice, Quinton knew Aanya hadn't looked at the pictures, let alone confronted Greg about them. That aggravated Quinton a bit, made him question why she enlisted his help in the first place. Still, Quinton smiled at "blue ball thingies." He whispered, "BOSU balls, pretty lady."

"I don't know what you're talking about," Greg said.

"You know, they're like, half-ball shaped. Really wobbly… dang it, what are they called?"

Quinton's smile faded. He felt like a hacker prying in on the private conversation of a married couple. Although he wanted to make Greg his student and teach him the art of bitch-slapping, collecting intel on him and Aanya wasn't part of the plan.

He mulled over removing his earpiece, until he heard, "Look, I don't fuckin' know what they're called, Aanya."

"What the…" Quinton said, his forehead tightened, bottom lip slack. "He talkin' to her like that?"

After a short pause, Aanya said, "I guess you're in one of those moods again."

"Whatever. Let me see that."

"What?" Aanya asked.

From his angle, Quinton couldn't peep inside Greg's car, so he had no idea of the "that" Greg was talking about. He pushed the earpiece in further, hoping to figure it out.

"In your purse," Greg said. "There. Those supplements you bought."

Supplements?

At least a minute passed without anyone saying a word. Quinton tapped the steering wheel, listening, waiting—literally on the edge of his seat.

"This shit better work," Greg said. "I can't believe your stupid ass hasn't gotten pregnant, yet."

Quinton's bottom lip dropped. *No this fool didn't!*

"Babe, I'm trying. I've been seeing an acupuncturist twice a week who specializes in fertility." Quinton heard the strain in Aanya's voice.

"Then you should've gotten pregnant by now! Right? It's been two years and what do we have to show for it, huh? Nothing! Definitely not a son, Aanya. Where's my son?"

"I… don't know. I'm… sorry."

Quinton felt himself steaming up, balling his right hand into a tight fist. He always knew Greg as an arrogant asshole, but domestic abuse never crossed Quinton's mind. He wanted to teleport into Greg's car and shield Aanya from the emotional beat-down and misdirected blame for not getting pregnant—a colossal dick move from the biggest dick of them all.

"Don't be sorry, be pregnant! All our friends are having kids, and all I hear is 'when are you two having one?' I'm so tired of hearing that shit."

The radio blasted to life, drowning out Greg a bit. Quinton yearned for Aanya to shed her meek side and put some bass in her throat, throw the pictures in his face, clap back—anything. She needed to shut him down.

But she didn't say a word in her defense, or, at least, he couldn't make out her soft voice over the radio. Big mouth spoke loud enough, though.

"For the last time, I want a son, Aanya!" Greg cried. "Understand? You haven't done anything else for me since we got married, so you think you can handle that?"

The car backed up. Quinton dropped the headpiece in the cup holder. He wanted to sprint toward Greg's driver side, rip the door open, crush Greg's larynx between his hands, then smash Greg's forehead through the windshield. For good measure, he would throw Greg onto the pavement while impaling his size 11 Converse shoe ankle-deep into Greg's ass. The sorry muthafucka deserved half as much for talking to Aanya like that.

Wishful thinking. The target of his murderous daydream sped off, made a quick right, then vanished.

Quinton stared at the spot where Greg had been parked, fuming. An hour ago, he thought he'd bug Greg's car, follow him around for a while, then catch him slipping again with another random sidepiece. Instead, he got a glimpse into Aanya's private hell.

Leaning into the car seat, still seething, Quinton knew he was the only one capable of exterminating the virus in Aanya's life. If it took cornering Greg one-on-one, maybe beating his ass in public, or worse, that would have to do.

CHAPTER 17
LISA

"Who are you texting?"

Lisa gave Greg the evil eye. "Oh, I'm sorry, are you my daddy now? My daddy lives in Texas."

Greg glanced out the window. "Lockjaw, the way you've been sucking me off the past few weeks, I'm Big Daddy to you, now."

Lisa slapped his arm. "Shut up! Told you not to call me that! You make me sick."

"I'm not playing, Lisa. Who are you texting?"

She smacked her tongue, but still tapped the cellphone screen, refusing to look Greg's way. "Nosy ass. If you must know, *Daddy*, I'm texting Sandy, Craig Meyer's wife. She's helping us with reunion stuff. I told her I would drop some decorations off, so I'm letting her know I'll be by soon." Lisa sent the message, then turned to Greg. "Satisfied?"

"Hmph."

Greg stared like he was trying to peek into the dark corners of Lisa's mind. She said, "What? Why are you looking at me like that?"

"Just can't figure you out. We're about to meet my cousin, the man who's going to kill your husband. But you're texting somebody about reunion stuff. Like it's nothin'."

"What's to figure out? We put a lot of work into this reunion. I want it to be perfect."

Greg repeated, "You want it to be perfect, huh?"

"Uh, yeah. What's wrong with that? Just because I'm doing this thing with you and Patrick, doesn't mean the rest of my life stops."

"Wow," Greg replied with a smirk. "Cold as hell, girl. You're so casual about all of this." He rubbed her thigh. "Kind of a turn on, though."

Lisa rolled her eyes. "Everything turns you on. That damn steering wheel turns you on. That baseball field turns you on. Air turns you on! Pervert."

He laughed. "Yeah, whatever. You love it. Where's the mark today, anyway?"

"He said he was going to the gym." Lisa's phone buzzed. "Well, what do you know? The 'mark' is calling me right now. Why is that fool calling, though? I never answer. Decline." She looked up. "See, that's—aw! Boy!"

The sight of Greg's mini Tower of Pisa shocked the phone out of her hands, and she dropped it between the passenger seat and cup holder. While she messed around with Gerald's call, Greg's sneaky ass had somehow leaned the chair back, unzipped his pants, and unveiled his package of hard Grade A pink meat.

"What?" He cradled it, wearing a stupid, Joker-like smile. "We have time."

Lisa had a thing for Greg's bold "I-don't-give-a-fuck-where-we-fuck" nature, but minutes before finalizing a hit on her husband? She couldn't go there, especially within view of the campus church.

"I'm not sucking you off, so zip it," she said, jabbing her hand between the seats. "See, now I can't reach my phone."

"Reach on this." He wiggled it. "C'mon, Lockjaw."

"Greg! Really, what the hell's wrong with you? Patrick will be—"

"Here any minute. Damn." He zipped up his pants. "That's him coming now."

Lisa saw a car creeping toward them. They were parked at CSU Marina Bay, near the baseball field. With baseball season over, Greg had correctly predicted a near-empty lot, the perfect site for a low-key meetup.

Lisa brushed off her trapped phone for later. She noticed a shift in Greg's mood. He had moved the seat back up, his posture now upright, almost military. Greg's cool and calm exterior had cracked, and for the first time, she saw a scared man.

A black Acura with chrome rims parked next to Greg's SUV. Greg opened the driver door. "Stay here."

Patrick wore a cutoff T-shirt and shorts, like he came straight from a basketball court. He looked like a stereotypical stone-cold killer, but with Calvin Klein model looks. He stood the same height as Greg's six-foot frame with a dirty blond buzz cut, square jaw, and high cheek bones. Slim, toned, and grimy. Patrick could definitely "get it."

As they bro-hugged, Lisa noticed Patrick staring at her. She felt a wave of heat across her face, a spike in heartbeats. No more games. Shit got real.

Greg slid into the driver seat, Patrick in the backseat behind him. Greg said, "Lisa, this is my cousin, Patrick. Patrick, Lisa."

Lisa turned in her seat. "Hi," she said, unsure about whether to smile like in normal greetings, or look as pissed off as him.

"Sup," Patrick said.

"Pat, once again, it's good to see you, cuzzo. I was—"

"I'm not tryin' to make small talk," Patrick said, cutting him off. "Let me see my money."

"Oh," Lisa said, taken aback. "Like that, huh?"

"Yeah. I'm not wasting my time. So what's up?"

"Okay," Lisa said, heart pounding. She glanced at Greg. He looked like she felt—jittery.

Lisa reached for the purse by her feet, retrieved a manila envelope, and handed it to Patrick. He flipped the envelope and stacks of hundred-dollar bills fell into his hand, each with a rubber band around it. Lisa managed all of the household expenses, and Gerald was clueless about the extent of their credit card debt, including the cash advances. He trusted her with everything; the fool had no idea he'd financed his own funeral.

"Thirty-five hundred for a down payment, like we agreed," she said. "I already gave your cousin his cut."

Patrick didn't answer right away. He flipped through the bills, then placed them back in the envelope. "We good."

Greg said, "Told you she's serious, cuz."

"I see that. Now, why you wanna do this?"

"Why? Because I'm over it. I'm done with his ass, and I want him dead. Period."

Patrick blinked a few times and looked stuck, like he didn't expect Lisa's dry response. "What, is he cheatin' on you or sumn'?"

"No."

"Beat you?"

"Hell no."

He shifted in his seat. "Is he on that shit?"

"No! I just want him gone, all right?"

Patrick glanced at the rearview mirror, as if trying to find more answers in the eyes of his cousin. Greg sat like a quiet spectator, a slight grin at the edge of his lips.

"Dude sounds like he's aw' ight," Patrick said. "Matta' fact, from what Greg said he kinda square."

"Yeah." She nodded. "He is. So?"

"So, I wanna know why I'm poppin' a square dude who ain't done shit to you?"

Agitated, Lisa said, "You want to know why?"

"I asked, didn't I?"

"All right, I'll tell you why." Lisa lifted her knees on the seat so she could face him better. "I can't stand the sight of that man. Everything about him disgusts me, from the way he snores, to his fat ass belly, to his funky, lizard feet. I can't take it anymore."

The men laughed.

Lisa said, "I'm serious. On top of that I can't have kids because of him."

That comment grabbed Patrick's interest. "Why? What he do?"

"This fool got a vasectomy before we married, but didn't tell me about it until like two years after the fact."

"What the fu… why'd he do that?"

Lisa threw her hands up. "How the hell do I know? Just a poor excuse for a man. He's a weak waste of space and I'm better off without him."

"Plus, once you get the money, you won't have to work at all, right?" Greg said, winking at her. "At least, not for a while, since you like not working. Live that good life."

"Shut up, fool," she said.

"Uh huh," Patrick said, nodding. He tapped his knee, an intense glare burning from his eyes. "So, it's really all about the money, huh?"

"Isn't it always?"

Patrick cracked a grin. "True. Why not divorce?"

"Look, I don't have time for all that! Divorce drags on too long and they're expensive. I'd rather have money and be a widow than be divorced and broke. Simple as that."

Patrick's grin turned into a smile that seemed to envelop his entire face. "I heard that. Tell you one thing, cuz, you were right about her."

Greg glanced at the rearview mirror. "I told you!"

"Can we stop with the twenty questions and get on with it, please?" Lisa asked, feeling antsy. "I have a plan."

Patrick rubbed the stubble on his chin. "Okay, Queen B, let's hear it."

"Finally." Lisa pulled a brochure from her purse and handed it to Patrick. "Here's the hotel where we're having our high school reunion."

Patrick flipped it open. Greg kept his face forward, still glancing at the rearview mirror, but refusing to turn around. Patrick said, "The Bayfront Hyatt? Never been there."

"There's a three-story public parking lot on the corner of Broadway and Pickney, right across the street from the hotel. On the top level, there's a broken light by the staircase. Underneath that broken light is a corner parking spot. It's hella dark in that corner, including the staircase. Like pitch-black."

Patrick studied Lisa. "Okay."

"I've checked out that light a few times in the past week," Lisa said. "Still broken."

Patrick shoved the brochure in his pocket. "What 'chu getting at?"

"What I'm getting at is, I'm gonna park there early the morning of the reunion and leave my car to keep that spot. We all have to be there early to prepare and stuff, anyway."

"Aw 'ight."

"Reunion starts at seven, goes until midnight. At around ten, I'm going to send Gerald to get something out of my car."

"To get what?" Greg asked.

"Whatever, I don't know! I'll think of something. I just want him at the car where Patrick will be hiding out. In the staircase."

"Uh huh," Patrick said, his head-nod extra slow.

"Then what?" Greg asked. "Smoke him while he's reaching in the glove compartment or something?"

"Noooo, do it *before* he opens the door. I don't want any damn blood and brains all over my car seats." She turned back to Patrick. "And take his wallet so it looks like a robbery."

Patrick chuckled. "You crazy as hell, girl, but I like that. I'm going a different route, though."

"What do you mean?" Lisa asked.

"Let's just say I have access to some shit that'll make it look like he had a heart attack. All it takes is a needle. If you ever checked out the show *Dexter*, then you know what I'm talkin' 'bout."

"Oh, okay," she replied, processing his plan. "Grab him from behind, stick him in the neck, then…"

"Yeah. It works fast. No mess and they'll think he died of natural causes and shit. Can't be detected. No blood. Real clean. Nobody's asking questions afterward, either."

"Okay, I like that. He does have high blood pressure, so that could work. Not the way I imagined, but it's better."

"Good. Tell you what: I'll scope out this parking garage and let you know if it's a good plan."

"Great," Lisa replied.

"I don't know, man," Greg said, wuss written all over his face. "Kinda risky, right? I mean, what if somebody walks to their car at the same time? And what about video cameras?"

"They don't have video cameras in that lot," Lisa said. "I checked."

"Still, I see all kinds of shit going wrong," Greg said, morphing into a bitch-made punk before Lisa's eyes. "Hell, won't he bleed after you stick him? What if she doesn't get that spot? What will scoping it out on a weekday do for you? There's gonna be way more people on a Sat—"

"Stop acting like a lil' bitch," Patrick said, stealing the words off the tip of Lisa's tongue. "Let me worry about all that. This ain't my first time. Aw'ight?"

This ain't my first time. Patrick's outburst shook Lisa, reminding her that a man's life meant nothing more to Patrick than the amount of money offered for it. Like a child mumbling under his breath but still knowing better, Greg said, "Okay, man. Whatever you say. That's all on you."

"Watch yourself, fam," Patrick said, his glare on Greg. "I told yo' ass we'll be cool once this is done. Until then, you still owe me."

Greg said nothing more.

Patrick pulled out his phone. "Anyway, baby girl, I already got your number from Greg, so I'm gonna text you through the burner. Send me a picture of this dude when I do."

Buttered up from his "baby girl" remark, Lisa smiled and said, "Okay. I'll be waiting for your text."

"Cool," he said, shooting a sly grin back at her. "You sure you want this done the night of the reunion?"

"Yes, but around ten. We put too much work into the party and I want to have a good time, catch up with everybody, ya know? I can deal with being a widow later."

Patrick nodded. For the first time, Lisa felt like a stack of BBQ ribs on a grill, and that glint in Patrick's eye made her think his sexy ass wanted a piece. Lisa could see herself giving up a slice.

"I'll check out the spot, then let y'all know what's up by Thursday." Patrick pushed the door open. "All right, baby girl, I got you. I'll text you later today."

"Sounds good."

He stepped out with the envelope. "Lata'."

Lisa waved at Patrick, watching him walk back to the car. She noticed a frown aimed at her from the man she had zoned out.

She frowned back. "What?"

"You know what," Greg said, trying to sound hard again. "I see you working that voodoo on my cousin."

"Psst, like I need to work. I just want this to go as smooth as possible."

"Yeah, okay."

They watched Patrick speed off. Once Patrick finished the deed, Lisa would properly thank him. Until then, she had to settle Greg's whiny ass down and keep him happy.

She slapped Greg's thigh. "Boy, you know I ain't trying to go there with him."

"Better not." Greg exhaled a long sigh. "That's a real gangsta. Only person on this earth that I fear."

"Yeah. I can tell."

Greg turned to her. "I was talking about you."

Lisa smiled. "Oh, is that right?"

"That's right. So, how do you feel, gangsta? No turning back now."

"I feel pretty good, which surprises me. I think it's all going to work out. I'll keep playing the" —she threw up the quote sign with her fingers— "'good wife.' Hell, maybe I'll give it up a few times before he kicks it. Like his last meal."

Greg laughed. "He's probably been getting some on the side already. Like you."

"Gerald? Oh, please. Nobody else sleeping with his sorry, fat-belly ass. He's too whipped on me, anyway."

"Damn. You are cold as hell, *Baby girl*."

"As cold as Gerald's body on reunion night."

CHAPTER 18

GERALD

She came.

Standing by the water fountain, Gerald saw Yara stepping off a treadmill. He stopped his iPhone's 90s playlist and yanked the headphones out of his ears. In a tank top and leggings, her body looked hourglass, the same as when he would leak saliva off his lips when she rocked shorts and skirts in high school. She wiped her forehead with a small towel, then draped it over her shoulder. While she knocked back a container of water, Gerald surrendered to Yara's ethereal power, fading into a familiar daydream.

Man, I can't believe she's really here. Maybe she can help me with—

"Excuse me, sir, are you done with the water fountain?"

"Oh," Gerald said, shaking off his thoughts and landing back on earth. He stepped away, allowing the young woman access. "Sorry about that."

As he walked toward Yara, she looked his way. Her megawatt smile boosted Gerald's mood higher.

"Hey," he said, trying to stay cool and poised.

"Hey, you," she replied, that thick ponytail set between her cleavage like a black dagger protecting her precious body.

"I'm glad you came. Good to see you again."

"Thanks for the free pass. It was just the push I needed to get back in the gym." She glanced at Gerald's shirt. "My goodness, it's like you're trying out for a wet T-shirt contest."

Gerald laughed. He looked down and grabbed the ends of his white T-shirt; he'd forgotten the bullseye of sweat. "Yeah, I was hitting the punching bag. Letting off some steam."

"Looks like a lot of steam."

"Yeah, I tend to sweat a lot," he said, embarrassed. He grabbed the towel sticking out of his pocket and wiped his face. "Have you, uh, been here for a while?"

"About thirty minutes, mostly on the treadmill."

"Oh, okay. I was in the back. Kinda in a zone, headphones on and stuff."

"No wonder I didn't see you."

She was looking for me. "Yeah. I was, uh, about to hit the showers and get a bite to eat. Are you still working out?"

Yara stepped back to allow an older couple to pass. "No, I'm pretty much done. Trying to ease myself into it, you know."

"I got you. I was thinking about picking up a sandwich and having a little picnic by our favorite bench. Beautiful day out. Care to join me?"

Her eyes lit up. "A picnic? Sure. That sounds like fun."

Wow. Two for two. "Okay. Just gotta shower and change clothes. Meet you back here in about ten, fifteen?"

"Sounds like a plan."

Gerald strolled to the locker room feeling like a natural-born boss. No subliminal nit-picks from Lisa to ramp up guilt, either. That side of his conscience vanished the moment he saw Yara on the treadmill.

They met in the lobby and picked up sandwiches from the deli next door. After grabbing a blanket from the backseat of his car, they set up shop next to the empty "Yarald" bench, their favorite tree providing the shade.

Yara slipped out of her flip flops, got comfortable; Gerald did the same, no shoes, only socks. Like before, he glanced at her manicured toes. Perfect from top to bottom, as always.

She said, "This is really nice."

Gerald unwrapped his sandwich. "Thank you for joining me."

"You're welcome, sir. Thank you for lunch."

"No problem."

Gerald propped his back against the tree while Yara sat cross-legged beside him. They tore into their sandwiches next to a wide body of California water under a light-blue sky. A family of otters frolicked near the rocks. As always, the ocean scenery and melody of marine life captured Gerald, but this time, his childhood crush sat next to him.

"Lot on your mind?" Yara asked. "You look a little zoned out."

He wiped his mouth with a napkin. "Always got stuff on my mind."

"I bet a lot of it has to do with Lisa, huh?" She gasped, pressing a fist against her mouth. "I shouldn't have said that. Omigod, I was out of line. I'm sorry."

"Don't worry about it," Gerald said with a shrug. Placing his half-eaten sandwich in a small paper bag, he gazed across the water. "You and I have a lot in common, Yara. I liken us to ships in the ocean. No land around, no destination... just... floating."

"Yes, that's exactly how I felt after Philip," Yara replied. "I still feel like that, sometimes. Like lost, I guess."

"Exactly. Hey, tell me something: If you could go anywhere in the world, where would you go?"

"Where?" She sounded surprised. "Um, well, Philip was stationed in Italy once. When I flew out to visit, we went to a place called Cinque Terre. I'd go back there, but—oh! I would really love to visit Cape Town in South Africa."

He smiled. "Cape Town, huh? What about Egypt or Somalia?"

She shook her head. "I've already been to both places when I was a kid. Why do you ask?"

"Just curious. I'd like to visit Europe, but Cape Town sounds good, too." He exhaled a breath. "I wouldn't mind hitting up Mexico City to work on my Spanish." He chuckled. "Yeah. Getting away sounds… good."

"Uh huh." Yara placed a hand on his forearm. "Are you all right?"

Her touch was soft, and he imagined Yara transferring much-needed energy into him. Glancing at her hand, Gerald said, "Ever since I saw you yesterday, I've been thinking about escaping, just getting away."

"What, a little vacay with Lisa?"

Staring deep into Yara's dark-brown eyes, with no fear, he said, "Not with her."

She didn't look away, didn't flinch. "Oh. Is there something you want to tell me?"

Gerald scooted away from the tree, then lay on his back, watching the leaves above rustling in the wind. "Yara, I feel like I can tell you anything." *Here goes.*

He dropped all defenses and opened up to Yara, like he hadn't done with anyone, including Quinton. Flipped himself inside out and held nothing back, granting unlimited access to old and new enigmas clogging his head and scars still darkening his heart. Yara lay on her side, strands of her hair grazing his elbow. Gerald felt her intense stare, her lips parted and eyes wide as he ripped off pieces of his psyche and laid them all out, unfiltered and uncensored. He didn't realize how much he needed Yara's ear again to unveil himself, and like their time at the restaurant, it felt good to have a female confidant.

Before his outpour became a one-way flood, he pumped the brakes and eased back a bit, thinking he said too much. Yara turned toward the water, and he toward her. He said, "There I go again, blabbing away."

Yara didn't respond, keeping a distant gaze on the horizon. Gerald studied the contour of her jaw, bronze skin, eyes no doubt clones of Nefertiti from ancient Egypt. She seemed to have a ton on her mind, too, and Gerald thought maybe he had piled on at least half of it during his makeshift therapy session.

Gerald said, "Look, I'm sorry if…" Before he could tiptoe through his words, he noticed a tear rolling down the side of her face. "Hey, are you okay?"

Yara wiped her cheek with the back of her hand. "No. Like you, I'm *not* okay."

The outpour resumed, but this time, it came from Yara. What Gerald had unlocked within himself somehow did the same for her, and Yara flooded him with her own secret demons. In a role-reversal that Gerald didn't see coming, his lips also parted, eyes as wide as small plates.

He remembered an old adage Mama Durston used to tell him and Quinton. She would say some people are like houses. The interior and exterior could look immaculate to the outside world, but the basement may be in complete disarray, or the whole foundation cracked. As Yara unlocked her "basement," allowing Gerald to peek inside, he heard Mama's voice loud and clear. From what he could tell, he and Yara needed a thorough overhaul, starting with their own cracked foundations and cluttered basements.

Their mutual cleansing chewed up three hours. No judging, no accusations, just a much-needed emotional release. They lay on their backs—him with hands behind his head, her with fingers interlocked over her chest—while trying to find the sky through a mesh of branches and leaves. Gerald felt like a damp towel, twisted and wrung of every water droplet. Drained, but relieved.

"You okay over there?" he asked, still looking up.

She sighed. "I'm better now. What about you?"

"As good as I can be. Hell, you know more about my life now than anyone, including my brother."

"You have the same honor. My sister doesn't know anything about the things I've done lately. I'm really surprised at myself for opening up to you like this. Only my therapist sees this side of me. And Gerald?"

"Yes?"

"You're a good man. A *real* man. You not getting promoted, your weight gain, or whatever excuse she's used to degrade you, doesn't make you less of one. Lisa obviously has a twisted idea of what a man is."

Gerald stared at the band gripped around his ring finger. "She always made me feel that way, at least since we've been married.

Like I'm not good enough. And I'm always trying to make up for past mistakes, like that damn vasectomy I got."

"Completely forgivable, by the way," Yara said. "It's not like you cheated on her."

"Yeah, but I know I should have told her." Gerald turned on his side. "I'm sorry that happened to you, Yara. I can't even begin to understand how a man could cheat on you."

"Men are simple creatures. They cheat for all kinds of reasons."

"Not *all* men. Even though Lisa treats me like crap sometimes, I've never cheated on her. Never even occurred to me."

Yara smiled. "I can see that about you. You seem very committed."

"Yeah. I guess I am. But, now I'm like why? She clearly doesn't appreciate me. I mean, not really. She's more about the material stuff than what I can offer from"—he fist-bumped his chest— "here."

"You already know I think she's an idiot."

He touched Yara's hand. As much as they shared the past few hours, his hand on hers seemed natural. "And so is... *was* Philip. He didn't appreciate you, either. It's so messed up how you found out about him cheating. I really feel for you. Can't even imagine."

"It's been tough." Her voice cracked. "*Really* tough. What he did almost destroyed me." She managed a chuckle. "That's one of the reasons why I pump myself with meds. Then when he died, I..."

Her words trailed off. Gerald saw the bubble of tears forming again, her eyes glassy. "Hey, it's okay," he said. "I'm here. And for the record, I would never, *ever* do that to you."

"And I would never be Lisa."

Again, Gerald faded inside her magical aura, trapped by hypnotic invisible chains. Her beauty made no sense, especially up close. After so many years, he still couldn't find the right words to encapsulate that "something" about her. She looked like a tangible melody, a timeless Prince song. And yet, Gerald also saw a wounded bird with tattered wings.

Still, remnants of joy glistened from her wet eyes, and they shined on the man in front of her. Yara had reminded him he was still a man—and a *real* man makes the first move.

Screw it. I want this. I want her.

Face flushed and heart pounding so hard he thought it could crack a rib, Gerald leaned his head toward Yara until his lips found hers. It started with a cautious lip-tap, then progressed to a slow dance. As they sank into a deeper groove, his hand on her waist, hers on his cheek, Gerald struggled to restrain his lust. She gave a little tongue, he gave a little back. A vampire's hunger brewed inside, bound to unleash in a frenzy on his prey. Lowly Gerald, Mr. Half-a-Man, lay lip-locked with the hottest woman on the planet. Fireworks exploded from each brain cell in Gerald's head—and in his *other* head.

Gerald killed the loud screech of Lisa screaming in his conscience, kicked her aside and let a woman named Yara take over. He never understood the concept of soulmates until now. Yara made him feel things he never felt with Lisa. *I can't believe this is happening.*

As he neared the peak of spontaneous combustion, Yara pulled away.

Gerald said, "What?"

Yara nodded toward the other end of the grassy field. Gerald raised his head and saw two kids, about seven and nine, running toward the "Yarald" bench, one of them holding a football. A young man walked a few steps behind. While floating through the clouds with Yara, Gerald had forgotten he was still on earth, lying outside in a public place where anyone could see, including children.

"Sit down and let your brother tie your shoes," the man said.

As the younger child sat on the bench, feet dangling off the ground, he waved. Yara and Gerald waved back.

"It might be too much PDA for the kiddies," Yara said with a smile.

"Yeah, you're right," Gerald replied. "Besides, I need to catch my breath."

"Ha. You're cute."

He sat up and stretched his arms high. Yara did the same.

"Gerald?" Yara said, resting her head on his shoulder.

"Yeah?"

Yara paused for a few seconds before she asked, "After all I've told you, you don't think any differently of me, do you?"

Yara definitely dropped a few bombshells during their heart-to-heart, but to Gerald's surprise, he didn't give a damn about the closet full of skeletons. "Not at all," he said. "I'm not judging you. I mean, you were going through a lot. Pain can drive people to do extreme things."

"Yes." She tightened her grip around his arm. "But I passed extreme a long time ago. Some of the things I've done are downright... evil. Part of me was trying to numb the pain and anger after he died, but another part—"

"Hey, you don't have to explain anything to me. That's all in the past. At least, I hope it is."

She smiled. "It is. I promise."

"Good." He kissed her forehead. "Now, pretty lady, we've been out here for hours again and believe it or not, I'm hungry. Again. And I gotta go to the bathroom."

She laughed. "Me, too. How would you like to try my famous tuna casserole?"

"Your famous casserole? What, you have it in your car?" he teased.

"No, silly. My sister's house." Yara winked.

Sister's house, huh? Long subdued, the devil in Gerald took the wheel, speeding toward a long highway of sin. But he didn't care.

"Sure. I would love some."

CHAPTER 19

GERALD

After a mini tour of her sister's one-story house, Yara and Gerald sat at the kitchen counter, finishing off her infamous tuna casserole. Conscious of a tuna breath after-effect, they laughed after each asked the other for gum at the same time. Once again, they fell in sync, an ongoing theme of the story they were writing together.

Yara found a pack of mints in a kitchen drawer and handed him a few. Then they migrated to the bedroom.

After a quick stop in Yara's bathroom, Gerald stepped out and said, "Dang, girl, you have your own pharmacy up in there."

"I know that, Gerald," Yara said, her face deadpan. "We already talked about this at the park, remember?"

"Oh, I'm sorry. I was making a stupid joke. I didn't mean—"

"It's okay," Yara said, now with a warm smile. She checked her watch. "Speaking of which, it's about that time to take my daily dose and stay sane. Can you grab the bottle that says Lexapro, please?"

"Sure." Gerald found the bottle near her toothbrush holder. He glanced at the label with her name in bold, a dosage of 10mg. It said, *Take once a day*. He handed the bottle to her. "Does this drug help?"

"Well, yeah," she replied, popping a pill. "I wouldn't be taking it if it didn't. It evens me out. I'm more in control and less moody, like that calm, steady feeling we both get when we're by the water."

"Hmm, that's good. Maybe I should get me some."

"Oh no, you don't want to do that. The meds can mess with your sex drive."

"They don't appear to have messed with yours," Gerald said with a wink.

Yara laughed. "True."

Framed pictures drew Gerald to the armoire. A picture of her parents stood in the middle with a notebook next to it—the same notebook in her hands when he first saw Yara at the bench.

Gerald said, "Ah, the famous notebook. I can't believe you write poetry and your Johns in here."

Yara threw her head back and slapped both knees, erupting a loud laugh. "Johns. Good one. It's kinda like a diary, so I put everything in there. The encounters with my 'Johns' help with my poetry. Call it inspiration."

"Inspiration," he repeated. He cracked the notebook, but didn't open it all the way. "May I?"

Yara said, "Go ahead. I'm an open book to you now."

Gerald flipped to the first page and found a hand-drawn table with several columns and rows. Most of the names had notes beside them. "Dang, so meticulous. I love your handwriting, too. Wait, *this* guy? Get outta here!"

She nodded. "Everything is true."

"And all of them BB. Crazy." He leaned forward, reading the notes in the "Misc" column. "'Sounds like a drunk hyena when he cums?' What the hell does a drunk hyena sound like?"

"Like him! That was the best way to describe it. It was like a slow, drawn out, high-pitched howl or something."

Gerald screamed, but the hilarity continued. Each row sounded like an X-rated SNL comedy skit, sparking a laughfest between them.

"This dude had a two-incher? How the hell does that work?"

"Ha, barely! I'm not lying, either. Full erection." She extended a pinkie finger. "This big."

"Wow." Gerald kept reading. "Oliver! I remember him." The comments beside Oliver's name made Gerald's face ball up. "Ew, you threw up on him the second time?"

"Noooo. Not *on* him. I did get sick, though. Oliver was the last one. It could've been more, but I'm done with it all. I was off my meds for a bit and that left me to make some very questionable decisions. But I started talking to my therapist again and taking the pills. Slowly, I began feeling more like myself again. That's why I've been writing so much poetry." She paused. "Then I saw you."

Then she saw me. Warm tingles peppered his insides. He had forgotten what that felt like until Yara reminded him.

He played it cool, though, didn't reply. But one name dissolved his laughter and killed the fun. He didn't see any reason to make jokes about him, so before Gerald closed the notebook and set it back on the shelf, he said. "Now I have a better idea of what happened to Marcus Obohu. And why."

Yara shrugged. "I didn't know she would go that far."

"But are you happy she did?"

"That's a good question," Yara said, staring at the ceiling. "I don't know."

"I mean, that's kinda the outcome you were looking for, right? To make him pay?"

"Yes, but... I... I really didn't think it through. I just wanted someone to feel how I felt, you know? I wanted to make a point."

"Well, you did. Big time. I'm not surprised at the names, though. Everybody at Monte Clara High wanted to bang you."

She chuckled. "Maybe. But I don't think they use the word 'bang' anymore, Gerald."

"Told you I bring the 90s back."

"Yeah, you do." She looked down. "So, now that you know my dirty business, are you disgusted or angry with me?"

"No."

She tilted her head. "Why not?"

Gerald stared at his childhood crush. Initially, her string of confessions shocked him, each reveal more horrifying than the last. But, for some reason, he felt nothing but compassion for Yara.

"Like I told you before, I'm just not. You were going through a lot of hurt and anger. Wives will be mad, though, if and when they find out."

"Oh, I'm sure they will. You know the saying 'what's done in the dark...'"

"Yeah. Regardless of the outcome, I'm glad you're back in therapy. And you have a friend in me."

Yara held his hand, but still looked down. "I never thought anyone would understand. Thank you."

"Welcome. You ever see that movie *Silver Linings Playbook*?"

"No."

"The main female character's husband was killed in an accident and she kinda lost it, you know? Then she started sleeping with a bunch of guys to fill the void."

"Thanks for trying to make a point, but I'm sure my situation is a little different."

He shrugged. "Same concept. An out-of-character reaction to a tragedy."

"Okay. I guess."

"Say, why wasn't my name in the book?"

"Because," Yara said with a puzzled look, like she couldn't understand why he would ask such a question. "You're not like them. They're all pigs. You're not."

"Lisa thinks—"

She slapped his arm. "Hey, no cursing in my room."

He rubbed the side of his bicep, acting like he endured the worst pain ever. "Ow! What? You know I don't curse!"

"Stop whining, you big baby. You said the L word. That's not allowed in here."

"Oh." He nodded. "Right. My fault."

They sat quiet for a few seconds, staring at different areas of the room. Then Gerald said, "By the way, I want to thank you, too."

"Thank me for what?"

"For everything. For being there, our talks, our walks, opening up to me, allowing me to open up to you. All that stuff."

"I'm happy you feel you can confide in me."

He nodded. "Likewise. I've never felt so relaxed with anyone before. I didn't think that was possible with a woman as beautiful as you."

"Never felt so relaxed, huh? Well…" Yara scooted closer. Dropping her voice to a whisper, she said, "I can make you feel even more relaxed."

Gerald swallowed. *Oh shoot.*

The rhythm of Gerald's heartbeats double-timed. A thump within his crotch pushed against the zipper of his pants. Yara's eyes conveyed the kind of thirst long vacant in Lisa.

The teenage version of Gerald would've spewed a sperm bath on himself at the mere thought of a tryst with Yara. Though now a married man, he detached from guilt and yielded to temptation.

He savored the soft, moist texture of Yara's lips once again, trekking deeper down an untraveled road toward marital transgression. His evil side urged him to rip off Yara's clothes and throw her onto the bed, but he handled her with the delicate care that a real woman required.

"Wait," Yara said, pulling back. "We shouldn't do this."

Gerald took Yara's hand, noting genuine concern in her eyes. "I think we should. I *want* to do this."

"Gerald, are you sure? After everything I told you at the park? You know I—"

"It's okay. I don't care about that. I only care about you."

A smile stretched each end of Yara's face, as if Gerald pumped life back into her. After a few minutes of slow-grinding his lips on hers, Yara pulled away and removed her blouse, tossing it onto a nearby chair. Gerald salivated at the sight of grapefruit-sized "twins" jiggling underneath her purple silk bra. A moment later, the bra dropped to the floor.

"Dayum," Gerald whispered. Full and supple breasts with nipples like two chocolate morsels. Perfect symmetry and one hundred percent lickable quality. Way better than he imagined, even in his wildest, wettest dreams. As if on high alert, his buddy "Willy" reached grown-man status in seconds.

Yara helped him lose the shirt, causing his belly to do its own little jiggle. Gerald cut the light as they decorated the floor with their clothes.

As they maneuvered to missionary, Willy thumped against her knuckles and wrist. "Omigod, really?" she said. "That woman is a fool."

Gerald smiled, his ego pumped up a notch. Packing heat at a concrete nine-and-a-half inches, Gerald cosigned that comment.

While swiping his tongue around Yara's nipples, he circled two fingers between her thighs, massaging slippery labia folds. She arched her back, a soft hum harmonizing with the urgent slurps of his lips and tongue playing with each breast. Sexual buildup and a nearly lifelong fantasy of Yara underneath him had officially collided. Although he hoped for porn star stamina, Gerald knew a premature firing was imminent.

With that scary thought at the forefront of his mind, he held his breath as she eased her hips against his, slipping Willy inside her private center.

"Oooooh," Gerald whispered, creeping in deeper until he couldn't slip and slide any further. He drowned in the feeling, every nerve in his body charged and amplified, testing his will to hold strong while high on Yara's nectar.

Gerald had never taken a hit of ecstasy before, but he once watched a documentary of teenagers popping the pills, their eyes drooping and sometimes rolling back, caught up in what looked like carnal rapture. Gerald always wondered how that elevated state of euphoria felt. Inside his dream woman, now he knew.

Squeezing the comforter with both fists as if gripping for dear life, Gerald contracted his abs while trying every Jedi mind trick possible to keep from blowing the lid off. When he felt like exploding, he pulled back a bit, careful not to dip too much, too fast. But Yara killed Gerald's pedestrian bump-and-grind, Shakira style. She pancaked Gerald on top of her by latching onto his shoulders and humping against him.

"Awwwww," he moaned, trapped by Yara's MMA lock and frenzied hip thrusts. He tried to keep up the pace, but the more he plunged, the faster she pumped back, her hips lifting in a bridge and pushing him upward.

Gerald's tongue slipped into her mouth, about the same depth as Willy in his new wet crawl-space. No place to go but where her sugar walls led him, forcing deep strokes. Clamped down.

Damn!

Despite her stronghold, Gerald managed a clitoral massage with one finger. Strumming her sacred string evoked a melodic whine from Yara's vocal cords, kicking her hips into overdrive. Flesh slapped against flesh, pound for pound—his grunts mixing with her high-pitched cries.

Gerald held on for as long as he could.

His pelvis tensed. With a rebel yell loud enough to make the neighbors come knocking, he double-pumped one last time until a wave of spasms ripped through him from head to toe.

Shots fired.

Within seconds, Gerald's whole body went limp, including Willy. Gerald buried his damp forehead in a pillow. *Damn*, he thought, heaving in large volumes of air. *I came too freakin' fast.* He knew he couldn't smother Yara for long, but didn't want to reveal his shame, either. Then he realized she had stopped her hip action, too.

"Omigod," Yara said, also gasping, "I can't believe I came so fast."

Gerald snapped his head up. "You came, too?"

"Yes. Not many men work the clit like you did. That was incredible."

Well, damn. On his first try, a maneuver that Lisa hated worked on Yara. Proud, he said, "Me and Willy was just trying to do a lil' sumn', sumn'. All part of my plan."

She laughed. "Willy? You goofball. Well, a lil sumn' sumn' accomplished, Mr. 90s."

He smiled, staring into the face of a gorgeous woman he satisfied in less than two minutes. "So," he said, with a quick peck, "it must mean something that we had orgasms at the same time, huh?"

Yara replied by caressing his cheek and planting her lips on his, a slow groove smooch, ripe with passion. Gentle and sweet, contrasting the maniacal "kisses" between their hips a few minutes before. As Gerald tasted her once more, a megamix of opposing emotions—touch of fear, some anxiety, smidgen of guilt, mountain of self-confidence—balled up in him. Such a weird state of mind; one he'd never experienced before, but welcomed entirely.

They lay holding each other, the cloud of post-coital bliss still wrapped around Gerald's head. As he stared at the ceiling, he felt himself crossing over, transforming under Yara's beacon of light. Shed his old skin and now shiny with a new coat. From that moment, he vowed to do anything for her. Damn the consequences.

"Are you okay over there?" Yara asked.

"Never better." Gerald kissed her forehead. "I feel brand new. Reborn."

"Me, too."

"Soooo, I guess I'm an honorary BB, now?" He winked at her.

Yara smiled, then sighed. "I guess you are. Kinda."

"Yup. I guess I am. I feel like doing something… I don't know… crazy. Something I've never done before."

Yara propped up on an elbow. "Like what you're doing now?"

"No." He placed his hands behind his head. "Crazier than this."

"Well, it's funny that you say that, Gerald. I have an idea I'd like to run by you."

"Yeah?" Gerald turned to her, saw a wicked smile. "That's good 'cause I have an idea, too."

CHAPTER 20

LISA

"Who are you and what have you done with my husband?"

Gerald strutted toward the bathroom, buck-naked. "Your husband's right here. Just a side you haven't seen in a while." He winked back at her.

"Correction," she whispered, "haven't seen ever."

As she took in deep breaths, still spread-eagled in the middle of the bed, Lisa wiped the sweat off her forehead with the sheets. The hard base vibrating against her chest slowed to a normal pace.

Her mental marbles still a little scrambled, Lisa tried to make sense of how the "missionary man"—with an all-too-familiar time-limit of four minutes and a one-position-only skill set—conquered her side, front, and back for thirty non-stop minutes. When she woke up around 5:00 a.m. to use the bathroom, Gerald was still in Dreamville, hog-snorting in bliss as usual. She couldn't fall back asleep with the pig noises squealing and squawking out of Gerald's mouth, so she played around on her cell phone until a naughty idea flashed in her head. She figured, *What the hell?*

Gerald only had a few days left of light before fading to black forever, so why not wake him up with a head clinic and her goodies before sunrise? Especially since she had barred him for months.

Lisa went into sex bandit mode and gently pulled down his shorts, reintroducing her lips and tongue to a part of Gerald she hadn't touched in a while. Once his thick flesh swelled inside her mouth, the hog snorts stopped and a few sporadic moans took over. She planned to suck him off for a few minutes, then mount the pony and ride him until she milked it dry—the perfect way to end the drought. At least, *his* drought. She assumed Gerald would shoot his load within two minutes, tops.

She never expected Gerald to morph into a porn star. Gerald hit it proper until he exorcised two seismic orgasms out of her, 10.0 on the "Dickter" scale, as he used to say when they were younger and more like rabbits. Feet in the air, then ass in the air, even a little hair pulling—Lisa howled and growled until she was out of breath and spent, like she'd just finished a high-intensity kick-boxing class.

To top it off, Gerald's surprise act ranked better than any rump-a-thon with Greg.

As she eased out of bed and marveled at Gerald's newfound endurance, a part of her wanted to know where the hell it came from.

Lisa whipped up a quickie breakfast of scrambled eggs and toast while Gerald showered and dressed. A vase of roses stood in the middle of the dining table.

"Roses I got you still going strong, I see," Gerald said, sitting down at the dining table. "And yet another wonderful surprise—breakfast before work. What prompted this?"

The insurance money I'm going to get when you're gone. "Nothing."

"Nice!"

Lisa handed him a plate of food. "Where did all that energy come from? You haven't been back in the gym that long."

He laughed. "Babe, it's been a few months since… you know. I'm way backed up. What did you expect?"

"Not that."

"Well, you got me, too. I don't know, this is kinda strange."

"What's strange?"

"This hot-and-cold routine. Like you cooking breakfast for me last weekend, acting all nice. Then the next day, you went back to ignoring me again. *Then* I get the main course meal in the bedroom this morning."

"What do you mean? I haven't been ignoring you."

"Yes, you have. You've barely spoken to me all week, aside from asking what time I'll be home. And you're always on the phone texting your reunion buddies, like I'm not even in the room."

Lisa swallowed her food, unsure how to respond. Ever since she'd finalized the hit on Gerald, she'd been a little jumpy, checking her phone more than necessary to make sure the plans were still on track. No turning back now.

"You know how I am about this whole reunion thing. We only have a few days left and I… *we* want everything to be perfect. It should be a" —she made a gun gesture with her hand, index finger pointing upward, cocking her thumb— "blast."

"I'm sure it will," Gerald said with a chuckle. "I know how much work you and your little committee have put in."

Out of the blue, Gerald set his fork down and placed his hand on top of Lisa's. She looked at his hand on hers, then back to him. "Why are you looking at me like that?" she asked.

Gerald scooted his chair closer to her. "Babe, from this day forward, I want us to be honest with each other. I've made mistakes, but you have, too. I think the past few years we've been kinda running away from our issues, so…" He shrugged. "Let's try to do better and communicate more. For us."

For us? Sure, for a few more days. Lisa suppressed a laugh.

But as he waited for a response, puppy dog eyes tried to tug at the hard strings attached to Lisa's cold heart. To her surprise, the strings bent a little. She still had an ounce of sympathy left for her husband. Even a frigid heart has a region of warmth. But not enough.

"Okay," she replied, trying to sound as genuine as possible. "From this day forward, a new beginning. Absolutely."

"Good." He kissed her forehead. "Love you."

Her face flushed, Lisa struggled with an unexpected spurt of mixed emotions. She held strong to her facade and uttered the same three words that had become a foreign language to her: "I love you, too."

Gerald went back to his food with an upbeat pep. "Man, this is the best morning ever. A little nookie, breakfast, my wife loves me." He jammed a piece of toast in his mouth, mumbling, "Can't get much betta dan dat."

Lisa caught a glimpse of chewed pieces of bread smacking inside his mouth and looked away. Type of shit little boys do—talking with their mouths open, one of many Gerald-made thorns in her side. But in a rare moment of self-restraint, she kept the disgust to herself.

"Oh, by da way," he said before a guttural swallow, "since we're being honest. You'll never guess who I ran into near the Wharf not too long ago. You finished?"

"Yes. Who?"

He checked his watch, then picked up both plates. "Yara Bassili."

"From high school? Your old crush?"

"Everyone's crush."

"I saw that she's coming to the reunion. What, she lives here now?"

"Yeah. After her husband passed, she moved in with her sister." He ran water and a sponge over the plates before placing them in the dishwasher. "We had lunch and everything."

"You had lunch with her?"

"Yeah. We ate and talked for a while. Just catching up."

"Catching up?" She cut her eyes at him. "What did you two have to catch up on?"

"Well, we did have a class or two together. We spoke for a couple of hours, actually. And man! She is still gorgeous. Even more now."

A heat wave rushed across Lisa's face. "What did you say?" She stood up. "Why are you up in here talking about another woman? And why the fuck did you have lunch with her, anyway?"

"Wait," Gerald said, picking up his briefcase. "Are you jealous? I thought you didn't get jealous? Hmmm, ain't that somethin'?"

A simple question, but it tripped her up—not only that he asked it, but how fast her blood burned from Gerald drooling over another woman. As she processed her hypocrisy, she noticed a smug grin under a sly glare, teasing her.

"It's not about being jealous," Lisa said, a calm tone now in her voice. "I had no idea you had lunch with her."

"I called you after we finished, but as usual, somebody didn't answer their phone. Why are you so upset?"

"It's just… okay. You had the nerve to call another woman gorgeous in my house."

Walking toward the front door with Lisa on his heels, Gerald said, "First of all, this isn't *your* house. We're just renting it. Second, I'm telling you, now, right? Improving our communication, being upfront? No harm done. I don't question you when you go to your reunion meetings, do I? Because I trust you."

Lisa placed a hand on her hip, mouth open, but the words clogged. Tripped up again. She couldn't say a thing. With Greg plugging up her holes on the regular and Patrick prepped to widow her, she knew she didn't deserve an ounce of trust.

Finally, she said, "Look, I—"

Gerald pressed his lips against hers, muffling what little she had to say. A sweet peck followed, tailor-made from a husband to his wife. To Lisa's surprise, she accepted. Welcomed it, actually, gave some back, too. He parted from her with that same smug grin, a wicked yet playful glint in his eyes.

Gerald grazed his lips against Lisa's ear. "Tonight I'm gonna hit it so good you'll say to yourself, 'Why the hell did I hold out on him for so long?'" He kissed her again. "Have a good day, gorgeous."

Damn. He had switched from an erotic whisper to a sweet farewell, igniting tingles from head to toe. Lisa watched her marked husband step outside and close the door, still wrapping her brain around it all. Surreal. He looked like Gerald, and sounded like Gerald, but it ended there. The tall order of swag with a side of cocky swallowed Gerald up and spat out a new man sporting a slick tongue and magic stick.

What in the world just happened?

Breaking away from the hazy fog that Gerald left behind, Lisa stepped back into the kitchen and ran the dishwasher. She was usually still in bed when Gerald left for work, but two orgasms and breakfast had her wide-eyed and alive, ready to tackle the day.

First, she checked the Facebook reunion page and found a long thread of comments and comedic memes referencing a new Blue Devil YouTube video. She clicked the link and saw another silly video with its slideshow of unearthed throwbacks, hilariously narrated by the mystery mascot. The video had been shared over a hundred times and generated a wealth of enthusiastic banter, with comments like, "I can't wait for the reunion!" The power of social media at work. Like Craig said, the phantom Blue Devil was the best thing that could have happened to the reunion.

Lisa brimmed with pride as she noted the new attendance numbers, up to 143. The reunion was on track to be one for the record books with an epic grand finale. And Lisa helped make it happen.

Lisa's purse vibrated. She dug around inside and retrieved her cell phone, noticing a "1" from the burner app. She logged in her secret PIN and saw a text message:

Checked out the spot last night. We good.

Lisa stared at the message. *We good.* Two simple, life-altering words.

In a few days, her world would flip on its head, jump-starting a massive charade of a wife in mourning. But while caught up in the fantasy of the good life, she never processed the practical realities of doing it all on her own. A life without Gerald.

The screensaver on her laptop started up, and a digital image of Gerald and Quinton floated across the screen. Decked out in suits with bowties, the fraternal twins looked identical—same smile, same chocolate skin tone, same build—except Gerald was thirty pounds lighter back then and Quinton rocked cornrows. Twin stacks of handsome, no question. But not head over heels with Gerald and not too fond of Quinton, either, even back then. For the first time, it sank in that Patrick would be cutting off Quinton's other half forever.

Lisa shook off the vines of guilt that threatened to take root. Quinton's loss of a brother was a small price to pay for a fast track out of a soul-sucking marriage. Lisa had married the kind of man she despised the most—a weak ass pussy. The "yes dear" type who let everyone walk all over him. In the beginning, his temperament was an asset—a fairytale wedding, an epic honeymoon, unlimited budget for shopping and self-pampering—the works. All she had to do was ask. But over time, the iron links of marriage wasted away, became too brittle, and the "almost-love" mutated into disgust and pity.

Yet, as she focused on the parade of digital images on her screen, Gerald formed a one-man parade in her head. She couldn't help but replay their early morning rumpfest, feeding the burn building between her thighs. Ever since his argument with Quinton, Gerald found his inner devil, and it all spilled over into the bedroom. Somehow, he had flipped a switch and found his swag.

Where has this Gerald been hiding all these years? Maybe he's turning over a new—

"No, I can't do this!" Lisa cried, shaking off the residue of sympathy for her soon-to-be late husband. "What's done is done. No turning back."

Lisa stood up, stretching her arms above her head. She couldn't allow herself to feel anymore, only for show—just enough to pump up Gerald's ego so he could have a sense of peace in his marriage before he kicked it. As Lisa stared at a picture of Gerald and his mother, she steeled herself up and said, "Don't worry. You'll be seeing your son soon."

By 6:00 p.m., daylight savings had ushered in the early black skies of the fall season. Gerald had texted about hitting the gym after work, so Lisa had a few hours to kill before slipping her wifey mask back on. She wondered about Greg. Hardly a day went by without him setting up an appointment for their next "rendezscrew."

As if they shared some type of telepathic connection, Lisa's phone buzzed. Frowning, her bottom lip dropped when she read Greg's message through the burner app. "He can *not* be serious." Her finger suspended over the phone, considering her response. Finally, she texted back, **Give me fifteen minutes.**

Delayed by the usual after-work traffic jam, it took Lisa nearly thirty minutes to arrive at the three-story parking structure downtown. She drove up to the top level. Like Greg's text said, an open field of empty spots lay before her. She saw a few cars scattered about, but none parked in the pitch-black corner that Greg had reserved for his SUV. She eased her car into the stall beside him.

"About time," Greg said, his window rolled down halfway.

"Just be happy I came."

"Not yet, but you will." He chuckled. "Man, you weren't kidding about how dark it gets in this corner. Gerald won't see Patrick coming."

Greg's comment launched Lisa into fantasy mode: Somewhere nearby was a potential crime scene with Gerald lying in the middle. Although Patrick claimed he wouldn't use a gun, she still imagined a pool of blood oozing out of Gerald's bullet-ridden body, flowing into a drain.

A chill rushed through her. Lisa could see him. Sprawled out. Lifeless. Alone.

I can't wait for this to all be over. Once done, she could kick Greg's smug ass to the curb, but for now, Lisa had to play the part of his little fuck toy to keep him happy.

"You getting in or what?"

"Oh." After breaking away from the gruesome imagery, Lisa climbed into the passenger seat and closed the door. The scent of Greg's cologne welcomed her, but lacked its usual magnetic pull. "I guess I zoned out for a second."

"I can see that. Hey, you sure you're all right? You look a little out of it."

"I'm okay," Lisa said, turning to look at him for the first time. "I'm starting to feel a little weirded out about all of this, I guess."

"Weirded out?" Greg faced her with a fire in his eyes she'd never seen before. "Okay, what the fuck does that mean? You changing your mind?"

"No, no," Lisa replied, trying to recover her hard exterior. "It's just starting to hit me that this is all going down."

"You damn right it's going down! And you can't back out. My cousin…" He shook his head, peering out the windshield. "He's not someone to play with. I'm telling you, he'll wipe out you, me, *and* Gerald. If you're changing your mind—"

"I'm not changing my mind, okay?" she snapped, determined not to look soft. "Reunion night, he dies, and when that insurance check comes in, we'll all get paid."

"Good. That's what I want to hear." Greg licked his lips. "I'm so damn hot for you right now." He nodded toward the backseat. "I wanna fuck you on the same spot where your husband will die."

Lisa climbed into the backseat, then faced him. Gave Greg that look, the one she knew he liked. Legs spread like wings, she slid a hand inside her panties. Greg watched the show, that same smirk still painted on his face.

"What are you waiting for?"

"Yeah," Greg said, before he cut the light, "that's my girl."

CHAPTER 21

YARA

"Do you think you've made progress, Yara?" Dr. Kazarian asked through the desktop computer.

"Yes, I do. For the first time since Philip passed, I don't feel this…" Yara paused to search for the right words, motioning with her hands, "this… all-consuming hatred."

"That's encouraging. You're doing the right things to heal. Moving in with your sister helped to cut the chains that held you down in the abyss, so to speak. Now that you're back on your meds, and writing poetry again, I think we've turned a corner. I absolutely loved your latest poem, by the way. Thank you for sharing."

Pumped with pride, Yara replied, "You're welcome, Dr. Kazarian. And thank you again for listening to it."

"It was my pleasure." Dr. Kazarian placed her arms on the oak table and interlocked her fingers. "Before we conclude, I'd like to talk about your relationship with this Gerald gentleman." The tone in her voice shifted. "I'm a bit concerned."

Yara leaned back into the leather chair recliner, tapping the armrest. She regretted telling Dr. Kazarian about her lunch date with Gerald. Clearly she hadn't done a good job convincing the doctor of her platonic intentions.

"Why are you concerned? I told you I went to high school with him."

Dr. Kazarian cleared her throat. "I don't think it's healthy to spend so much time with married men. This is becoming quite a pattern, Yara."

"I told you I'm not having sex with any of them," Yara lied. She caught a frown on the doctor's face, and Yara knew she wasn't buying what Yara was selling.

"Becoming emotionally attached can be just as harmful as a physical relationship. You're making such great progress. I'd hate to see you suffer a setback."

"I understand your concern, but it's all harmless. Besides, they approached *me*. I was just trying to be nice, probably to make up for ignoring them in high school." She shrugged. "They're old classmates, nothing more."

"And Gerald?"

Yara's lips parted, but she cut herself off, stopping the build-up of lies. Some things were best left unsaid. She had placed Dr. Kazarian on a need-to-know status, only revealing bits and pieces of her story. Her psychiatrist would never understand what compelled her to sleep with those men, or the motivations behind her end game. And she would definitely have something to say about her affair with Gerald.

Yara looked out the window, gazing at the rose bushes in her sister's pint-sized backyard. She replayed her first time with Gerald—their naked bodies touching, his perpetual sweet side, the butterflies she felt. Then the rose. Gerald had reached outside the window and pulled a rose for her, but his romantic gesture turned into an epic fail when he cut his finger on a thorny stem, blood leaking down his hand. They shared a good laugh, though.

"When we meet next week, I'd like to further explore where you went just now."

Yara blinked away her thoughts. "Excuse me?"

"I asked about Gerald, but you didn't say anything and went blank, like your mind ran off somewhere. I also noticed a little smile. Wherever you went, I believe Gerald took you there."

Yara looked down, trying to scrub whatever the doctor saw from her face. "Okay, we can explore where I went next week." *Or not.*

"Good," Dr. Kazarian said. "Now remember, Yara, Gerald is a married man. Try to minimize contact with him, please."

"I will," Yara said, all smiles. "Thank you for everything."

"You're very welcome. Talk to you soon."

"Byyyye," Yara replied, waving.

After signing out of SKYPE, Yara went stone-faced and quiet. Dr. Kazarian didn't know it, but Yara had said her last goodbye. She no longer required the good doctor's services.

Yara propped her feet on the desk, grabbed the mouse, and clicked the Facebook tab. Greg Stephen's home page popped back up on screen, his profile pic a headshot of him and wife Aanya cheesing for the camera. Beautiful picture. Gorgeous couple. And fake.

Poor, clueless Aanya. Yara remembered what it felt like to be head-over-heels in love with her husband, oblivious to the betrayal and deceit perpetrated behind her back. Greg's profile picture alone told the bold-faced lie, and was nothing more than a dolled-up billboard trying to sell a phony product —their happy marriage.

Like the other male rodents that chased after her, Yara knew Greg's true side.

Yara clicked one of the last messages from Greg, mainly comprised of bold claims about the nasty shit he would do to her. Another message bragged about his goods while trying to seal the deal with Netflix and a hotel.

Thirsty pervert.

Greg had contacted her via instant messenger, and to no surprise, his messages went from the usual "how ya doing" to dick pics in record time. Greg had been next on her list to become an honorary BB, but once she started seeing Gerald, she cut off all contact with Greg and the other little boys disguised as men. Mr. Playboy didn't respond well to the silent treatment, and the thirst intensified. Yara could almost hear him crying and whining through the computer.

Though she was trying to reform her evil ways, she still had room left in a cold space of her heart, specifically for Greg Stephens. Someone had to teach his dumb ass a lesson.

She pulled the keyboard towards her. "I'm sorry you haven't heard from me. Got really busy. How about we hook up the night of the reunion?"

Yara clicked Send, then picked up her phone to text Gerald. I just sent him a message on Facebook, she typed. He thinks we're hooking up the night of the reunion. LOL

Within minutes, Gerald texted back: Good. We'll see who's the boss and who's the bitch then.

CHAPTER 22

QUINTON

"Where's the rest of it?" Quinton said, after counting seven twenty-dollar bills and a ten. "I told you three hundred dollars."

"I know, Daddy," Darla said in a whiny voice. She flipped her blond hair toward the back, perking up the two new bubbles not far from Quinton's chin. "I only got half right now. I told you I maxed out my credit card to get my babies. You like?" Hands on her hips, she wiggled the extra "baby fat," the twins stretching her halter top to its max.

Nothing new. From bee-sting lips, to back alley Botox, to asses that doubled in size, Quinton had seen it all before. *Stupid ass*, he thought. *Got two kids and she maxed out her credit card for fake titties.*

Quinton handed the money back to her. "Come back when you get the rest."

Darla stood still with her mouth cocked open as if stuck, eyes blinking. She looked like a robot that had shut down from system overload, unable to compute the new data in her processor. Quinton could hear the words screaming in her head: *How dare this man turn down an ultra-fine woman like me with titties the size of volleyballs.*

"What are you saying?" she said, crossing her arms and covering up her newly enhanced chest.

Quinton placed his camera equipment back in the closet behind him. "I'm not taking professional headshots for a hundred and fifty dollars. When you have all the money, we're good to go. Now if you'll excuse me, I have other projects."

Darla, still trying to compute rejection, rearmed herself the way only a woman with a thick hourglass could.

Darla sashayed over to him. "C'mon, Daddy, let me pay you another way, like we did before." She grabbed his hand. "You know you want these all up in your face."

Quinton turned to the green-eyed Heather Graham look-alike. Another wannabe, but a primetime freak, too. No doubt, of all the thirsty hoes he tangled in his bed sheets, Darla pushed freak mode to new heights, every hole of hers unguarded and open for "jizzness," swallowing even. More triple-X than PG-13, she had taken full advantage of Quinton's dick discount, all for some damn pictures she hoped would pave the way for her appearance in a glossed out magazine or ratchet rap video. But when she found out her "tittie bitties" couldn't make the cut, she sold out and went plastic, then had the nerve to come back to Quinton with half the dough.

No matter how well she rocked the mic, Quinton knew he had to stop accepting pussy as a legit form of currency. At least, for now. Chickenheads tried to play him too much.

He pushed her hand away. "Take you and them silicone pimples out of my face. For real, unless you got the money, you ain't getting shit from me. A nut ain't paying my rent."

Again stuck, Darla did her best impression of a statue. Her over-inflated double whammies couldn't whammy Quinton enough.

But she still didn't catch the hint. "Did I st-st-stutter?" Quinton asked. "You can get ghost now."

Darla whipped around and stomped toward the door, her heels nearly punching holes in the floor. "Ugh! You're one dumb asshole!"

"Yeah, that's what they say." He sat at his desk, his back to her.

Darla yanked the front door open. Pissed, she missed the first step and stumbled outside, screaming a hailstorm of cuss words. Quinton whipped around to see ass and heels tumbling to the ground.

Quinton laughed. "That's what you git!"

No amount of sexy could erase the image of Darla pancaking the concrete. Still, Quinton stood up to help her, but Darla shot to her feet before he reached the door.

"Fuck you!" Darla screamed.

"Not today," Quinton said, closing the door in her face. A minute later, he heard her revved up Mustang bolt out of the parking lot. But like the others, he knew she'd be back. "Betta have my money, too."

Free from female detractors, Quinton returned to work. He uploaded a completed set of digital picture files into a Dropbox account for another client to access and download, one who paid their debt in full. With no photo shoots scheduled for the rest of the day, he burned one and started a new project, an overhaul of a local fitness instructor's busted website.

A 90s Neo Soul channel on Spotify bumped D'Angelo's "Brown Sugar" through the desktop speakers. As Quinton played around with the HTML files, he muddled through piles of mental garbage in need of a swift cleanup, like the dirt he had on his sister-in-law. Quinton hated that Lisa was playing his brother, and hated even more that Gerald didn't know, but Gerald was being a first class dick. Still, it bothered Quinton. Mama wouldn't stand for her two boys barely talking to each other.

If the mess between him and his twin didn't wreck his nerves enough, somehow D'Angelo's lyrics molded a picture of Aanya that inflamed his conscience like the slow burn on his Marlboro cigarette.

Ever since he last saw her in the park, that face and smile, which he adored so much, became permanent fixtures in his daydreams, disrupting his focus on projects that paid the bills—like now. He owned the smoking gun on her sorry husband, but what good was that when Aanya refused to respond to his calls and texts? Quinton was more than ready to become the proverbial shoulder.

He glanced at his cell, thinking he might have missed a message while messing around with Darla. As usual, nothing from Gerald or Aanya.

Why the fuck hasn't she responded yet? Pissing me off, for real.

Unable to place his mind on the task at hand, Quinton pushed the chair back and lit another cigarette, taking in a puff. He relocated to the futon and grabbed his iPad, deciding to smother his senses with stupid YouTube videos. Jill Scott took over the silky smooth delivery from D'Angelo with her song "Running Away."

Someone knocked on the door. Frowning, Quinton said, "Who the hell is that?"

He hit Pause and placed the iPad on his desk. Had to be Darla, either with the rest of the money or still determined to renegotiate with the promise of pussy droplets splattered around the room. Quinton took one more puff, then mashed the cigarette in the copper ashtray, nowhere near in the mood for Darla's theatrics.

He cracked the front door. "Look! I... oh. Damn."

"Hi."

Aanya stood on his doorstep with a smile that looked forced. Quinton opened the door wider and stepped forward. The mystery woman had finally decided to show her face. He thought the ass in him would chew her up in a tirade, but Aanya's sad eyes muzzled him a bit.

"Sorry about that," he said with an even tone. "Thought you were someone else."

"It's okay," Aanya said, moving a strand of hair away from her eye. "Sorry to stop by without calling first."

"Where have you been? I know you got my messages."

"I did," she said, looking down at her Ugg boots. "I just..."

"You just what?"

When she looked up, Quinton saw the face of a woman searching for a lifeline. Her mouth moved, but no words followed. Then Quinton watched as she closed the gap between them, slow, cautious.

What the...

He stood his ground, body heat spiking, but no flinching, no backing away. Without saying a word, her body spoke loud and clear. His did, too.

Aanya pressed against Quinton, chest on chest, lips on lips, forcing him to backpedal. Quinton closed the door as she shifted into a famished aggressor, tugging at his white tee while digging her tongue in his mouth. Quinton's head told him to slow her roll, but the other head commandeered and took the reins.

He pulled the t-shirt over his head and threw it on the floor, her red-coated nails grazing his pecs. A million questions rode the tip of his tongue—along with the slobberfest from their mouths smacking into each other—but as Aanya's sweater also hit the floor, exposing a silky white bra fresh out of a Victoria's Secret catalog, he kept his trap shut for fear of killing the groove.

Man, he thought, the back of his leg bumping the futon, *I'm glad I kicked Darla out.*

He kicked off his sweatpants and fell onto the futon. As he scooted back toward the pillows, he enjoyed the strip show at the foot of the futon. Aanya hooked her thumbs inside her leggings at the waist, then leaned forward and pushed them toward her ankles. She kicked her boots, panties, and leggings under a nearby chair off to the side.

Quinton took a quick survey of her temple. So damn beautiful… that glow, her curvy body and all its minor flaws. Smooth skin, even-toned. Hourglass waist, little pooch belly, neatly trimmed bush. All woman, nothing manufactured. Real.

"Dayum," he whispered, heart pounding. Seeing her as more of an erotic display than a cheap X-rated peep show, Aanya had Quinton's heart *and* head, turning him on in a way that dumb bitches like Darla couldn't.

Aanya eased onto the futon knee-first, both hands behind her back. "This is me now," she said, unsnapping the bra strap. "What you see is what you get."

"And I want what you got."

The bra fell on his shin. Nipples hard and pointing at him, Quinton shot her a smile of approval. On the small side, they were more like oranges than grapefruits, but plump. Just right.

The fabric of his boxer shorts pushed upward like a tent, so Quinton lost the boxers and made them an ornament on his desk, still watching Aanya as her gaze stuck on Big Daddy. Her eyeballs almost ejected from each socket, mouth as round and wide as an opened manhole.

Quinton smiled. Big Daddy always inflicted momentary paralysis on the ladies once revealed.

"You remember Big Daddy?" Quinton asked, grasping the meaty middle.

"How could I forget?" Aanya replied. "To this day, that's the most man I've ever had inside me."

Quinton beamed with pride. "Then what 'chu waiting for?"

She crawled toward him. Big Daddy grazed her rib cage, bending backward as she pressed forward.

"It's so warm," Aanya said, his hard flesh pressing her left breast.

He chuckled. "That's just a sample."

"Um hum. Sample, huh?"

She straddled him, lip-tapping Quinton's neck first, then waltzing into a slow kiss while running her hands through his dreads. Her nipples rubbed against his chest with Big Daddy hard as titanium. Succumbing to a primal desire, Quinton had some sense left to reach for a Trojan, but as Aanya gripped the shaft and eased him inside, he seized up and self-control collapsed. Felt so good, he broke his safe sex rule by dropping the packet on the floor.

"Aww, yeah," he whispered, now nine inches deep, exposed and raw. He watched Aanya gasp and her eyelids droop, bliss draping over her.

Quinton didn't expect his afternoon to veer off into him naked with another man's wife. He could barely fathom the surreal sight of Aanya literally on his sack while rocking her wedding ring. Greg fucked up big time. He practically dropped her off at Quinton's front door.

Quinton gripped each of Aanya's butt cheeks and they rocked with each other, same rhythm, same speed, creating an orchestra of moans and hisses that complemented Maxwell's well-timed slow jam "Til The Cops Come Knockin'." Cupping her breasts, Quinton enjoyed a private lap dance while exploring the contours of Aanya's wet walls. Aanya nibbled her bottom lip, riding the deep stroke. Her hair was a perfect mess, strands across her eyes, mouth, cheek. Sexy. As. Fuck.

"Ooh," she moaned, hands pressed on Quinton's chest as she clamped down on his pony.

Aanya's hips moved faster and her moans grew louder, morphing into a siren-like tone. Quinton interlocked his fingers with Aanya's, staring at her as she trembled, loving the sight of a woman in the throes of pleasure as she gnawed her way to climax. Quinton teetered at his peak, but like a gentleman, held back from erupting and waited for the lady to get hers first. Another Quinton rule, and one he planned to keep.

Aanya whipped her head forward and unleashed a high-pitched crackly whine. She bent Quinton's fingers backward, gripping his hands so tight that sharp spikes of pain shot through his knuckles.

The last wave of body spasms made her twitch like a pop locker, and he kept their fingers intertwined to steady her, never letting go.

"Omigod!" Aanya reverberated her cries to a higher power in spurts. Seconds later, her breathing slowed, hips grinding to a halt. She wiped her brow with the back of her hand. "That was so intense. Did you come, too?"

Ripples fired from Quinton's inner thighs, tightening his gut. Through clenched teeth, he grunted, "Not… yet."

The moment he said those words, he pushed his hips upward and a geyser exploded in Aanya's canal. He lifted his head off the pillow, muttering a series of growls that vibrated inside his throat.

Spent, Quinton plopped his head back on the pillow, looking up at the ceiling fan. "Woooo!" he cried, still breathing hard. "Damn, woman!"

She laughed, then furrowed her eyebrows, as if processing a new thought. "Quinton, were you waiting until I came?"

He nodded. "Ladies first, right?"

The look in her eyes told Quinton he had touched her where it mattered most. Aanya said, "You are so sweet. You always were."

Quinton learned at an early age that if you made the woman's needs a priority, a man could get almost anything out of her.

Aanya planted a soft kiss, then cuddled her naked body next to Quinton. Curled up under his arm, she rested her head on his chest while Quinton watched the fan blades spin with Maxwell serenading their gradual descent from the sweetest high. Quinton suppressed the urge to blaze one.

"I just realized you had music playing," Aanya said. "Maxwell. Nice."

Quinton pulled her close, taking in a flowery fragrance that scented her hair. "Shoot, with all that noise you was making, no wonder you couldn't hear the music."

She slapped his chest. "Shut up. I wasn't that loud."

"Just messing with you."

"Ha ha."

Aanya turned onto her side to face Quinton; he did the same. With Aanya only a breath away, he skimmed her over, as if for the first time. Round eyes, full lips. Brown skin painted by angels. Lovely. At that moment, Quinton realized she never wore makeup. Ever. When girls used their faces as a canvas for mascara, eyeshadow and lipstick in high school, Aanya always stayed chemical free, and still looked better than 85 percent of them. He wondered about waking up next to that face each morning.

"You're so beautiful," he said, tracing the curve of her hip with his palm.

She sighed, then looked down. "I wish I could see what you see."

Quinton frowned, stunned by her self-doubt. That flirty, confident girl he'd fallen for way back when had cowered up and vanished. Greg had trampled her self-esteem.

"You still are," he said, staring deep into her eyes so she could feel his conviction. "You always have been… one of the most beautiful women I've ever known."

Her smile, once vacant, again tried to take root. "Thank you, Quinny Binny. I just find it so hard to believe, considering all the beauty around you." She gestured at the pictures littering the walls.

"Trust me, these chickenheads have nothing on you."

"You're sweet," she replied, but Quinton noted traces of doubt still trapped in her eyes, and he wasn't convinced she believed him. Before he could say another word, Aanya sat up. "Omigod, what have I done? I haven't been with another man in years."

Quinton propped up on his elbow, confused. "Wait, you're not feeling guilty, are you? You did see the pictures, right?"

"Yes, I saw them."

"And you're kicking Greg's ass to the curb, right?"

Aanya gathered her discarded clothes, avoiding his eyes. "It's complicated, Quinton."

Quinton almost let a cuss word slip out. Aanya had said his real name again, back to a formal exchange. And she hit him with "it's complicated," one of the weakest excuses ever said to avoid facing a problem. He never expected those words to come out of Aanya's mouth. Her words punched a hole in his spirit, reminding him that another man still held stock in a relationship with Aanya, while Quinton was just a spectator who got lucky.

"Aanya, what the hell is complicated? Your husband has been kicking down women all over town. What did he say when you confronted him?" He never mentioned Lisa.

Aanya slipped back into her panties and leggings. "Do you mind if I use your bathroom?" she asked, standing up.

Not only did she sidestep Quinton's query, she was rushing to dress herself. The shift in mood puzzled Quinton and ticked him off a bit. Still, he put a leash on his tongue.

"Naw, go 'head," he replied.

Quinton put on his sweats and waited, still confused by what had just transpired. Minutes later, Aanya emerged from the bathroom, fully clothed, having transformed back to the woman who popped up uninvited at Quinton's front door. She sat down across from him and put on her Ugg boots.

Reading his mind, she said, "And, no, I haven't confronted him, yet. What, you think I should just act like the jilted wife, slash his tires, and show up at his job or whatever?"

Quinton glared at her. "No, but… damn, it's like that, though? Wait, we just gonna sit here and pretend what just happened didn't happen?"

"No, I know what happened," she said. "And it was wonderful."

"Then why are you in such a hurry to get out of here?"

"Because," Aanya said, strands of hair concealing parts of her face, "this is a lot to process right now. My world has been turned upside down. My marriage is over." Her voice cracked. "I have a lot of things I need to figure out."

"I can help you with all of that," Quinton said, taking her hand. Seeing the strain on her face, he lost the desire to grill her.

Aanya leaned forward and planted a kiss. "You've done enough. What happens next is on me."

Quinton watched as she stood up to leave. He followed her toward the door. "When can I see you again?"

"I'll see you at the reunion," she replied.

"You're still going?"

"Of course. I think I need a night of fun, seeing old friends. My mind needs to be somewhere else for a while."

"I heard that. Well, if you need anything, you know where I am." They played the awkward dance, looking away, then at their feet, searching for the right parting words. No real protocol for goodbyes after infidelity, especially if both parties catch feelings.

"Just so you know," Quinton continued, "I won't do or say anything. That's between you and your husband. I just…" He scrambled to extract the right words that had bottlenecked in him, crammed at the tip of his tongue—anything to let her know he wanted more. But he couldn't articulate what "more" meant, so he kept it simple. "Whatever you need, I'm here."

"Thank you," Aanya replied. "And what happened here, I have no regrets."

"Me, either."

"Good." She nodded. "That's good. So, see you at the reunion?"

"That and beyond, I hope."

"Okay." She kissed his cheek. "See you then."

"Bye."

Quinton closed the door, trying to recover from the whiplash of Aanya's hit and run. She had treated him like a fast food drive-thru—came by, got what she needed, and dipped out. She used him to channel the hurt and exorcise her demons, spurred by a thirst for revenge. He was happy to provide some jump-off relief, and wouldn't mind playing that role for a while, but something didn't sit well within him. He still wanted more. So much more.

Although Quinton told Aanya he would stay out of her business with Greg, he knew he couldn't. He had tasted the fruit that belonged to another man—a fruit that belonged to him *first*. Now, he had gotten back in too deep. Literally.

He lit another cigarette. "Fuck this. I have a feeling ol' Greg's going to know all about me."

CHAPTER 23

GERALD

She got them.

The ends of Gerald's lips crept up each side of his face upon reading Yara's text. Crazy. Another piece had fallen into place, and Gerald felt more charged and alive than ever, ready to move full-speed ahead. "Looks like this is really happening," he said, shoving the phone back in the pocket of his slacks. "Man, this is going to be fun."

He resumed his walk toward the glass door of his nine-to-five, an extra pep in his step. Without fail, "Nia Long" greeted him from behind the front desk with her million dollar smile.

"Good morning and happy Friday to you, Alicia," he said, walking up to the counter. "How are you?"

"Morning, Gerald. I'm fine. And it looks like you're doing great once again."

"Always. Beautiful day, isn't it?"

Before Gerald disappeared down the short pathway to the cubicles, Alicia said, "Okay, wait a minute."

Gerald stopped in his tracks. "What's up?"

"You're what's up!" She leaned back in her chair, crossed her arms. "What in the world is going on with you?"

"What do you mean?" Gerald asked with a fake frown, stepping closer to the counter.

"I mean, you've been in such a good mood lately. I don't think I've ever seen you this happy—oh!" She snapped her fingers. "You have a high school reunion tomorrow, right?"

Gerald placed an elbow on the counter, smiling. "Yup. Looking forward to it very much."

"I can tell! Excited to see all your old girlfriends, I bet."

"Naw, no old girlfriends except for the wife. But I am excited. It'll be good to catch up with old friends, have fun." He set his case down, pulled out his phone. "Everybody's waiting for the big reveal, too."

"What's that?"

"Somebody's been dressing up as the Blue Devil mascot and posting funny videos." He clicked on the Facebook reunion page and played the latest clip for her.

"That's freakin' hilarious!" she cried. "You don't know who it is?"

"Nope, no one does, yet. We'll find out tomorrow. There's a five hundred dollar prize for the first person who correctly guesses their identity."

"That's so cool! I hope you're this upbeat after the reunion. I like the new Gerald."

"I'm just trying to be more like you," he said with a wink. "All sunshine and stuff."

"Like me?" She gave him the side eye. "I'm only Ms. Chipper because of my job."

"Suuuuure. You're always upbeat. It isn't just the job."

She nodded. "You're right. I get it from my mama. But really, there's got to be something else going on. What's the deal? Inquiring minds want to know."

Gerald collected his thoughts. "I guess I'm starting to live my life with a new attitude. Shedding my old skin, you know? I'm like that Taylor Swift song. All the crap in my life I'm trying to—"

"Shake it off?"

"Exactly. You know, 'cause haters gon' hate, so I'm gonna…" He wiggled his shoulders, then swiped each one with the back of his fingers.

Alicia threw her head back and belted out a cackle, the first time Gerald witnessed a crack in her always professional customer service demeanor. As if catching herself, she slapped a hand over her mouth. She looked around and said, "Oops."

Laughing, Gerald said, "It's cool. I won't tell." He waved. "Talk to you later."

Gerald entered the kitchen to get a cup of coffee, and found his nemesis peering into the refrigerator. *Aw, hell.* "Morning, Greg."

Greg grabbed a yogurt and shut the fridge. "Oh, hey Gerald. Just the man I was looking for. I need you to stop by my office for a quick chat."

Let's get this over with. "How about now? That's if you don't mind me bringing my cup of Joe in there."

"No, I don't mind. Just don't spill it on yourself." He laughed.

Gerald smiled. "I won't."

Gerald followed Greg to his office. He noticed a few spy eyes peering out from several cubicles, including the Gossip twins. To them, Gerald probably looked like a caught kid walking to the principal's office. Gerald made a silly face behind Greg's back to lighten the mood.

They stepped inside. Greg said, "You can close the door."

Gerald did what Bossman told him. "Okay."

"Still making faces behind the boss' back, are we?"

"You saw that?"

Greg sat down and gestured for Gerald to do the same. "I see everything."

"No disrespect," Gerald said, crossing a foot over his knee as he sat. "Just messin' around. So, what's up?"

"Just wanted to check in. See how you were doing."

"Never better."

"Yeah, I can tell. You seem to be in a good mood."

"I am."

"Great, great."

Greg looked like he struggled to find the next word. Gerald asked, "Did you... need me for something?"

Leaning forward, Greg interlocked his fingers on the desk. "I just wanted to tell you that you're doing a great job. I've enjoyed... I'm enjoying working with you."

"Okay," Gerald replied, one eyebrow thrusting upward. "I appreciate that. What, are you leaving? You just got here."

"No, not at all. I just—"

"I mean, this sorta sounds like a goodbye or something."

"No, absolutely not. I just wanted to let you know I appreciate your work."

"Ooookay," Gerald said with a side eye and grin. "Well, thank you. Feels good to be acknowledged."

"You're welcome. And Gerald, I gotta tell ya, I thought you and I would start off on the wrong foot. But that's not the case. You've been nothing but professional."

"Of course. Wouldn't be a good look if the manager and director didn't get along."

"Very true."

"Yup."

The word exchange stopped, replaced by synchronized head nods and muted mouths with nothing else to say. After a few seconds of dead space, Gerald said, "Is that it?"

"Um, yeah. I'll be in and out of the office, so I probably won't see you the rest of the day."

"I get it. Director stuff."

"Right. So…" Greg stood up. "I guess I'll see you at the reunion tomorrow night?"

"Yes, you will," Gerald replied, standing up with him. "The wife has been putting in a lot of work with this thing. She claims it's gonna be the best reunion ever."

Greg paused, like the gears that worked his lips stuck. Gerald found his facial tics odd. Finally, Greg said, "I'm sure it will."

They shook hands. Gerald noticed Greg's eyes shift away, breaking eye contact. That cocky air bubbling around him seemed to shrivel up.

"Cool," Gerald said. "You need anything else?"

"No. Unless…"

"Unless what?"

That trademark half-smile resurrected. The kind that always looked like it came with a knife to the back as a package deal. Slick, slithery, sneaky.

Finishing his statement, Greg said, "Unless you have intel on the mystery person behind the mask. The pot is now five hundred dollars!"

Gerald threw his head back, laughing. "So, *that's* why you called me in here! Man, I have no idea. Lisa and her little reunion clique are tight-lipped."

"Well," Greg said, acting like a disappointed little boy who missed the ice cream truck, "I had to try."

Gerald walked to the door. "At least we'll see the whole class of 2005 almost, which is crazy. That last Facebook post said something about 85 percent of the class is scheduled to come."

"Yeah. Old smash buddies and everything, huh?" He smacked Gerald's arm.

"Yeah, right," Gerald replied. "That's all you. Have a good one."

Greg returned to his desk. "You, too."

Gerald brushed off the powwow with Greg as nothing more than a bizarre one-on-one with someone still feeling himself too much. He stepped out and headed to the wasteland of cubicles. With his favorite 90s pop station bumping from Pandora on his computer, Gerald started his work, acting like a new jolly member of the team.

After a full day at the office, Gerald arrived home to find Lisa on the living room couch with a cardboard box by her feet and a stack of raffle tickets on the coffee table.

"What's all this?" he asked, setting his briefcase down.

Lisa stood up. "Little prizes we'll be giving out."

To Gerald's surprise, she kissed him, a gesture she hadn't initiated in years. Leaning against the kitchen counter, he said, "Had a strange meeting with your old boyfriend today."

"Gerald, I told you…" Lisa shook her head. "Never mind. What was it about?"

"He wanted to tell me that I'm doing a good job."

"What's strange about that?"

"I dunno. He was acting weird. It felt like a goodbye or something. Kinda thought I was getting fired, but I didn't, so…" He shrugged. "Oh, well. He's still a dick."

"Umm hmm, right. So, how about we go out to eat tonight, then maybe a movie? My treat. Isn't there, like, a new Avengers or Thor movie or something?"

"Ha, you're funny," Gerald said, chuckling. "You cooked all week, now you're taking me out to dinner and a movie? Shoot, I feel like a king."

"You wanna go?"

"Of course."

"Good. I made a reservation at Cafe Mare for seven p.m."

"And my favorite Italian restaurant, too? Nice. Looks like it's gonna be a great night."

"Um hmm." Lisa headed toward the bathroom. "Why don't you get ready? I'm going to freshen up."

"I haven't showered, yet. Wanna join me?"

"I already took a sh… you know what?" She took the ends of her shirt, pulled it over her head. "C'mon, boy."

CHAPTER 24

LISA

After months of planning and preparation, reunion night had finally arrived. Lisa and the rest of the committee had spent most of the day setting up the hotel banquet room, transforming it into the perfect capsule for memory lane.

A night to remember. In more ways than one.

While finishing up the banquet room, she had received confirmation from Patrick about the hit. As planned, she parked her car on the top level of the garage, underneath the broken light. While riding an Uber back to the house, Lisa realized that in just a few hours, while enjoying the fruits of her labor with other 2005 Monte Clara High alumni, she'd send Gerald on his final errand.

But first things first. At home, Lisa decided to play the wifey role one last time.

Before getting dressed for the reunion, Lisa initiated a little fun in the bedroom, Gerald's "last meal." Gerald jumped at the chance for a quickie release, and Lisa got hers, too. Since she reopened her legs for business to her husband, he had somehow conjured up and maintained a deviant alter ego, not stopping until her body rocked from a cascade of tremors.

Ten minutes later, she lay on her back, staring at the ceiling and hauling in volumes of air. As she recovered, Lisa realized something that she never thought possible: the last few rumps with Gerald, her ill-equipped husband with no swag, topped every guy lucky enough to sample her goodies. Best sex she'd ever had.

After showering, Gerald rocked a new sport jacket, collared shirt, and jeans, while Lisa wore a teal V-neck blouse and black pencil skirt. While rubbing lotion on her legs, she watched Gerald surveying his GQ-style handiwork in a full-length mirror. With a fresh haircut and clean-shaven, he looked suave, smooth, and handsome. Sporting a sly smile, Gerald wore a shield of confidence on top of a shroud of pride, enough to keep her gaze on him longer than usual. Her eyes now wide open to him, she had discovered a sexy side of her husband she never noticed before.

But after tonight, the man in the mirror would disappear forever. A chill crept inside her, and unanswered questions sprouted like beanstalks in Jack's fairytale.

She tried to blink away the fight brewing inside her. *No, it's too late for this. I can't go back now.*

"I'm diggin' those legs."

Lisa sat up straight, placed her hands on her thighs. *I need to stop worrying. But what if something goes wrong? Do I really—*

"Hey, you okay?" Gerald asked.

"What?"

"I said, are you okay? You look kinda out of it."

"Oh." Lisa saw him staring back from the mirror. "I'm fine. Just thinking." Lisa stood up, almost stumbling against the nightstand. Gerald reached for her, but she waved him off. "I'm okay. I just stood up too fast."

"You sure? I—"

"I'm fine," Lisa said, stepping toward the closet, avoiding his eyes. "I'm gonna get my shoes. I'll get yours, too."

Gerald backed off. "Thanks."

Inside the closet, Lisa grabbed her gold high heels off a shoe rack. Pushing his clothes aside, she noticed his half of the closet looked a little bare.

"Hey, did you get rid of some clothes?" She grabbed his Kenneth Coles, the only pair on the rack. "And some shoes?"

"Oh, yeah. Salvation Army run. Got rid of a few clothes that don't fit anymore. Motivation to lose more weight. Besides, you always said I needed a new look, right?"

All right now. A reincarnated Gerald. Brand new, transforming before her eyes. He had already upped his game in the bed; now, he tweaked his fashion sense, reaching grown man status. In the process, he somehow pushed the buttons that made Lisa want to hit the sack on her back again.

A little discombobulated by his new ability to get her moist, Lisa couldn't determine if her heat stemmed from the twisted thrill of sexing a marked man, or that Gerald simply brought sexy back. Still, Lisa knew she had to snap out of it because primal urges for Gerald blurred her focus.

Dressed to impress, they headed out. Always the king of chivalry, Gerald opened the car door for his queen. "Here ya go, my lovely lady."

"Thank you," Lisa replied, easing into her seat, the ends of her skirt grazing up her thighs. She caught Gerald stealing glances at her stems before closing the passenger door.

Lisa ran through a mental last-minute to-do list. Only one task stood out.

As Gerald walked to the driver side, Lisa scrolled the messages in her burner inbox. Still nothing from Greg nor Patrick.

She dropped the phone in her purse. "Damn it."

Gerald turned onto the main road that led to Highway 1. The radio station, 105.7 Kiss FM, kicked off the Saturday night street party. After a few minutes of him in deep denial about his skills as a rapper, Gerald said, "So your, uh, what 'cha call it? Itty Bitty Reunion Committee? You all did a great job with everything. I'm impressed."

"Thanks."

"I mean, the prizes, the number of attendees, slideshow. Man." He smacked his tongue. "And the memorial. I can't believe we lost three classmates already. I'm still shook up about Marcus Obohu. His friggin' wife shot him *in the head*. That's so crazy."

"Um hum, I know. Tragic."

"Yeah."

As if he suffered from Tourette's, their one-way convo braked left when Gerald jumped back into his nursery rhyme rap routine, pounding a fist in the air to the beat on the radio, which suited Lisa fine. Despite her quest to stay the course as the good wife, especially on his last night, Lisa couldn't find the energy for a smile, much less idle conversation.

But with Gerald being Gerald, he couldn't keep his gums from flapping for too long. "I gotta say," he said, "you look beautiful."

A little surprised, her heart warmed up a bit from the only b-word that women wanted to hear. "Thank you," Lisa replied. "You look nice, too."

"Appreciate it."

Lisa stared out the passenger window, watching people become specks, then fade away as sunset darkened the sky. She wondered about the personal business of each passerby, some with a lazy crawl of a walk; others with a clear agenda propelling them forward. She bet none of them carried the same kind of load pushing down on her conscience—a load that seemed to grow the closer they got to the hotel.

"Babe, you sure you okay? You look like you have a lot on your mind."

She took a second to answer, then said, "I just hope everything goes well tonight."

"Oh, it will. Don't worry. But…"

"But what?"

Gerald turned the volume down. "I don't know. I was a little disappointed when you guys disqualified spouses of your committee from winning that five hundred dollars. I understand, though. I have a good idea who Blue Devil is, too. Bobby Coffield. Remember him?"

"Yes."

"He was always the pep rally dude, wearing masks, make-up, all that stuff. The class clown. I can see him making those videos."

"Hmm."

After a short pause, Gerald asked, "So, am I right?"

She frowned. "Are you right about what?"

"Hel-lo? Am I—"

With an icy glare that could slice his skull in half, Lisa fired back, "Boy, don't you *hel-lo* me!"

Gerald raised a hand, palm showing. "I'm sorry, babe," he replied, changing his tone. "I wanted to know if I'm right about Bobby. Is he Blue Devil? C'mon, you can tell me. It's not like I can win the mon—"

"Look, Gerald, I don't know who it is, all right? Stop asking me."

"Huh?" Gerald glanced at the road, then back at her, twice. "What do you mean?"

"I mean, I don't know!" Lisa cried. Releasing some pent-up steam, she closed her eyes for a moment, then exhaled a breath, calming an unstable twitch. Her little secret now out of the bag, she said, "Look, Gerald. One day this video pops up on the reunion page and I get an email from the mystery mascot about posting more videos. I thought it was great for marketing, so I just went with it."

"But you made it seem like you knew the identity from the jump."

"Well, I lied."

"Wow." He slowed behind an SUV at a red light. "So you never found out who's behind the mask?"

"No! The big reveal is supposed to happen via SKYPE at ten o'clock, too. We've hyped the unmasking as the highlight of the night. But… now I'm not even sure if this stupid Blue Devil is gonna show up."

The light turned green and Gerald sped up, changing lanes. "Well, shoot. Now, I really wanna know who it is."

"You're not the only one. Everyone's trying to win that prize money, too. I'm just really nervous because I've emailed Blue

Devil several times the past few days to make sure we're still on track for tonight, but haven't heard back."

Gerald placed a hand on her thigh. "Look, I highly doubt the mystery person would go through all this trouble just to disappear the night of the reunion. I think you'll be fine."

She allowed his words to trickle inside her. He made a good point. "I never thought of it that way. You're probably right."

Still, Lisa tried to suppress an uneasy flutter in her gut. She thought the car ride to the reunion would kick-start an upbeat mood. But as Gerald exited off the highway, beatboxing a song from the radio—and apparently in higher spirits than her—she felt the opposite. The true source of Lisa's jumpy, combustible nerves had little to do with a damn get-together of ex high schoolers from over a decade ago, or even the so-called "Blue Devil." It started to sink in that only one person in the car would return home alive. A small part of Lisa, like a glitch in her once stoic conscience, rebelled against the plan, pushing her to abort the whole thing.

Gerald pumped up the radio. She glanced at her marked husband and for once, cracked a smile. Gerald bobbed his shoulders in a zombie-like way, a stupid little dance he'd done for years.

My God, he doesn't have a clue.

Home-cooked meals and more sex in one week than they'd had in months made Gerald a happy husband in his last days, her goal all along. She'd turned in an Oscar-worthy performance as the good wife, but a dull sore had formed, darkening her spirit. Lisa knew she would miss him. More than she thought. After all, she wasn't *that* evil.

As they turned onto the street that led to the hotel, Lisa said, "I think you should settle things with your brother tonight. You don't talk about him much anymore."

Gerald sighed. "Yeah, I know. I'll need to get a few drinks in me first."

"Whatever it takes. Just make amends."

"You never seemed interested in us making up before," Gerald said, turning to her with one eyebrow poking up. "You don't even like him."

"I know, but... just... look, he's your only brother. "

"Okay. Yes, ma'am."

Gerald pulled up to the hotel entrance. "Here ya go, my lady," he said. "I'll park the car and meet you inside." He leaned toward Lisa and planted a kiss. "Everything's gonna be all right. I have a feeling."

Lisa turned up a weak smile. "Yeah. I have a feeling, too."

CHAPTER 25

QUINTON

"Here we go."

Quinton pushed the glass doors and walked inside. Although pimped out in a blazer and jeans like a model for one of his own photo shoots, butterflies swarmed his gut, mostly because of his eventual run-in with Gerald and Aanya. He hoped the festive mood and shots of "drank" would soften up Gerald so they could squash the beef. Regardless, he had decided to drop a dime on Lisa. Stupid bitch. Bottom line: Gerald needed to know about his skank wife.

The answers for his Aanya dilemma didn't come so easy.

Several weeks had passed since Aanya stood at his door befuddled, freshly removed from a bed she had transgressed with a man not her husband. No stranger to breaking matrimonial chains, Quinton didn't mind playing the temporary side-piece as partial payment for a model's portfolio. Hit it, quit it, then end up a freaky afterthought. "Came" with the territory. But Aanya was different. Anchored in his dreams, she had graduated from high school crush to the only lady on Quinton's radar, the sole woman to have a hold on him since puberty. Possibly, "The One." Somehow, Aanya had poured a part of herself into the gaps of his unfulfilled heart.

Quinton didn't plan to cause a scene tonight, but now that Aanya knew about Greg's dirt, he figured she would handle it, either on the low or all out in the public's eye. And when shit went down, Quinton would step in to pick her up, knock him down, or both.

The hypocrisy made Quinton chuckle inside, though. He plotted to rat out Lisa for messing around with Greg while doing the same thing with Aanya behind Greg's back. The players involved had created a loop of infidelity that angered and amused Quinton at the same time.

Quinton navigated the hallways, following the signs on the wall toward the reunion. As he approached the double-door entrance, he felt a buzz against his thigh.

"Aw damn," he said, pulling his phone out of his pocket. Message on the screen warned it only had 10 percent juice left. So caught up in work and the reunion, Quinton forgot to charge his phone.

Quinton couldn't stand a dead phone. Made him feel naked. He wanted to sprint back to his car for a portable charger, but that meant hiking up to the top level of the parking garage across the street.

"I'll get it later," he said, entering the room. "Damn." He scanned inside. "A lot of people in this piece." Through the masses, he saw neither Gerald nor Aanya.

Someone on the microphone said, "On behalf of the reunion committee, I would like to welcome everyone to Monte Clara High's ten-year high school reunion for the class of 2005. If you haven't recognized me yet, my name is Craig Meyer, your former class president."

A clamor of handclaps filled the air—at least from those with hands free of clear plastic cups that Quinton figured held cheap wine. At the first table, he recognized Deb Plato. They hugged, then after signing the guest book and some small talk, Quinton pasted an adhesive label on his blazer that boasted his name and a fly senior mug, the first and last school picture pimping his trademark short dreads.

"Hey, Quinton," a voice said, one he knew all too well. Lisa sat behind another table looking at least a seven-and-a-half out of ten. Dash of makeup, red lipstick, emerald eyes that harmonized with her outfit. Not bad, but still a trick. Quinton couldn't wait to snitch on the bitch.

"Hey," Quinton replied, mean-mugging her. "Where's Gerald at?"

"He's in there somewhere."

"I'll find him," he said, eyeing her hard. "We have a lot to talk about."

She eyed him back. "I'm sure you do."

Before he walked off, Lisa said, "Hey, don't forget to enter our 'Who's The Blue Devil' contest." She tapped a small plastic box with a slit on top. Quinton wrote "Aanya Stephens" on a red raffle ticket and dropped it in the small hole.

As if on cue, Craig announced, "We'll be giving away a few small prizes each half hour by calling out random names, but make sure you submit an entry for the 'Who's The Blue Devil' contest. Five hundred dollars, people! Personally, I still have no idea who it is, but from what Lisa Townes-Durston told me, that person is here right now."

A collective "ooooooh" settled around the room. Quinton lifted his head, still trying to pinpoint the two people that mattered most. Nothing.

"By the way, an awesome slideshow is showcasing old photos on that screen right over there, and the real Blue Devil will reveal him or herself at ten o'clock via SKYPE!"

Since Quinton couldn't see Craig from where he stood, he followed the heads that turned the same way. A large screen hung on the wall over a small table, wires hanging down toward a laptop. Although at an angle from his spot, Quinton could peep out a slideshow of still pictures fading in and out.

Craig continued, "There are servers bringing around food and wine. My brother-in-law is the deejay, and he'll be setting up soon. We have until midnight, so let's mingle with old friends, fill up our bellies, and get fuuuucked up. Enjoy!"

The room erupted in laughter and more applause. Quinton nodded, impressed by the scene of his senior class representing in full force. Although he felt some type of way about his sister-in-law, Quinton couldn't knock her reunion committee's hustle. They went all out.

As expected, Quinton ran into a logjam at every turn, caught up in a hailstorm of hugs and one-on-one exchanges with folks he hadn't seen since he wore the old cap and gown. He and his former classmates switched between conversing, laughing, and watching the slideshow, which consisted mostly of high school pictures. One special segment starred high school sweethearts who eventually married, and included pictures of Gerald and Lisa, among others. He snickered at a prom picture of Greg standing behind Aanya.

"Dayum!" Quinton heard someone say out loud. "Who is that?"

Quinton turned toward the entrance. "Dayum."

It felt like the room paused when Yara Bassili entered. Laced in a black dress that hugged her hourglass figure and stopped mid-thigh, she drew everyone's gaze like a high-powered magnet. Several dudes standing next to their ladies tried their damndest to keep their eyeballs in their heads, but it was impossible not to stumble, stop, and stare—male or female. Off the charts fine, the epitome of "slayage." Quinton had photographed some of the finest women in California, so perfect-ten looks were nothing new. But as Yara walked in, he still cursed under his breath at the sight of her, all grown up and runway flawless.

A woman that fine surely had a man, but Yara had arrived solo. Quinton figured a pro athlete or some other deep pocket baller had taken Philip's spot, and would make a grand entrance later. No doubt Gerald would fall hard all over again once he saw his all-time crush.

Quinton took a swig of beer. After a series of hugs with former girlfriends no longer in the same league, Yara stepped to the tables. As she bent over to sign in, she arched her back, her cheeks pressing the tight fabric of her dress like a pair of heart-shaped imprints. More heads turned, and Quinton heard room chatter shift from folks recapping the past ten years and guessing the identity of the Blue Devil, to the long-haired devil in the little black dress.

Yet, while all eyes zeroed in on her, leaving a trail of dribble on the bottom lip of each man she passed, Quinton lost interest and turned the other way, back on the lookout.

He only had eyes for one woman.

After about twenty minutes of trying to scope out Aanya and Gerald, with no luck, Quinton bumped into one of his old homeboys, Paul, at the memorial table. Like everyone else, they caught each other up: Quinton on his life as a photographer-graphic designer-playa; Paul on his adventures in the Marines. They then paid their respects to the classmates who passed.

"Damn," Quinton said, reading Marcus Obohu's obituary. Scented candles illuminated a soft glow against each framed black-and-white picture of the deceased. "Can't believe Marcus is gone, man. That was my dude."

"Yeah," Paul said, facing a picture of Philip Hampton. "I was thinking the same thing about my man here."

Quinton glanced at Philip's picture. "That's cool they included Yara's husband, even though he didn't graduate with us. Heard he died in Afghanistan."

"What?" Paul said, eyebrows furrowed. "Philip didn't die in Afghanistan. He committed suicide here in the States."

"Oh, damn, for real?"

"Yeah. We bumped into each other a few times while we were both active. I heard Philip was discharged before he completed his service, though. I think he was forced out or somethin'."

"Why?"

Paul shrugged. "I don't know. He loved the service, man. But whatever happened to him while he was overseas, it's probably why he took his life." Paul shook his head. "I heard he was struggling with some personal shit."

Mama Durston's face flashed in Quinton's head, resurrecting an incurable ache that he'd carried since the moment he first saw Mama in the hospital, tubes coming out or going in parts of her chest, nose, and arm. He never handled death well, especially the death of a loved one.

Wanting to escape the morbid talk, Quinton said, "Anyway, man, I need to find my bighead brother, so I'll get at you later."

"I saw Gerald not too long ago by the back door." Paul pointed toward a corner of the room. "I think he's outside."

Quinton saw an open door, folks walking in and out. "Oh, wow, didn't even notice that. Thanks, man. Good to see you."

"You, too."

They dapped, then parted ways. Quinton snatched a cup of wine from a server's platter, then headed toward the back door, trying to avoid yet another random alumni corralling him.

He stepped outside onto a wooden deck, the sight of the bay under a dark sky before him. A whisk of air brushed against his cheek and cooled his skin, a stark contrast from the heat inside the packed banquet hall. The "chill" crowd hung out here, either staring at the water, planting seeds for a late-night hookup, or burning a few. Quinton wanted to join the smoke crew, but pledged to leave the cancer sticks alone tonight. Not around Aanya.

"Q."

Gerald leaned against the wooden railing with no one within ten feet of him. The perfect solo spot.

"Hey, bro." Quinton walked up to his twin, placing his cup on the railing. "Been looking all over for you."

"That right?"

"Yeah. Looking sharp, bro."

"Thanks. You, too."

Quinton glanced around the sparsely populated patio. "Why you out here in the corner by yourself?"

Gerald shrugged. "Just needed some fresh air."

"Oh." Quinton paused, struggling to find the right words. Then he decided to jump to the point. "Look, man, I hope you're not still mad at me about Mama. How can we squash this?"

Gerald looked away. "You missed her funeral, Q. Didn't see her much at the hospital, either, even when she asked for you. You know what you did was messed up."

"I know, man, I know," Quinton said, resting an elbow on the railing, tired of repeating the same old argument. "Not a day goes by where I don't regret it."

"You *should* regret it." Gerald faced his mirror image, then to Quinton's surprise, he took a sip out of Quinton's cup. "But, you know what? One thing about Mama, she always forgave. She wouldn't want her boys fighting. So…"

"So… that means we good? I mean, since you're drinking from my cup and all."

Gerald nodded with a grin. "We good."

They hugged. "Thanks, man. Missed you, bro."

"You too, Q."

"Look, I gotta find somewhere to charge my phone," Quinton said. "Roll with me real quick. I need to talk to you about somethin'."

"About what?"

"Fool, just come with me. I'll tell you in the lobby."

Gerald frowned. "Okay, but let me hit up the bathroom first. You know what wine and hamburgers do to me."

"Man, I didn't need to know all that!" Quinton said, pushing his twin's shoulder. "All right, meet me after you're done. Don't forget, now. It's important."

"I won't," Gerald promised.

"Hold up," Quinton said, "Have you seen your crush Yara yet?"

"No, but the real question is, have you seen Aanya yet? Because I have. She asked about you."

"What, you talked to her? When? Where?"

Gerald threw his head back, belching out a loud laugh. "Calm down! Saw her a little while ago in the lobby. Oh! She told me to tell you to meet her there at 9:30. My bad. Said she tried to text you."

Quinton looked at his watch. "That's now! Man, why didn't you tell me?" He turned to head back inside.

"I'm telling you now. Hey!" Gerald grabbed Quinton's elbow. "You hittin' that?"

Quinton's lips parted, but the words evaporated with the fall breeze. He looked into his brother's eyes, shot him a wink, then kept it moving.

Behind his back, Quinton heard Gerald say, "You a dog, Q."

Quinton bee-lined for the front lobby. When he got there, he found Aanya standing near the glass doors, staring into her phone.

Quinton slowed his pace. "Hey, pretty lady."

She looked up. "Hi, Quinton."

Wearing a black jumpsuit with heels, she had a classy, throwback style all her own. "Been looking for you since I got here," Quinton said, licking his lips. "I'm liking what I'm seeing, I can tell you that much."

"Thank you. You look handsome."

"Thanks." He suppressed an urge to lean in for a kiss.

She placed her phone in her purse. "How about we go outside?"

"Sounds good to me."

Quinton pushed the door for her. Outside, they walked down the block a bit, out of the flow of reunion traffic and hotel patrons.

"I tried to text you," she said.

"Yeah, Gerald told me. My phone's dead."

"Oh. Well, thanks for meeting me."

"Are you kidding? I wouldn't want to be anywhere else. I thought I'd never get you alone."

"I know. So many people in there."

"Yeah. Where's Greg?"

"Talking to one of his old basketball buddies."

"Uh huh." *I bet he ain't now.* "So, what's up?"

"Look, Quinton." She folded her arms against her breasts, staring at the pavement. "I'm sorry, but... I made a huge mistake."

Quinton cocked his head sideways. "What are you talking about?"

"I never should have come to your place that day. I never should have gone that far."

"Hold up," he replied, feeling an uptick in body heat. "Why are you flipping on me like this?"

"Please, Quinton." Aanya looked toward the hotel entrance, still refusing eye contact. "This is hard for me. I care about you. I really do." Her eyes finally found his, tender yet unflinching. "But I love my husband."

"Oh, okay," Quinton replied, his temperature rising. "The same husband you hired me to spy on, huh? The same husband fucking around on you? C'mon! I—"

He cut himself off as an older man and woman ambled toward them. So caught up in the moment, he had no idea where they came from. Quinton somehow suppressed the tremors rippling inside him and concocted a smile that matched theirs.

After they passed, he turned to Aanya. "Look," he said after a deep breath, "Greg is a serious dog, you understand? Always has been. I know the type. I told you she wasn't the only—"

"I'm pregnant."

Quinton froze, those two words shutting him down. "Pregnant?"

"Yes. I found out this morning. We've been trying for years and it finally happened. I've never seen him so happy."

"How can you be sure the baby's his?" Quinton asked.

A cloud passed over Aanya's face, a confused look, then panic. Her eyes thick with denial, finally, she said, "It's not your baby, Quinton. We only had sex once."

"Last time I checked, once is all it takes," Quinton fired back.

Aanya stood with her mouth open, as if she were still trying to process his paternity theory. "I... no, it's not yours. It can't be."

"Whatever you say. Damn, did you even confront him about the pictures?"

Aanya paused. She looked defeated. "No."

"Wow. Talk about turning a blind eye. You don't plan on telling him about us, either, huh?"

She shook her head. "And Quinton, if you care about me, you can't say anything to him. This baby is Greg's and I want my child to grow up in a home with two parents. I want my marriage to work. Please don't ruin this for me."

Quinton could barely recognize the spineless woman standing before him, much less process the words coming out of her mouth. She sounded like someone under duress. "Can't believe this. If you think he's gonna stop screwing around just because he has a baby on the way, then… you know what? Whatever." He threw his hands up in surrender. "You two deserve each other. And you don't have to worry about me anymore. At least I got my money's worth."

The hard glare in her brown eyes told Quinton he cut her deep. But she'd cut him even deeper, so he couldn't find a reason to give a fuck.

"I know you're upset," she said, "and I'm sorry that I hurt you. What we shared will always be special to me, but… I think this baby will help Greg see where he belongs… where *I* belong."

"Yeah, okay. You just better hope that kid don't come out with an abundance of melanin. Have a good life, Aanya."

"Goodbye, Quinton." She walked back into the hotel, no break in stride. While his whole body simmered, a small part of Quinton hoped her senses would kick in, then 180 back to him. But she turned the corner, never looked back, and disappeared.

Reaching for a cigarette, then remembering he didn't bring any because of her, Quinton cursed under his breath. He had opened up to Aanya more than any other woman, and had gotten sucker-punched. His pride could not swallow the nonsense of Aanya running back to a man who treated her like a third-class ho.

He checked his phone, but forgot it had died a long time ago. No phone, no smokes, and he needed both of them right now, especially since it looked like a booty call night. Only a few minutes before ten, he shook out of his statue stance. "Fuck this, I'll meet up with Gerald later," he said, crossing the street and heading toward the parking garage. "I need a smoke."

CHAPTER 26

LISA

I'm ready.

Two simple words never screamed so loud. A chill skipped down the curve of Lisa's spine, killing her trip down memory lane with her old sidekick, Rhonda Jackson. While Lisa stared at the message, she slipped into a soundproof vacuum as Rhonda blabbed something about the prize she'd won. Lisa had gotten caught up in the social affair, laughing and carrying on like everyone else, acting carefree. Patrick's text reminded her that the reunion was nothing more than an alibi.

"Lisa!"

"What?" Lisa cried, louder than she intended. Back in the present, she noticed heads turn her way.

"Well, excuse me," Rhonda said, hands up. "Damn, girl, you all right?"

Lisa shoved the phone back into her purse. "I'm sorry, Rhonda. I just got a text that kinda messed me up."

"Everything okay?"

"No. I mean... yes, it'll be fine. It's personal, though." Lisa looked around. "I need to find my husband."

"Funny you should say that." Rhonda nodded in the direction of the memorial table. "Look over there."

Cutting through the traffic of revelers in her line of sight, she saw Gerald talking to Yara Bassili by Philip's tribute, of all places. Lisa had a brief run-in with Yara earlier before Oliver McCluster bulldozed into the conversation, acting all clingy and possessive like he was her boyfriend.

Lisa stared at them, a twinge of jealousy setting in. "I'll talk to you later, Rhonda," she said, making her way toward the pair.

Lisa watched Gerald and Yara interact with each other, and a part of her didn't believe what she saw. In high school, Gerald could barely hold his own with a member of the opposite sex, much less a girl like Yara. But the script had flipped. Yara appeared to hang on his every word, smiling like she truly gave a damn about what he had to say. As she touched his forearm, Gerald stood poised and tall in front of her, never breaking eye contact, that new cool swag brimming off him. They seemed so in sync, and Lisa felt herself steaming up.

As Lisa tried to advance on them, she ran into a roadblock of folks thrusting their chipper selves on her with hugs and more chatter. Lisa got sucked back into that vacuum of garbled mumbling, where the only voice Lisa could hear came from within, telling her that time was running out. Gerald had a date with destiny and he was going to be late. She broke from the small pack of wolves that swarmed her, ready to send Gerald on his final errand.

Yara whispered something in Gerald's ear, then stepped away, returning to the field of male predators on the prowl. Gerald now stood alone at the table, his back to Lisa. A tap on his shoulder, a whiny fake request to run to her car, and the ball would roll. Simple.

But as she drew closer, her breathing became labored, chest tightening. *No!* Without thinking, Lisa veered to her right.

"Ow!"

Face-planted against someone's chest, the top of her head knocked a chin. A voice cried, "Double ow, Lisa!"

Lisa stepped back and looked up. Craig, her reunion committee partner, towered over her. "Oh my God, I'm sorry."

"No worries," Craig replied, rubbing his chin.

"I… I was just…" Lisa covered her face with a hand. *What is wrong with me?*

"Geez, you okay? You seem a little flustered."

"I'm fine. I was just…" She took in a deep breath. "I'm good."

"You sure?"

Lisa turned back to the memorial table. Gerald was gone. Vanished into the crowd that fast.

"Lisa?"

"Yeah, yeah," she said, turning back to him. "I'm good. Really."

Lisa noticed his eyes shifting downward, then up, as if undressing her. He said, "Hey, I'm glad we literally ran into each other. I don't think I said it yet, but you look nice tonight." His eyes took another trip around her cleavage. "*Very* nice."

Really? Oh my God, whatever. "Thanks," Lisa said with a dry tone. She had noticed other guys with thirsty looks, but never expected thirst from Craig, especially with his wife, Sandy, standing not ten feet away conversing with a man Lisa didn't recognize.

"So," Craig said, "where ya headed, besides my chest?" He laughed at his own corny joke.

"I was going to…" She froze. *Damn it.*

The sight of Greg posted up in the hallway muted her. Still a bit disoriented from what she assumed to be a mini panic attack, Lisa finished with, "To the, um… just outside for a moment."

"Oh, okay. We're still on to unmask the Blue Devil, right?" Craig looked at his watch. "It's almost ten."

Greg stared at Lisa from afar. No Aanya in sight. Except for a few stray folks in the hallway, most of the reunion crowd had packed themselves inside the banquet hall, deep in party mode, awaiting the Blue Devil reveal.

"Lisa?"

She shook. "Yes, yes. We're on."

"Good. I'm going to make sure the computer and projector are hooked up and ready to go. You'll be back right at ten?"

Greg stood with an icy demeanor, and she wondered if he had seen her punk out with Gerald. But at that moment, watching him watching her, knowing all about the secret message that spoke from his eyes alone, Lisa wanted no part of Greg anymore.

"Did you hear me?"

"Yes," Lisa said, breaking away from Greg's hypnotic latch. "Meet you at ten."

Craig placed a hand on Lisa's shoulder. "Are you okay? You seem a little out of it."

"I'm fine! You know what?" She pushed his hand away. "I'll be back."

Ignoring the parade of stares, she headed to the restroom, away from the crowd and its endless banter. Greg stood watch next to the ladies' room, the look in his eyes as cold as a Detroit winter. Face forward, neither she nor Greg said a word as she passed, but out of the corner of her eye, she caught Greg tapping his watch.

"Whatever," she whispered.

Lisa hoped to find refuge in the bathroom, but Yara stalled that plan. The sight of her humming a tune while holding her phone made Lisa's face twitch. *Great. Not her.*

"Oh, hi there, again." Yara looked up and greeted Lisa with a smile, then returned to her phone, texting whomever. Cute silver butterfly earrings bounced against her cheeks.

"Hi," Lisa replied.

Yara placed her phone by the sink, then checked herself in the mirror. No matter how much Lisa tried to suppress it, Yara triggered the acidic taste of jealousy in Lisa—the same as when Lisa would watch Yara sashaying through the school hallways, a holier-than-thou air about her.

Lisa refused to engage further, but as she walked to a stall behind Yara, Lisa took a quick inventory of Yara's fashion game, from her French-manicured toes, to her thick, dark Pocahontas hair. She wore criss-cross high-heel sandals and a sleeveless dress, her figure more slender than in high school, but as sleek as the curve lines of an electric guitar. Forever the Egyptian Barbie, Lisa plotted to keep Gerald away from her, then remembered he would never see her, or anyone else, ever again.

"Lisa, I have to say Gerald is looking pretty suave tonight," Yara said, staring into the mirror while finger-combing her hair. "You are so lucky. He was just talking about how much he loves you."

Lisa stopped in front of the stall, shocked to hear a woman of such caliber talk about her Gerald in that way. "He said that about me?"

"Yes."

Pleasantly surprised, Lisa's hard exterior softened, and she changed her mind about small talk. Lisa figured Yara was tired of people bringing up Philip, so she asked, "What about you? Are you seeing anyone?"

The width of Yara's smile could've covered the entire mirror. "There's a guy I'm interested in, yes. And if he's anything like your hubby, then he's a keeper."

Excuse me? Tongue-tied, Lisa failed to find any words in response. How had Gerald become the template for Yara's type of man? Lisa knew Gerald crushed on her hard, but the way Yara talked about him, it seemed like the crush was mutual.

Before she could reply, Lisa heard a beep. Glancing at her phone, Yara said, "And now he beckons, so I have to go. See you around, Lisa."

That's right. Go ahead to yours and stop talking about mine. "Bye."

As Yara stepped out, two more women stepped in, yapping and laughing. Lisa retreated to the stall without seeing their faces, finally finding the alone time she needed. Thoughts of her husband swarmed her head, driving her anxiety level up.

"Damn it," Lisa uttered. Sitting on the toilet lid, she rocked back and forth, wringing her clammy hands together while staring at the stall door, her heels tapping the floor. Gerald. Everywhere. Wrapped more around her heart and head than she realized. The jealousy that crested after seeing Yara with Gerald had unearthed a dormant side of Lisa, revealing a special spot that still harbored love for the one man who stood by her side for years.

Lisa closed her eyes, trying to reconcile the fray in her head. In her self-made cubicle with no one else around her, she could not escape the highlight reel of years spent with Gerald. From their high school sweetheart days, to their wedding and honeymoon, and to the passion-filled romp before heading to the reunion, the good times had completely edged out the annoyance and contempt that had driven Lisa to hatch such an evil plot.

Bottom line: She still loved her husband.

"My God," she whispered. "What have I done?"

She stood up and pressed her hands on the stall, but hung her head. Digging deep, Lisa's heart and mind finally bonded in synergy. She found her strength as she shredded all doubt. At odds with her original motive, Lisa knew she had made a grave mistake.

"I can't do it." She stood tall. "I won't."

She heard the two ladies leave. Now alone, Lisa gave herself a few minutes, then pulled the stall door. *I'll just tell Greg that—*

"Hey."

"Greg!" Lisa threw a hand over her chest, gasping. "What the fuck are you doing in here?"

Greg approached her, a cool stride coupled with his trademark smirk. Nothing in his walk showed that he cared a lick about trespassing into female-only territory.

"I wanted to see if you were okay," he said. The smirk stretched his lips wider. "Well? Are you?"

Lisa crossed her arms. "Damn, why's everybody asking that? I'm fine! And you didn't need to come in here to say that."

"My bad." Pushing the stall door behind her, he said, "You know, we can take care of some business in here. You sit on the toilet, I stand right there and..." He tapped his crotch. "You know."

Unbelievable. Lisa's bottom lip dropped, her hard glare aimed at the bitch-made jerk standing in front of her. Handsome, but somehow ugly at the same time—an asshole of the highest level. Everything about him turned her stomach now, and she wondered why in the world she involved herself with a married man who saw her as nothing more than a "cum bucket."

"Cat got your tongue, Lockjaw?"

Lisa shook her head. "You disgust me. You need to get out. Go find your wife."

"You sure?"

"Go!"

"Humph, okay." Greg backed up, still smiling. At the door, he said, "We should celebrate sometime, though. And good job on handling that thing."

She frowned. "What are you talking about?"

Greg winked. "See you later, Lockjaw."

With a chuckle, he stepped out, taking the invisible cloud of snobbish stink with him. Lisa glanced in the mirror, smoky eyes staring back at her, ashamed at what she saw... what she had become.

A buzz came from her purse. Retrieving the cell phone, she clicked the new email message that popped up on the screen. She read, then re-read the message. "What the hell is this?"

Lisa almost collided with Sandy as she exited the restroom. "There you are!" Sandy exclaimed. "We've been looking for you!"

Lisa checked the time on her phone. She had holed herself up in the bathroom for nearly ten minutes and it was past ten o'clock. "I'm sorry. I needed a moment."

"Omigod, Craig's going ape shit about this SKYPE thing! Nobody knew where you were. He's… hey, are you okay?"

Seriously? Again? "Yes, Sandy, I'm fine," Lisa replied, rolling her eyes. "Just a little confused by the strange email I received from my Blue Devil contact." She handed Sandy her phone. "Read this."

After perusing the email, Sandy reacted with a similar WTF response. "What in the world?"

"I know. What do we do?"

"After all the energy we've spent hyping this contest, Mr. Perfectionist will have a fit if we can't deliver this Blue Devil person," Sandy said. "So I guess we have to do what the email says."

"Right." Lisa brushed off fear and let the chips fall, completely separating from the alter ego that once thirsted for blood just hours ago. Finally herself again, she replied with a firm, "Let's go."

When Sandy and Lisa entered the banquet hall, they saw Craig standing at the front of the room, microphone in hand. "Woo, here she is!" he said into the microphone, sounding like the discovery of Lisa answered all his worries. He gestured for them to hurry over.

"Are we good to go or what?" Craig asked. "Did you hear from your contact?"

Lisa handed him the phone. "Read this."

As Craig held the phone, Lisa noticed most of the crowd had congregated around the large screen. Folks seemed anxious to get on with the main event.

"C'mon, I want my money!" someone yelled. "I wanna know who it is! Let's get this started!"

Laughter erupted. Lisa noticed Derek Johnson flapping his gums, the same loudmouth as that teenage knucklehead jock over ten years ago.

Craig ignored the rant, but glanced at his watch. "I don't know what this is about, but whatever. We'll see where this goes." He switched the microphone back on. "Ladies and gents, the plot thickens! We just received word that Blue Devil won't reveal his or her identity unless the following people come forward, so please, play along, okay?"

The room fell silent, except for a few random remarks among the crowd. Lisa sensed the change in mood, watching many of her fellow alumni with deer-in-the-headlights looks, waiting patiently for the shoe to drop.

Craig stood under the screen. "We'll need to make a little room here."

The people closest to the screen backed up in unison. Craig read the list of names from Lisa's phone.

"Okay. Yara Bassili. Colin and Diane Michaels. Oliver and Rachel McCluster. Quinton Durston…"

As people stepped forward, Craig instructed them to stand single file in two rows, military style. Some came forward immediately upon hearing their names, others took a while. Rachel McCluster clapped like she was a contestant on *The Price is Right*.

"Gerald Durston. Lisa Townes-Durston. Greg and Aanya Stephens…"

Lisa stood in the back row as Greg eased up next to her. Leaning over, he said in her ear, "All right, what is this about?"

"I don't freakin' know," Lisa replied, scanning the room. "Where the hell is Gerald?"

Greg's smirk returned. "Uh huh. I knew it."

"Knew what?"

He leaned closer. "Knew your ass was gonna chicken out. But that's okay. I handled it."

Lisa felt a wave of nausea. "Handled what?"

"I ran into Gerald while you were in the restroom. He was looking for you. I told him you'd gone to your car to get one of the larger raffle prizes and mentioned that you could probably use some help. So... he went over to the parking garage to help. And I texted you know who."

"What?" Lisa covered her mouth to stifle a scream.

CHAPTER 27
QUINTON

Quinton stomped toward the parking garage, heated. Aanya had the nerve to hire him to catch Greg cheating, but then when he did his job, she got pregnant, had an epiphany, and realized she should stay with her fuck-boy husband? She had taken five steps forward with Quinton, only to jump ten steps back to Greg.

She's one stupid... whatever. He couldn't bring himself to call Aanya out her name.

As he approached the elevator, he noticed a man leaning against the wall near the stairwell, smoking a cigarette and staring down at his phone. Quinton thought about bumming a smoke from him, but quickly changed his mind. Dude looked like a tweaker.

Monte Clara had developed a meth and heroin problem the last few years, and the population of addicts was booming, especially in that area. Quinton noted the guy's clean-shaven chin and low-cut blond hair. Definitely not some random homeless guy. Still, something about the dude seemed a little... off. Maybe it was the gray hoodie half-covering his head, or how he did a double take, his gaze holding a little longer than it should for a stranger at night. Ol' boy almost looked confused at the sight of Quinton.

Quinton readied himself in case the stranger tried to pickpocket him, or worse. Though, a part of Quinton wanted him to cross a line; he hadn't beaten someone's ass in years, and right now, he was more than ready to put his hands to work.

Dude blew a cloud of smoke. "Sup."

"Sup," Quinton replied as he passed, the cloud dissipating around him. He looked ahead, but still caught dude's every move from the corner of his eye.

Quinton punched the elevator button. While waiting, he shot a quick glance at where dude last stood. To Quinton's surprise, he'd disappeared. No trace of him anywhere, except for a cigarette butt on the sidewalk.

Alone in the elevator, Quinton ascended to the third floor, his head becoming a hazy fog of everything Aanya. She had latched onto him, his desire for her only matched by his hatred for Greg Stephens. Despite an endless inventory of panties dropping at his feet, no other woman cut him as deeply as his first love. After their time together, he'd carried false hope that Aanya would leave her husband for him. But the spouse never leaves. Quinton had taken the bait and like a fool, got caught up.

Shoot, I should just go home. The second that idiotic thought materialized, Aanya's oppressor stomped to the forefront again, sporting a villainous smile. That punk was way overdue for a day of reckoning, and Quinton was the man to give him one. He still had a chance to right the wrong in Aanya's life, even if it meant losing her for good. *I ain't going home. I have unfinished business.*

Quinton stepped out of the elevator. Cars clogged every parking spot. He couldn't see a soul in sight.

As he strolled to his car, Quinton noticed that the backdrop of downtown looked like a postcard from the top level, encapsulating the coastal allure of a fall Monte Clara night. Quinton glanced at the Bayfront Hyatt, situated at the epicenter of town. He wondered about his next move upon returning to the reunion—what to say, how to act. Until he crossed paths with either Greg or Aanya, he truly didn't know.

The area surrounding his car seemed darker than usual. Quinton clicked the keyless remote.

"Damn," he said, pissed that an SUV and a colossal pickup truck had sandwiched his car, parked too close on both sides. The truck left a little more room on the passenger side, so he opened the door and climbed in. While reaching for his portable charger and Marlboros in the center console, he caught a shadowy figure through the back window, hightailing toward his side. He didn't move like a man simply trying to get to his ride.

"Muthafucka," Quinton whispered, his instinct kicking in.

He backed out of the car, barely upright before a man lunged at him, holding a narrow object in his right hand. Despite the tight space, Quinton managed a front kick to the chest, then stumbled against the passenger door. The man backpedaled, but steadied his balance against the truck. Having attempted an ambush, his attacker ended up the victim of a surprise defense move.

A dim stream of light cast across the man's face, exposing his eyes. *I knew it*. The tweaker.

Quinton heard what sounded like a cuss word. High on adrenaline overload, his eyes widened. Time and space blurred from reality, but somehow moved at lightning speed.

"Best get the fuck away from me, tweaker," Quinton said, fists up. "I'm tellin' you!"

No response. The two men faced off, with Quinton barricaded between two vehicles. Quinton tried to make out the object the tweaker was holding. Not enough light where he stood, though, so Quinton couldn't see it, nor understand why he had been chosen for such a random attack. Considering the brain fog of a typical drug addict, their motives couldn't always be explained, but as the tweaker pointed his weapon at Quinton, the intent was more than clear.

Quinton felt the beats of his heart vibrating inside his throat. He could dart back inside his car, but would probably get caught from behind. Maybe try to scale the passenger door onto the hood of the truck? Too tight—he barely had enough room to move, let alone the time to pull off a ninja maneuver. Trapped, only one thing made sense. Little did the tweaker know, he had picked the wrong man to fuck with tonight.

All right, then, this is it. It's either him or me.

The tweaker charged again, right arm extended. Quinton backed up as far as he could, bracing himself. As his attacker advanced, he saw it. A needle of some type, sharp, long. Quinton raised his left forearm to deflect the blow, but the tweaker's wrist slapped against something, blocking him. The truck's CB antenna. It was mounted on the back and thick enough to stall forward momentum for a second, which was all the time Quinton needed.

Quinton threw an elbow to the left temple, then shoved him. The tweaker stumbled again, lost balance, then collapsed on his back.

Quinton smelled his escape. He could hop back into his car, lock the doors, and drive off. Or run past his wannabe shanker before he got to his feet. Either option meant emerging with his life intact.

But it also meant dude could try the same shit on someone else. Maybe even come after Quinton again.

Fuck that.

Quinton ran toward him. The tweaker rolled to his left to grab the weapon he'd dropped, but Quinton got to it first and kicked it under the SUV.

"Fuck you, Gerald!"

What? "How do you—argh!"

Discombobulated from hearing his brother's name, Quinton hesitated. The tweaker shifted to all fours and charged at Quinton like an NFL lineman, arms wrapped around his waist, propelling him backward. Quinton struggled to remain upright.

Quinton slammed against the back of the pickup, a sharp pain shooting between his shoulder blades, but he stayed on his feet. The fucker didn't let up, ramming his head into Quinton's belly, like he was trying to bulldoze into Quinton's ribcage.

"Arrrgh!" Quinton growled. "Mutha—"

A sprinkle of white, flashy dots peppered Quinton's field of vision, and then everything went black. He felt himself outside somewhere, leaning against… something. A man's body pressed against him. Fingers clawing at his face. Cars everywhere. His arms wrapped around the man's neck. The haze dissipated, almost as quickly as it appeared—and he remembered the tweaker. He must've unleashed a roundhouse punch against Quinton's eye socket, sending him on a short trip into La La Land.

But somehow, Quinton maintained consciousness.

His mental marbles back, Quinton squeezed as hard as he could, the bones from the back of the tweaker's neck pressing against Quinton's bicep. The tweaker grabbed Quinton's leg, pulling Quinton away from the truck, lifting him. Quinton's feet dangled, but he locked down his iron grip, refusing to be manhandled and slammed onto the concrete. The tweaker was one strong son of a bitch.

Shit. Quinton's knees buckled. He tried to find traction, but not in dress shoes, too slippery. Tumbling backward, stuck in a vertigo tailspin, the scene around Quinton switched to him looking up at the dark sky.

But his arms were still locked around the tweaker's neck.

Quinton pounded the concrete, flat on his back. He heard a thud that sounded like a cinder block smashing the pavement. The tweaker lay limp on top of him, head buried under Quinton's arm. Out cold. Quinton breathed a sigh of relief, then shoved him off.

Quinton had no idea how long they went at it, but it seemed like forever. For the first time, Quinton noticed the rapid rhythm of his breathing, his chest rising with each haul of air. Salty beads of sweat slid down his cheek into his mouth. He wiped his wet lips with the back of his hand, yet savored the swift change in his predicament— from a life and death struggle, to him finally at a state of stillness, peering into the black sky. But that didn't last long.

Quinton checked himself over, running a hand over his chest and face. Felt chafed skin on his forehead and tasted blood. His eye throbbed and a dull ache spread across his back. He needed a mirror, but from his brief self-assessment, Quinton didn't detect any permanent damage.

The tweaker lay on his side, still as a rock. He wouldn't be rolling up on Quinton, Gerald, or anyone else, not anytime soon.

As if struck by a bolt of lightning, Quinton jumped to his feet. A sense of gloom shrouded over him. "Gerald."

The tweaker had said his brother's name. Knew who he was, his location, obviously what he looked like. Dude had been lurking in the shadows waiting for Gerald, thinking he was Quinton. He probably wasn't a tweaker at all.

He didn't know why his brother had a target on his back, but Gerald was clearly in danger. Quinton knew he needed to get back to the banquet hall as fast as he could.

CHAPTER 28

LISA

"Any luck locating Gerald?"

Lisa shook her head. She, along with everyone else, had already scoured the room. After several texts, then several calls, she enlisted the help of Craig and a few others, checking the lobby, the deck outside, hallways, even the men's bathroom. No sign of Gerald. Quinton was MIA, too.

She also searched within her conscience, refusing to hear a little voice that reaffirmed what Greg had already told her: He sent Gerald on his death walk. That was the plan all along, her idea, her show. It shouldn't have felt like a shock. But in her heart, Lisa couldn't accept that Gerald might be gone. He was probably somewhere with Quinton, hashing things out like she'd encouraged him to do. At least, she prayed for that outcome.

"Well, great," Craig said, looking ready to throw the microphone across the room. "We're missing, like, three people who were just here, Lisa!"

"I know!" Lisa snapped back.

Craig glanced at the row of people who had lined up at the front of the room. "Wait, where did Greg go? Aanya?"

"He said he needed to check his voicemail," Aanya replied. "He'll be back. So, no one's seen Quinton, either?"

Murmurs spread across the room, heads looking around at each other. Amid the mass of confusion, Lisa tried to project a calm facade and quell a panic attack.

"Okay, really, what's going on?" Oliver asked, standing beside Lisa. "Why are we up here? Anyone?"

"Yeah, can we move this along?" Colin said. He had lined up as well, along with his wife Diane. "C'mon, it's already after ten."

Lisa didn't answer. She noticed a few stares directed at her, including from Aanya. Stuck in the solid grip of a dark secret, she let her eyelids drop, finding a brief escape in the black. For all she knew, Gerald was reaching for her car door while Patrick hid in the background, waiting. Her breaths grew deeper, lungs on the verge of collapsing. *Oh God.*

"Okay, may I have your phone again, please?" Craig said.

Lisa blinked several times, trying to process Craig's words and his hand reaching out to her. "What?"

"Give me your phone. I'm gonna email your contact and just say we're all here. Hell, if they ask, I'll just say we have a few folks in the bathroom or something."

On autopilot, Lisa handed him the phone. She could've sworn someone asked for the millionth time if she was all right, but she ignored him or her.

"Oh," Craig said, holding Lisa's phone closer to his face, squinting. "New message. It says, 'Don't worry about Yara Bassili and Gerald Durston showing up. They're off to a better place.'" He stopped. "Whoa. I don't know what you got planned, Lisa, but that sounds kinda creepy. I'm emailing back that everyone else is here."

What in the world? Yara? Lisa's knees knocked together, buckling. The words didn't register; nothing made sense. It seemed the entire room stood still.

A loud ringtone chimed from the screen above Craig's head. The message, *Blue Devil is calling* flashed under a blank avatar that faded in and out. Lisa felt a lump in her throat. Her contact.

"Okay, here we go," Craig said into the microphone. "We're about to solve the mystery!" He nodded to his wife, Sandy, who stood by the laptop.

Lisa thought her heart would catapult out of her chest. Sandy's keystrokes showed on the screen, so as the white arrow pointer clicked the Answer button, Lisa peeked over at Aanya. Still no Greg.

The so-called Blue Devil appeared in a virtual box, mask and all. Slightly shrouded in the dark, it looked like something out of a 90s horror flick.

"Here I am," a gruffy voice behind the mask said.

The room erupted in handclaps. As the applause died down, Craig said, "Thank you for showing up, Blue Devil! Now, without further ado, let's see who the hell you are!"

"Okay," the voice said. A hand appeared, gripping the chin. "You ain't ready, though."

The mask came off. Lisa covered her mouth as she gasped. Someone said, "What the hell?" Whoever said it, they yanked the words right out of her head and mouth.

Laughter followed, mostly from the person in the SKYPE spotlight, the face revealed. In the flesh.

"'What the hell' is correct, sir. Good evening, everyone."

CHAPTER 29

GERALD

"Gerald Durston, is that you?" Craig asked, squinting. "It's kinda dark in there, but... wow! It *is* Gerald! How about that! You were just here!"

"Yes, I was," Gerald replied, his proud smirk beaming.

"Nice!"

Facing his tablet's webcam, the expressions of the people closest to the screen were so clear that Gerald could make out facial lines. Although Gerald couldn't see everyone, the number of people that fit within the limited range of the camera surprised him. He felt like he was standing on a terrace while they all stared up at the Almighty, waiting for a speech from "Your Highness." Gave Gerald a sense of power, like he stood above them all.

Gerald took a quick visual sweep of the room. "Great job rounding everyone... wait. Where's my brother? And... Greg Stephens?"

"No one knew where you were, so Quinton went looking for you. Greg just went to make a phone call."

"A phone call. At this hour?"

"Yeah, that's what he said," Craig replied. "Right, Aanya?"

"He's just checking his voicemail, that's all," Aanya replied.

"Uh huh."

Behind Craig, Gerald spotted Lisa standing near the edge of the screen, almost out of view. Lisa's face rivaled a cartoon character, animated to an exaggerated extreme, obviously shocked to the core. To Gerald's delight, her stance appeared unbalanced—she wobbled, threatening to tip over any minute.

It worked. He had pulled it off.

Gerald said, "Hello, wifey-of-mine. Surprise! Hey, I... Damn... Babe, are you all right?"

"She can hardly speak. Poor thing." Craig glanced at Lisa, then back to Gerald. "Wait, didn't you two plan this together?"

"Not at all," Gerald replied. "Funny thing is, my wife made it *seem* like she knew the Blue Devil's identity, while I acted like I had no idea. But she was in the dark like everyone else, including my twin brother." He noted Lisa shaking her head, mouth agape.

"Pretty slick, sir," Craig said, nodding. Turning to the crowd, microphone still in hand, he asked, "Did anybody guess Gerald Durston?"

Gerald could make out a few heads moving right and left, scanning for the chosen one—the winner of the $500 pot. But no one said a word or raised their hand. Only shrugs.

"Anybody? Well, I'll be." Craig faced the screen. "Not one person. Looks like you got us, Gerald. Guess we'll have to figure out something else to do with the money."

"Guess so," Gerald replied.

Craig placed the microphone on the table. "We can hear you loud and clear, Gerald. I assume you can hear me without the mic if I speak loud enough?"

Gerald gave him the thumbs up.

"Okay. So, everyone wants to know: Why did you wear the mask and make those videos? And why did you call us all out here? What did you mean by 'off to a better place?'"

"What does Yara have to do with this?" Lisa demanded, coming alive. She stepped to the forefront, eyes scorched and arms folded across her chest. "And where are you, anyway? It looks like you're in a car or something. Are you okay?"

Gerald said, "Whoa, whoa, one at a time. And yes, I'm okay." Muffled chuckles erupted from the seat next to him, but Gerald stayed focused. "True, I'm in a car. We're not driving right now, though."

"We?" Lisa asked, giving Gerald the side eye.

Yes, we. Although dimly lit, Gerald could see frown lines sprouting off Lisa's forehead.

"Where are you going?" Colin Michaels asked. Others bombarded him with questions on top of questions, including more about Yara.

"Slow down!" Gerald cried. Several folks laughed, but Lisa mean-mugged hard.

"Okay, okay," Craig said.

Gerald cleared his throat. "Look, I know some of you are scratching your heads right now. I have a few things to say that everyone will want to hear, trust me. Don't cut me off, okay?"

"The floor is yours," Craig said.

"Good." Gerald adjusted his back against the car seat. "Ah, look who's here, everyone! Glad you could join us, Mr. Stephens."

Heads turned. Greg snaked toward the front and stood next to Aanya, his mouth and eyes like big circles. "Wait, what the fuck is going on here?"

"Language, Mr. Stephens," Gerald said. "You're right on time. To answer the questions about why I made the videos… I did it for Lisa, my beautiful wife. She was frustrated with the attendance numbers, and since I hate seeing my wife unhappy, I thought up this crazy idea of dressing like our school mascot, cracking a few stupid jokes, then posting videos on Facebook with old high school pictures. I disguised my voice, of course. Shot the videos before work, sometimes right after, then edited them later. I wanted to help her drum up interest."

Lisa moved closer to the screen and center-stage, where Craig stood. Gerald figured she wouldn't try to blend back into the crowd anymore, especially after Gerald tugged on her heartstrings, talking about making her happy and all. Sure enough, he saw the shadow of a smile on her face.

"You did this… for me?" Lisa asked. Gerald nodded.

"So, this all started because of Lisa, huh?" Craig glanced at her. "The man loves his woman!" He turned back to Gerald. "Well, the videos definitely got people talking. It's one of the reasons so many are here. Who knew you were such a comedian."

"Thanks. The pictures made it easy."

"Yeah, your commentary on the pictures was pretty funny. How did you change your voice like that?"

"This cool app I downloaded. You can become anyone, really."

"Nice!" Craig said, looking impressed. "Where'd the pictures come from?"

"Saved them from Mr. Pete's photography class in 10th grade. Quinton and I loved that class, and I was always snapping pictures on school grounds, most of the time without anyone knowing. I even 'borrowed' some from Mr. Pete's hard drive. Don't ask me how I did that." Gerald winked.

"Lips are sealed," Craig replied, winking back.

"Drumming up attendance was only one of the reasons for this grand scheme, though," Gerald confessed. "Reason number two was... oops." Gerald pressed a fist against his lips, acting embarrassed. "I said number two."

Sprinkles of laughter spread throughout the room. As he'd hoped, Gerald held his audience captive, cracking a few one-liners while teasing with the promise of a sweet surprise. Had them exactly where he wanted, teetering on the edge.

Gerald continued, "The number two reason is because I wanted to surprise my wife, Lisa, with a little sumn' sumn'." He pulled out a diamond ring. "Can you see it?"

Gerald heard a few aaaaah's and watched Lisa's face stretch in slow motion. *Got her again.* "I know, babe, I know," he said. "Lisa and I are approaching our wedding anniversary and I knew—"

Gerald stopped at the sound of handclaps and a few whistles. They seemed to applaud the lucky lady, Lisa, now standing in a bright spotlight, covering her face with her hands. She had become the woman of the hour, a treasured honoree of Gerald's chivalry.

Gerald said, "Thank you, thank you. Like I was saying, I knew my wife wanted a ring upgrade, and I thought she would find it romantic if I asked her to renew our vows in front of everyone. I even made plans to whisk her out of the country for a second honeymoon after the reunion."

More claps and whistles, a few floor stomps. Louder than before.

"Okay, that's cool and all, but why did you call like ten of us up here?"

Greg spoke loud enough to kill the applause. Standing in the background with his head almost out of view, Gerald had anticipated Greg's loss of self-control the moment he saw his prison-faced mug on the screen.

"Relax, Greg," Gerald said, showing the palm of his hand. "I mean, Boss. I'm having a moment with my wife here."

"Yeah, well, let's get on with it. Finish saying what you need to say and tell us why the hell you called us up here."

"I agree," Craig said, trying to regain his role as the head emcee. "I'm curious about why we're here, too. What else do you have to say, Gerald?"

Gerald froze, ignoring the question. He leaned toward the screen, squinting. *There he is.*

Some folks turned and made room for Quinton. A grin spread across Gerald's face, but as his twin moved closer, it faded away. He noticed Quinton holding his side.

"Oh, my God," Aanya said, stepping around Greg to get to Quinton. She placed a hand on his cheek. "Are you all right?"

Quinton nodded. From Gerald's vantage point, it seemed like a thousand stares centered on his brother. His shirt appeared stained and the left side of his face puffy. But his smile outshined everything. The look in his eyes showed a man relieved at the sight before him.

"Q!" Gerald cried. "What the hell happened to you?"

"Wow, you all along, huh? Good one, bro, good one." He stepped closer, standing between Craig and Lisa. "I can't tell you how happy I am to see yo' ass up there. Please tell me you good."

"I'm good, Q. Don't worry about me. But are *you* good?"

"I am now. Some dude jumped me in the parking garage across the street. Fool tried to stab me, but I whipped dat ass."

A collective gasp echoed around the room. Gerald felt a lump in his chest. "In the parking garage?"

"Yeah. And what messed me up is… he thought I was you. Punk said your name."

Gerald took in a deep breath, placed a hand over his mouth. Tension bubbled to the surface, so strong Gerald thought it could rip through his skin.

"What happened to him?" Gerald asked.

"I took care of him. He ain't going nowhere, trust me. But I'm still trying to figure out how he knew you."

Gerald clutched his fist, the diamond ring digging into his palm. Face now like stone, he said, "I'm sorry, bro. I didn't know you would get wrapped up in this." His tone was deadpan, almost robotic. "I know why he thought you were me."

Quinton frowned. "What? Why?"

Gerald fixed his gaze on Lisa, who was standing like her feet had turned to cement. "Because of that ho over there, Lisa Townes-Durston." He nodded toward her. "Yeah, bitch, you."

As if synchronized on command, everyone within the webcam's view freeze-framed. A few looked around at each other, most of them congregating amongst themselves, saying words that Gerald couldn't make out—except from Craig, who spoke at the right decibel when he turned to Lisa and said, "Did I freaking hear what I think I heard? Is this a joke, Gerald?"

"No, it's not. Let's just say Lisa won't get a chance to renew vows with me. Or wear this ring." He dropped the ring in the cup holder. "*Or* go on the honeymoon. She'll be going somewhere else for a very long time."

Craig placed a hand on Lisa's shoulder, who looked seconds away from a tear flood, but too stunned to move. He said, "Gerald? Um, hey man, what are you doing? This really is a joke, right?"

"I said no."

"Then what the hell is this?"

With a casual tone, Gerald said, "I have this bad habit of butt-dialing." He grabbed his phone from the cup holder and clicked on an app icon. "But I'm not the only one who butt-dials. Hold on a sec."

A small support group converged around Lisa. Tears now streaming, she said, "Gerald? Baby, why are you saying these things?"

Gerald found an audio file. "Wow, seriously? Kill the dramatics, you lying slut."

The hostility he had toward Lisa, now unleashed, surprised Gerald, almost scared him. Not caring about a damn thing anymore, he pressed Play on the app.

Several people tilted their heads, ears open for the digitized voices emanating from Gerald's iPhone.

"Gerald," Craig said, his right ear on full display. "I don't understand. What are we listening to?"

"Just listen! I used an app to record this conversation I heard when Lisa butt-dialed me. But for those of you who can't quite hear what's going on, it's a murder-for-hire plot between my soon-to-be ex-wife, some guy named Patrick—the same guy that attacked my brother—and Mr. Playa Playa Greg Stephens."

"What?" Greg yelled, his face enlarging as he charged toward the screen. Amused by his spastic, mad gorilla response, Gerald watched Greg bulldoze past Craig. "Motherfucker! Bring your ass back here, you piece of shit!"

Like someone staring into a peephole, Greg's distorted face was too close, blocking Gerald's panoramic view of the room. Before Gerald could respond, Quinton pushed Greg so hard it forced Greg out of camera range. He cried, "You tried to have my brother killed?"

Folks screamed and scattered, backpedaling out of harm's way. Fists flew until Gerald could no longer see who hit who. Body parts flashed in and out of the screen. An orchestra of chaos obliterated the reunion decorum Craig spearheaded minutes before, and Gerald sat back, grinning.

Off screen, Gerald could still hear his brother. It sounded like Quinton had the upper hand, but within seconds, Nick Francis and Frank Giglitari, two ex-football players, played bodyguard and rushed the scene. Nick, a Marine muscle head, pushed Quinton backward into video range once again, forming a wall with his arms spread. His hair now untied and loose, Quinton's dreads slapped against the side of his face as he jabbed his index finger over Nick's arm toward Greg, who was still out of camera range. Gerald had never seen his twin in high-capacity set-it-off mode. Left Gerald with a jolt of pride to watch his brother defend him like that.

"Get away from me, man," Quinton said, pushing the arms of a man nearly twice his size. Nick maintained his self-made wall while Quinton turned to the screen, still high octane and hyped up for another round. "Bro, for real, you ain't fuckin' with us, are you?"

"No, Q. I—"

"Bitch, get away from that laptop!" Quinton cried to someone that Gerald surmised was trying to cut off SKYPE. "I'm talking to my brother!"

"Okay, okay." Craig came back into view, palms up. "Quinton, you don't have to talk to my wife like that."

"Shut up!" Quinton yelled, turning his rage on Craig.

They stood nose-to-nose with Nick's arms extended, keeping them apart. Gerald could hear Quinton exchanging words with Craig now. He took in the whole scene. The attendees had become bystanders, chattering amongst themselves and standing as wide-eyed and open-mouthed as him; yet, unable to pull away, probably for fear of missing something. No Lisa or Greg in sight. Tension still thick, Gerald could feel it, driving his heart rate up, as if a piece of what he was watching teleported through his tablet and into the car.

"Q, chill, bro!" Gerald cried. It took a few seconds for his twin to break from his stare-down with Craig, but Quinton eased back and turned to the screen.

Quinton appeared paralyzed and bewildered, frowning so hard he looked meaner than the rapper Ice Cube. "I'm good, I'm good."

For a second, Gerald imagined himself standing among the crowd, staring into a screen with zombie eyes, hearing his own chilly words. He probably would've been as tongue-tied as everyone else. But exposing the secrets of Greg and his side piece bolstered Gerald with an adrenaline rush of power. It felt good to grip Greg's pulverized nuts in a tight fist, then scatter the last bits of his cremated manhood around the room like confetti at a New Year's parade.

"Where's Lisa right now?"

"She's over there cowering against the wall," Quinton said, pointing. "Sittin' her ass down, looking guilty as hell. Crying and shit. I should beat her ass, too."

"Naw, Q, don't even try it. Besides, she's gonna get hers." He shook his head. "She tried to act all nice to me, cooking, sex, and what not. Knowing she put a hit on me. She's a special kind of evil. I saw through all that crap."

Frank, a cop, stepped back onto the "stage," the SKYPE camera on him again. "Gerald, these are some pretty serious allegations," he said.

"They're more than allegations, Frank. Greg Stephens and my wife tried to have me killed and it's all recorded. Simple as that."

Frank walked closer to the screen, blocking Gerald's view of the room. "We should talk about this in person. Why don't we meet somewhere?"

"Uh, how about, hell no? I'm in hiding right now. Just make sure Greg and Lisa don't get away. But don't worry, your buddies will get a copy of the evidence."

More muffled laughter erupted next to him, so Gerald placed an index finger on his lips. At the same time, a subdued Greg reemerged. He slowly walked toward the screen and stood next to Frank. "Gerald, man, listen, I-I don't know what you think you heard, but I'm telling you, it's not me."

Begging. Sad, especially from Greg Almighty. Going down in flames that he created but still trying to douse the fire with oil. Gerald almost felt sorry for him. *Almost.*

Aanya's face appeared in the far right corner, which surprised Gerald. He assumed she left to escape the heat she now shared with her sorry husband. Gerald admired her quiet, yet stubborn ride-or-die nature, despite what she heard.

But he knew how to snap the grip Greg had on her. For good.

"Greg, Greg, Greg. Tsk tsk, I thought you see everything? Betcha didn't see this coming, huh? Oh, if you haven't figured it out yet, I quit."

"Gerald, I… okay, look, buddy. What had happened was—"

"Did this fool just say 'what had happened was'? Really, Greg?" Gerald lost it, almost dropping his tablet. "Dude! I know you're smashing my wife. What you call her? Lockjaw? I have audio of her sucking you off. You sound like a broken police siren when you ejaculate, by the way."

"Gerald, that's enough," Craig said, popping up on-screen out of nowhere.

"No, it's not. And I'm not talking to you." Gerald turned his attention back to Greg. "All right, *Greg Stephens*. Balla Shot Calla. You can act all innocent if you want, but I have you on tape, dumb ass. But don't worry. My twin will take care of Aanya when you go away. My wife ain't the only one who's been screwing around. Ain't that right, Q?"

Another series of gasps and curse words spread around the room, becoming the reunion's soundtrack. Gerald heard someone cry, "Okay, this cannot be real!"

Someone else said, "The best reunion ever!"

Leaning toward the tablet, Gerald watched Greg malfunction. Pure comedy. Like Greg's mental processors couldn't compute Gerald's data and his whole face crashed.

Any sign of Aanya vanished, at least from Gerald's point of view. Quinton came back into view as he and Greg faced off. Then they both turned their heads in unison to where Aanya had stood.

"Aanya!" Greg cried. "You fucked him? I knew it! Get back over here, you bi—"

Quinton chin-checked Greg with a closed fist, laid him out on his back, arms and legs fully extended in an X. "Stay your ass down. And the baby might be mine, bitch!"

"Damn!" Gerald cried, his mind doubly blown by what he heard and saw.

He watched his twin shake out his right hand, then step over Greg's body while glancing down at the carnage. Giving him the respect of a mafia boss, Nick and Frank eased back, letting Quinton approach the screen untouched.

Cradling his hand, Quinton said, "Bro, I need to roll before I kill somebody up in here."

"I'm coming with you," Frank said, standing behind Quinton. "We need to talk more about this attack. And Gerald, I suggest you come in soon, too."

"Oh, count on it, but not now. Just look after my brother for me."

"I will."

Gerald watched Nick and Frank pick up Greg, then carry his limp body out of camera range. A part of Gerald wanted to jump out of his shoes from witnessing his brother's knockout of the year, but he kept an icy composure and said, "Q, is Lisa still by the wall?"

"Yeah, she—oh." He tilted his head. "Her ass tryna dip out."

"Whatever. Let her. She's not going to get very far, especially since I emptied all our accounts."

"Good. I'm gonna try to catch up to Aanya. I'll call you later."

"All right, man. Great punch."

As Sandy stood by her husband, Craig said, "We let this nonsense go on long enough. Gerald, I hope you got what you wanted."

"Not yet. Especially since your wife, Sandy, is in danger, too. But of a different kind. Also, Diane Michaels and Rachel McCluster, wherever you are, you're gonna want to hear this."

"What do... okay, enough of these damn games. Turn it—"

"Wait," Sandy said, pushing Craig to the side. "What do you mean? Why am *I* in danger?"

Yara poked her head into the tablet's camera view. "Because your husband is a piece of shit."

"Yara? Where did you come from?"

Yara took the tablet from Gerald. Her turn to drop bombs. "I've been watching all along."

"Let's just turn this off." Craig moved toward the computer.

Sandy blocked his approach. "No. I want to hear this."

"Honey, this is all a farce!" Craig cried, grabbing her arm and trying to pull her away from the computer.

"Get off me!" *Whack!* With the quick hand snap of a ninja, Sandy smacked the soul out of Craig.

As if watching a scene from their favorite TV show, Gerald and Yara's jaws almost bounced off their chests at the same time.

Sandy acted like jacking up her husband's face never happened. She turned back to the screen. "Yara, what is going on? Why am I in danger?"

Craig rubbed his cheek. Had the eyes of a scared man about to enter the gas chamber. Again, Craig tried to lunge for the Power button, but Sandy stopped him.

"Because I had unprotected sex with your husband," Yara said, her voice calm. Standstill. More gasps. Loud whispers in the background. Craig looked like he wanted to crawl into the nearest hole and hide. "And I'm HIV positive."

CHAPTER 30

YARA

"Oh my God."

Yara watched the skin on Sandy's forehead furrow deeper, her sweet, bubbly side draining away like the blood in her face. Yara saw it, that switch in Sandy's eye—the last strain of love burning into black ashes of hate.

Yara knew the feeling well. She had the same reaction after she found out Philip, the man she adored, her first real love, destroyed her life forever with a virus he picked up from some tainted skank. When the Army became aware of Philip's HIV status, he began the process of a medical discharge, and rather than face the consequences of his actions, he chose to end his life, leaving Yara to fight new demons alone. The trauma of it all—from finding out Philip cheated and gave her HIV, to finding him in the bathroom with a self-inflicted gunshot wound to the head—devastated Yara and ripped her life apart. No goodbye, no apology. Nothing. All that remained was an unquenchable thirst for revenge on men like Philip.

Yara could tell from the look in Sandy's eyes that she had similar plans for Craig.

Craig's eyes connected with Yara's for the first time. He mouthed the word, "bitch," then turned back to Sandy. "Babe, she's lying," he said with a pathetic whine. "I don't know why she's saying these things, but it's not true!"

More gasps from the crowd. Before everyone's eyes Sandy was slowly morphing into the woman Yara had already become—bitter, pissed, hurt... and unstable.

"You initially called Rachel and Diane up here with me," Sandy said to Yara, somehow calm. "I assume you slept with their husbands, too?"

Yara nodded. "Yes."

Sandy picked the microphone up off the table and switched it on. "Rachel McCluster and Diane Michaels," she began in a somber tone, "If you're still here, your presence is needed up front urgently." She paused. "Bring your sorry husbands with you."

"Wow," Yara whispered, "She said that."

After a few minutes, Rachel and Diane appeared with their husbands. Sandy ushered them to the front so they could face Yara.

"They didn't hear you because they were leaving," Sandy said. "Tell them what you told me."

Yara wondered how many others had filed out after the ruckus Gerald started. No matter, she knew people loved drama. From the noise in the background and body parts still in view, Yara could tell the room had no shortage of nosy onlookers glued to the never-ending soap opera unfolding before them.

Yara glanced over at Craig and the other two men, Colin and Oliver. Fear carved in their faces while the wheels turned to cook up bold-faced lies.

Sandy said, "Why are you smiling? You think this is funny, Yara?"

"I didn't realize I was. No, it's not funny, it's tragic." She looked at Rachel. "But your husband's squealing when he has an orgasm is pretty funny." To Diane. "And so is Colin's two-inch excuse for a penis. I must say, I've never seen a birthmark on the head of one before." Back to Sandy. "Craig couldn't last longer than thirty seconds."

Cuss words hurled Yara's way, mostly from the wives. At the same time, she heard a bellow of "oooooh's" and laughter off screen from leftover alumni and their spouses turned fanatical spectators, enjoying part two of the Gerald and Yara SKYPE confessional. But her fellow women scorned failed to direct their anger to the true guilty parties—until Rachel McCluster finally turned to her husband Oliver and asked, "You really fucked her, didn't you? How could you do this to me *again*?"

Oliver, who was dripping sweat like a tourist in Costa Rican heat, whispered something in her ear. Before he could sweet talk his way out of the hot seat, Sandy said, "Damn it, Yara, tell them what else you told me! Is it true?"

Sandy's face begged for a punchline, a big-bang mega prank to end all pranks. Anything that said, "You've been punked, everyone!"

Yara knew she had to set them straight.

"My fellow classmates, yes, I am HIV positive and I slept with Craig Meyer, Oliver McCluster, Colin Michaels, and Marcus Obohu. Your husbands are what I affectionately call 'BBs' or BareBacks, since they don't like to wear condoms." She raised a wallet-sized picture to the screen, the same picture that used to hang from her rearview mirror. "My sweet, dear husband, Philip, gave it to me before he killed himself. He didn't even have the courage to tell me to my face he was carrying the virus. I learned the truth from his suicide note. Now, because your so-called husbands pursued me on Facebook, each of you might have it. Like Marcus Obohu, may he rest in peace."

The couples all seemed to represent different stages of grief and surprise. On the verge of collapsing into a heap of tears, Diane Michaels whipped around and disappeared from view, her husband close behind, reaching out to her.

Craig pointed at the screen, mouthing "I'm gonna fuckin' kill you," without a sound to back it up. When he turned around, a man shoved him. Strands of black hair covered his face, but Yara recognized him as the deejay, Sandy's brother. The men hit the floor, cuss words and fists flying. Cries rang out as chaos erupted in the background once again. A woman fell. Then a guy over her. Craig and Sandy's brother wrestled on the ground while people rushed to break them apart. A surround sound of jumbled noise, mostly from people screaming, emanated from the speakers.

"Damn, it's going down!" Gerald said, eyes wide.

She and Gerald glued themselves to the tablet, trying to scope out the bonfires of pandemonium igniting around the room. Then the screen went black as SKYPE disconnected.

"Aw, damn!" Gerald cried. "It was getting good, too!"

"Looks like someone finally cut us off," Yara said, handing the tablet back to Gerald. "I'm surprised it went on for that long, actually."

"Me, too. Dang it, I wouldn't mind seeing what's going on right now."

Yara smiled. As planned, she'd lifted the rug and exposed double lives, watching filthy married men try to scamper away from the truth like roaches in light. Mission accomplished. She didn't need to see anything more. "I'm fine," she said. "I got what I wanted."

"Yeah, me, too," Gerald replied.

After powering down the tablet, they sat quiet, staring out at the half-lit parking lot of a Marriott hotel, where they had "borrowed" free WIFI to drop virtual bombs on the class of 2005. She glanced at Gerald reclining in his seat. Yara could barely wrap her brain around the synergistic connection that had emerged from their oddball pairing. Blindsided and betrayed by two people who had vowed to love them the most, Yara and Gerald had forged an unshakable bond over their shared pain. But the hell their spouses put them through also invoked a united front, whetting Yara and Gerald's desires for good, old-fashioned payback. Sitting next to her new partner-in-crime in his darkened car, she couldn't believe they'd actually pulled it off.

"Crazy night, huh?" Gerald said, reading her mind.

"Way more crazy than I imagined it would be."

"Yeah. But 'two-inch excuse for a penis'? Really, Yara?"

Yara laughed. "I went there, huh?"

"You did." He gave her a fist bump. "We both went hard."

"Yes, we did. And I gotta tell you, Gerald, you played that mascot thing to perfection. If you hadn't told me during our picnic, I never would've guessed Blue Devil was you."

"Thank you, thank you. I had fun with the mask. I literally became someone else. I get my acting chops from Lisa, though." They laughed.

"Oscar-worthy performance," Yara said.

"Yeah." Gerald exhaled a breath he seemed to have held for a long time. "But, dang, Quinton almost ended up dead in my place. My brother..."

"But he didn't."

"Thank God. He clocked Greg into a new area code, too!" Gerald chuckled. "Hey, you know what I was just thinking?"

Yara adjusted her head against the headrest. "What?"

Gerald showed two fists, flicked an index finger and said, "Philip. You. Marcus. His wife. Craig. Sandy. Colin. Diane. Oliver. Rachel." Having reached the number ten, he reset the count on his fingers. "Me. Lisa. Greg. Aanya. Quinton... wow, that's fifteen people. Hell, the way everyone's been messing around, there's probably more potential carriers."

"You missed a couple," Yara said. "The skank that gave it to Philip, and Aanya's unborn child."

"Aw, man, that's right." For the first time, Gerald's mood dipped. "That kid could be my nephew or niece."

Yara covered his hand with hers. "I'm sure the baby will be fine. I've been taking my meds and my viral load is low. The chance that any of them contracted HIV is pretty slim."

"Tell that to Marcus Obohu."

Yara sighed. Marcus and his wife had become official members of an exclusive club that most people don't want to claim, courtesy of Yara's hypnotic appeal. Dirty dogs always end up with fleas, even when the "fleas" come from someone who looks as clean as her.

"I was in a bad place when I hooked up with Marcus," she confessed. "A *really* bad place. Philip had just died and I hadn't started my HIV meds yet. When Marcus contacted me on Facebook, all too eager to cheat on his wife, something inside me just snapped. I felt like I needed to teach the cheaters of the world a major lesson."

"You definitely accomplished that. From the looks on Craig, Oliver, and Colin's faces, I doubt they'll be having unprotected sex with anyone anytime soon."

Yara stared out the window. "I know I set this whole thing in motion, but… I really hope none of the wives get it. You, either."

"Yeah, I hear you." Gerald shook his head. "Man, talk about tangled."

"What do you mean?"

"I mean, our lives—all tangled together. By deceit."

"Oh. Yes, you're right." *Tangled.* Yara couldn't have described it better.

Yara sensed a shift in mood. So caught up in her selfish quest for revenge, she had ignored the voice of reason that wanted to keep Gerald out of her twisted plan. "Gerald," she said, looking down, "Are you having any regrets?"

He turned to face her. "About what?"

"You know." She shrugged. "This crazy plan we started, um, getting caught up with me. I wish—"

"Stop right there. I mean, yeah, I'm bothered that my brother was almost killed because of me, but as you said, it worked out. I'm grateful for that."

"I am, too. You should check on him."

"Yeah. I need to find out about Patrick, too. But as far as us?" He took Yara's hand. "I really don't care if I get it, as long as we're together. I'd much rather be HIV-positive and happy with you than HIV-negative and miserable with Lisa. Or dead."

Yara couldn't stop herself from smiling even if she tried. Despite Gerald's sweet declaration, she never wanted him to experience her private hell firsthand. She would do whatever it took to keep him safe. No more BB slip ups for him ever again.

Gerald caressed her cheek, then leaned in for a kiss. He tasted like their first time, but with a tinge of red wine on his lips. That boy whose nerves once rattled at the mere sight of Yara was long gone.

After what seemed like minutes of acting like frisky teenagers on prom night, a phone buzzed. Gerald came up for air and pulled his iPhone out of his jacket pocket.

"It's Q," he said, looking relieved. "He's with Aanya. Oh, dang... whoa!"

"What?"

"The police have Patrick in custody, charged with attempted murder," Gerald said, eyes wide. "That fool apparently confessed everything!"

"Whaaaaat?"

"Yeah! Looks like he flipped on Greg and Lisa, I bet to cut a deal. They should be arrested soon."

"You know, murder-for-hire is a serious crime," Yara said. "Lisa will probably do major time."

"Good." He shrugged. "She killed the love I had, so if she goes to jail, oh well."

"Oh, well," Yara repeated, a little turned on by Gerald's new bold don't-care attitude. She glanced at the dashboard clock.

"Okay, handsome, it's about that time. We should drop off the flash drive and head to the airport now."

"I'm ready if you are." He glanced at the mask behind Yara's seat. "Should I bring the mask?"

"No! Goofball. I think I've had enough of Mr. Blue Devil."

"Yeah, me, too," Gerald replied with a chuckle. "The ring will stay in this cup holder until we get back. Gonna sell it."

"Sounds good to me. Not my style anyway." She winked.

"Right. Hey, you have plenty of new material for your next poem."

She nodded. "Very true."

"Yup. So, you got the tickets and your passport, right?"

Yara shot him the side eye. "Really?"

"Just kidding. Time to go to a better place."

They left the parking lot and headed to the nearest police station. Gerald pulled up to a drop box near the station entrance and dropped off the package—a small manila envelope containing a flash drive of the entire murder-for-hire voice exchange, and a short handwritten letter detailing the cast of characters, including the target himself.

Back on the main road, Gerald headed toward the highway, following the signs to Monte Clara International Airport.

"Mexico, here we come."

CHAPTER 31
GERALD

"Hey, you changed!"

Yara returned to her seat next to Gerald in sweatpants, a hoodie, and sneakers. "You expected me to wear that dress and heels on the plane?"

"Of course not," Gerald replied, now in jeans and a sweatshirt, his go-to comfort attire. He moved her bag from the seat. "Just like looking at your legs, that's all."

"You'll be looking at my legs a lot very soon." She winked.

Gerald leaned in for a kiss. "I hope so."

Yara grabbed his hand. "You took your ring off."

"Yeah. I freakin' almost yanked out the joint, too."

"I bet. My goodness, look at the imprint. You don't even need a ring to show you're married."

Gerald raised his finger, moving his hand around. "Legally married, yes. But that's definitely gonna change." He inspected his finger closer. "You're right, though. Geez, it's like I need a tan in just that spot."

"Exactly," Yara said, laughing.

"I consider it more of a scar, now. A scar that will fade away very soon."

She nodded. "I get it. It took me a while to take my ring off. Hey, you talk to your auntie, yet?"

Gerald smiled. Yara had proven herself the queen of remembering the little things. "Yes, I talked to her this morning. I'll tell her about tonight after we get back."

"I pretty much told my sister the same thing in a voicemail a little while ago. What about your brother?"

"Yeah, I texted him while you were in the bathroom. We're going to talk sometime later today. The cops have been hounding him to get me to come in."

"You think we should?"

Gerald frowned so hard the skin tightened around his skull. "Are you kidding? And miss out on a getaway with you? Hell naw! We deserve this. Besides, they already have my evidence. And oh, guess what?"

"What?"

"Aanya is staying with Quinton tonight."

Yara rested her head on Gerald's shoulder, yawning. "Good for her. That's right where she belongs."

"Yup."

Gerald felt the smooth texture of Yara's hair against his chin, her familiar flowery scent suspended in an invisible cloud. As he chilled in his new happy place, Gerald watched the late night news on one of the TVs mounted above. Random snippets of Spanglish buzzed around them, clashing with amplified voices announcing flight updates over the speakers. Although after midnight, the high number of travelers bustling to their next stop seemed no different than a typical afternoon.

With his new flame nuzzling up next to him, Gerald once again sank into a deep lazy groove that only manifested with Yara by his side. An aura of peace overtook him, the same feeling he had while sitting on their "Yarald" bench, gazing out into the water, breathing easy, without a care in the world. Despite the hurdles ahead, he knew that with Yara as his co-pilot, he would encounter clear, blue skies.

In English, a ticket agent announced that they were about to board. She repeated the same announcement in Spanish. Gerald yawned, then said, "We're up next, beautiful."

"Awesome. We're officially one step closer to sun, sand, and bottomless margaritas."

"Roger that. Are you sure I can't pay you back for the tickets and hotel room?"

"No, I told you I have a ton of points. You keep forgetting you're unemployed now, Mister. I got you."

Gerald kissed her forehead. "I got you, too. Lisa thought I wasn't minding my money, but I have my secret stash. It'll probably last me about six months."

Yara smiled. "That's good, but don't feel like you have to spend all of your stash on me. Just continue to be sweet to me and we'll be fine."

"Shoot, that's easy."

Gerald stared at a commercial of a man sliding a wedding ring on a woman's finger. The facade of matrimonial bliss burned him from the inside. Shaking his head, Gerald said, "Man, and to think if not for Lisa butt-dialing, I would be dead right now. *Dead*. And my crime? Trying too hard to be a good husband."

Gerald's fingers folded into a tight fist as his body vibrated with a palpable rage. All at once, the gravity of it all fully hit him.

His wife, the woman he'd devoted almost half his life to, had set him up to be murdered—all because she saw him as a meal ticket. While performing "lockjaw" services on Greg Stephens, her lover and co-conspirator, no less. The betrayal had so many layers.

The ticket agent ran through his spiel about boarding procedures. As they stood and stretched, Yara tugged his arm and pointed upward. "Omigod, look."

Gerald glanced at the TV and saw what looked like jerky cell phone footage of an all-out brawl. The newscaster mentioned a hotel's name while giving a commentary on the action unfolding. It looked like a drunken fistfest. Yelling, screaming, censored cuss words. A woman in a skirt smashed a vase over a man's head, then somehow, they ended up on the floor, with her kicking at his crotch. The whir of bodies swinging on each other flashed in and out of the screen as the recorder attempted to hold the camera steady.

"What the hell?" Gerald said, his voice low. "That's our reunion! We started that!"

"Yes, we did," Yara whispered. "Look at them. Sandy is whipping Craig's ass."

"Well, Craig got what he wanted. That reunion was epic."

Yara laughed. "Do you think Lisa got caught up in that before she left?"

"Don't know and don't care." Gerald picked up their bags, his anger boiling over. Hate had corroded the protective shield he once harnessed for Lisa Townes. "Fuck that bitch."

Yara's bottom lip dropped while she stood frozen. A one-sided grin emerged, and she had a strange glint in her eyes, like Gerald's newly discovered bad boy side flipped all the switches to what turned her on. Digging into her purse, she pulled out the picture of Philip decked out in Rambo gear, one Gerald had seen several times. Then she balled it up and tossed it in a nearby trash can.

"Fuck him, too."

CHAPTER 32

EPILOGUE

(ONE YEAR LATER)

"She spat on ol' boy?" Quinton said, eyes wide.

Gerald nodded. "Yup. When she first put her stuff in storage here. The messed up thing is she didn't remember doing it at first."

"Damn, that *is* messed up."

"Yeah. I'm just glad I've never seen that side of her."

"Yet."

Gerald leaned back, a rolled-up area rug cushioning his elbows. "Yara's not that person anymore. She's been taking all her meds religiously since we've been together. Trust me, she's not trying to mess up her probation."

Quinton knocked back a sip of Powerade. "For your sake, I hope you're right."

"By the way, this conversation stays between you and me. Don't tell her I said anything about that dude."

"She ain't gonna hear anything from me, bro."

Legs dangling, they stared at Yara's empty storage unit. After an hour of hauling Yara's personal effects, they had posted up on the back of the U-Haul truck with everything neatly packed behind them, enjoying a much-needed chill moment. Quinton never anticipated a permanent detour to another state, beginning a new chapter with a divorced woman and their three-month-old son. He still couldn't believe the baby was his. After all those years trying to get pregnant, it turned out that Aanya wasn't the one with a fertility problem; Greg was.

"You know, Q," Gerald said, "after all we've been through the past year with the trials and media, I'm just happy we're back in a good place."

"Yeah," Quinton said. "But let me ask you something: All those dudes that ran up in Yara, that didn't bother you?"

Gerald stared into space. After a short pause, he said, "Yeah, it did a little. I told her it didn't, but it did. I was crushing on her so hard, whatever happened before me didn't matter."

"Hmmm. Whatever the case, your girl's lucky as hell nobody else got it." He shook his head. "The way everybody was fuckin' everybody, it could've been passed around like a damn blunt. Happy as hell you don't have it."

"Yeah," Gerald said, laughing. "No BB for me!"

Quinton didn't laugh. "Man, I'm serious. If anybody came up HIV positive, you know Yara could've been charged with a felony, right?"

"Actually… no. I read California is passing some law to make intentionally spreading HIV a misdemeanor now."

"What? For real?"

Gerald nodded.

"Well, damn. That's kinda messed up. To this day, I still think that's why Marcus Obohu's wife killed his ass. He probably gave it to her."

"Yara and I are convinced that's what happened," Gerald said. "And she really regrets the part she played in it. She's changed, man. Even though she never misses her meds, she refuses to have sex with me without a condom. Not only that, I've never seen anyone champion the fight against HIV like her. Hella motivated now, bro. Going to schools, organizing campaigns, taking donations, public speaking, all that. Shoot, you and I were at the HIV Awareness March in San Francisco not too long ago!"

"Yeah." Quinton's shoulders shuddered. "That was… kinda weird."

Gerald slapped Quinton's back. "It's cool, man. Everybody knows you're not gay. Appreciate the support, for real."

"It's all good."

"But!" Gerald threw up an index finger. "Let's not forget the whole citywide panic wouldn't have happened if *some* people knew how to keep their dicks in check! It ain't like Yara and I was pullin' drive-bys, shooting HIV darts at people, right? I mean, who knew Colin Michaels and his wife were swingers? And Sandy Meyer banging a college student, while Craig was sleeping with Yara? Really?"

Gerald had a point. Private lives usually stayed behind closed doors, but after the disaster at the reunion, panic mode about HIV status kicked into maximum overdrive. As a result, secret freak fests and identities of sidepieces slipped into the public domain—a Monte Clara Who's Fucking Who blacklist.

"Yeah, bro, you're right. Folks gotta wrap it up. Always."

"For real. People always talking about, 'I hope she don't get pregnant.' That's after going bareback and raw. Stupid. They forget about STDs that can make your willy look like a freakin' cactus."

"Cactus?" Quinton took another sip of Powerade. "You a fool, but I see your point. Yara didn't look like someone with an STD."

"See? That right there. How does one look like they have an STD?"

Quinton shrugged, realizing he'd made a dumb-ass comment. No one can self-scan a regular Joe-Schmoe with X-Ray eyes, detect a viral invader, then bark "HIV" like a police hound who located a suspect. But for some reason, too many I-know-everything Einstein's think they can.

Changing the subject, Quinton said, "You know, Patrick probably ran up in Lisa, too, right?"

Gerald slapped his knee. "Patrick! Man, that's a name I haven't heard in a while! I still can't believe you had that fool in your trunk." Gerald laughed.

Quinton shrugged. "What else could I do? I couldn't let him get away."

"He ain't getting away now. They gave him thirty years. Crazy."

"Hey, repeat felon."

"Yeah, and Greg got fifteen. Those two are in the same correctional facility. *That's* crazy."

Quinton said, "Patrick gonna get in that ass, if not already. But your ex got twenty, though!"

"Twenty years." Gerald ran a hand over the back of his head. "I'm still trippin' off that, too, but oh well. We should send Lisa a postcard from Portland."

"Hmmm. Yeah. Be like, 'This is what five hundred thousand dollars got your dumb ass. Enjoy your stay!'"

They laughed, finding humor at the expense of the wannabe

criminals. As they waited for the ladies to return with food, cracking jokes like best friends, Quinton felt the closest he'd been with his brother in years. He wondered what Mama would say as she peeked through the clouds at her two boys.

Quinton placed a hand on Gerald's shoulder. "I know one thing, though."

"What's that?" Gerald asked.

"No matter what, I'm just relieved she butt-dialed yo' ass."

"Me too, bro," Gerald said, swiping the back of his hand across his forehead. "Me, too."

Quinton hopped off the truck, stretching. He also ran a hand over his lock-less scalp, watching a Kia Optima drive up toward the gate at the opposite end of the parking lot. Inside sat two gorgeous women and baby Brandon.

Smiling, Quinton said, "They're here."

"Good 'cause yo tengo hambre." Gerald jumped off, copycatting Quinton's sky-high stretch and scalp rub. Quinton still marveled at his brother's new cut biceps and lean frame, courtesy of beast mode in the gym, a clean diet, and thirty-pound weight loss.

As the gate opened, Quinton said, "Crazy how things turned out with all of us, huh?"

"Surreal," Gerald said with a slight grin. "I never would've thought Aanya and Yara would end up soul sisters. But I tell you, bro, I'm happier than ever. Yara Bassili, *the* Yara Bassili is *my* woman. And beautiful Aanya Patel is yours. Our two high school crushes are driving up to us as we speak."

Quinton nodded, soaking it up. "For real, I'm officially off the market, and I've never been happier. Got me moving to be with her and shit."

"Hey, I'm doing the same thing."

Finishing off his Powerade, Quinton said, "Fool, your puppy-dog ass would follow Yara anywhere."

"Yeah, you are right, bro," Gerald said, staring at Yara as she parked. "Shoot, I'm still drinking her bath water."

Quinton smiled, rubbing his brother's back. "Me, too. Tastes like Kool-Aid."

"Shut up, fool," Gerald said, play-punching Quinton's chest.

Gerald didn't know it, but Quinton caught the same bug for Aanya. He never thought the word "sprung" and "Daddy" would enter into his vocabulary. Not anytime soon, anyway. But as Yara cut the engine and he glanced at Aanya playing with little Brandon from the passenger seat, he wanted nothing more than to stay in that circle, even if it meant moving to a new state.

Gerald's cellphone buzzed. He looked at it, tapped the screen, and slipped it back in his pocket.

Quinton asked. "Who was that?"

"Aunt Frieda. I'll call her on the way to Portland."

Did you enjoy this book?

If so, please leave a review on amazon.com :)

(Important: Please try to avoid spoilers and revealing plot twists when crafting reviews. Thank you!)

Stay in Touch!

Join my mailing list at:
www.jameswlewis.com

Find me on Facebook:
www.facebook.com/authorjames.w.lewis

TANGLED BOOK CLUB QUESTIONS
(Spoilers, so beware!)

1. Gerald represents the typical average-looking, "too nice" guy often overlooked by women. Why do some women have a hard time appreciating a good, hard-working man? Do women's standards change as they age and mature? Have you ever passed over a man that, years later, you wish you could have a second chance with?

2. Some people believe it's a bad idea to marry young, especially right out of high school. Can high school sweethearts last forever, or should young people seek out more life experiences before settling down?

3. Have you ever worked with a friend or associate who was promoted over you? How did their new position affect your relationship?

4. Quinton has had his share of the best looking women in Monte Clara. If a man has access to beautiful women anytime he wants, is it naive to believe ONE good woman can tame his wild oats?

5. Quinton believes Aanya is his soulmate, but she is married to someone else, who is clearly not worthy of her love. How hard would you fight to win someone back under these circumstances? Is it ever okay to break up someone's marriage, or is it better to stay out of it and let things play out?

6. Lisa and Greg enjoyed public "sexcapades." Has anyone caught you "smashin'" in public? Where?

7. After Aanya learns that Greg is cheating, she decides to stay with him anyway, for the sake of the baby. Is this the right call? Can/should infidelity be forgiven, or do you believe that "once a cheater, always a cheater?"

8. Do you know anyone who's used a private investigator to catch a spouse cheating? What was the result?

9. Philip cheated, gave Yara HIV, then committed suicide. She could not channel her hurt and anger toward her dead husband, so she targeted men who exhibited the same deviant sexual behavior as Philip (i.e., infidelity, "raw dog" sex). Was Yara's revenge plot understandable? Do you think she should be punished or go to prison for her reckless actions?

10. Do you believe people still have a lackadaisical attitude about the possibility of acquiring HIV and STDs in general? Is it reasonable to require a STD screening before you're intimate with someone? Would you be offended if someone demanded one from you?

11. Would you hook up with an old flame at your high school reunion, despite your relationship status? Have you? What's the wildest thing that's ever happened at a reunion you've attended?

BONUS QUESTION (inspiration for my upcoming novel ABSENTEE)

A man and woman agree that they don't want kids, but still have unprotected sex. She ends up pregnant and decides to have the baby. Do you consider the man a deadbeat if he chooses not to participate in the child's life, given that he was very clear that he did not want to be a father?

ANOTHER SPOILER ALERT!

If you have not read this book yet, you might want to skip this page since it reveals major plot points. I'm sure you don't want to ruin your reading experience.

If you have read the book... thank you. Again, I truly hope you enjoyed it. :-)

Now, it may seem far-fetched that anyone fully aware of his/her HIV status would sleep with someone unprotected, much less be devious enough to infect their partner on purpose.

And, a sensible woman would never-ever-ever secretly become involved in a murder-for-hire plot, right?

Well, fact truly is wilder than fiction. If you don't believe either scenario is likely, you may reconsider once you check out the REAL-LIFE headlines (from 2014 to 2017) on the following pages.

Crazy Cases of HIV Misconduct

Report - **Sex Roulette' Parties: An Insanely Risky New Trend Spreading HIV Like Wildfire**

Report - Dating sites and apps may be spreading HIV, a new study reveals

Report (CDC): **Half of gay black men will get HIV**

Abu Dhabi - **AIDS victim slept with many in UAE to 'destroy' men**

Akron, OH - Indictment could make Akron man the fourth Summit County resident charged under HIV disclosure laws

Atlanta, GA - **Find Out Why Almost Half of Atlanta's Newly Diagnosed HIV Patients Have AIDS?**

Australia - Transgender hooker accused of spreading HIV

Baton Rouge, LO - BRPD arrests man for intentionally spreading HIV/AIDS virus

Billings, MO - Charges: Billings woman may have infected hospital employee with HIV through bite

Busan, South Korea - HIV-positive woman arrested for prostitution in Busan

Cambodia - **Cambodian man on trial for infecting more than 100 with HIV**

Charles County, MD - **HIV-infected school aide accused of sexually victimizing 42 children in Maryland**

Chattanooga, TN - Rossville woman charged with criminal exposure to HIV

Chattanooga, TN - Man arrested for allegedly spreading HIV

Coralville, IO - Police: Coralville man charged with knowingly spreading HIV

Czech Republic - **30 Gay Men Face Decade in Prison for Having Sex While HIV-Positive**

Denver, CO - **Hospital Warns 3000 of Possible HIV Exposure**

Douglas County, GA - Man charged with knowingly spreading HIV

Elizabethtown, KY - E'town man with HIV charged with prostitution

Fort Myers, FL - Man sentenced to 25 years for knowingly spreading HIV

Fort Wayne, IN - Indiana man sentenced to 3 years for hiding HIV status

Greenacres, FL - **Cop accused of knowingly spreading HIV**

Herinco, VA - Henrico man accused of spreading HIV faces more charges

Hong Kong, China - 'It's not just a gay problem': head of Aids Concern Hong Kong says growing number of HIV cases a concern for whole of society

Houston, TX - **Search for more victims of HIV-infected man charged with raping baby, toddler**

Indianapolis, IN - **College wrestling star given 30-year sentence for spreading HIV**

Italy - **HIV carrier infected more than 30 women**

Jacksonville, FL - JTA driver accused of spreading HIV

Los Angeles, CA - **HIV-infected man poses as cop to rape 15-year old girl**

Kalamazoo, MI - New information in case of man accused of knowingly spreading HIV

Kampala, Uganda - Army officer on trial for spreading Aids

Macon, GA - Midstate men may have spread HIV to unsuspecting victims, indictment alleges

Manila, Philippines - 48 individuals found positive with HIV for April 2017 due to paid sex

Manitoba, Canada - Court upholds sexual assault conviction of woman with HIV who had unprotected sex

Memphis, TX - **Memphis minister headed to jail for knowingly spreading HIV**

Missouri - **Missouri woman charged with knowingly spreading HIV**

Missouri - Man With HIV Arrested After Seeking Sex On Social Media

Mulanje, Malawi - **Man defiles step-daughter, infects her with HIV**

Muskogee, OK - Muskogee High School employee accused of rape and spreading AIDS

Myrtle Beach, FL - Man arrested in connection with spreading HIV virus

Newburgh, IL - Daryll Rowe, hairdresser on Grindr, 'secretly gave lovers HIV'

New London - Murder suspect 'believed cousin had spread HIV through Native American tribe'

New York City, NY - **Dentist in Greenwich Village Faces Charges of Willingly Spreading HIV**

Nigeria - 1.7m Nigeria women, 380,000 children living with HIV

Nigeria - **Port Harcourt pastor infects pregnant woman with HIV during deliverance**

Orange Park, FL - Sexual predator accused of knowingly spreading HIV

Phoenix, AZ - **Woman runs over boyfriend after learning he has HIV**

Richmond, CA - HIV-infected man had sex with teen boy, Contra Costa DA says

Russia - Russian woman stabbed to death 'after infecting one of her partners with HIV'

San Diego, CA - San Diego Man Gets 6 Months Jail For Spreading HIV

Seattle, WA - US man ordered to stop spreading HIV

Scotland - Man with "Scottish accent" arrested over purposely spreading HIV

Sumter, S.C. - Police: Man charged with knowingly exposing at least one woman to HIV

Tampere, Nigeria - **Police Detain Sexy African Woman For Deliberately Spreading HIV In Finland**

Terre Haute, IN - Formal charges filed against Vigo Co. resident accused of knowingly spreading HIV

Toledo, OH - Man who 'didn't tell his mistress he had HIV' is charged with murder after the 51-year-old woman died of AIDS

Tulsa, OK - **Man accused of giving 15-year-old HIV while mentoring for Tulsa youth program bound for trial**

U.K. - Personal Trainer Sentenced over HIV Spread

U.K. - Man threatened to infect others with HIV in sauna

U.K. - Gay man accused of deliberately infecting people with HIV 'told victim he was being paranoid'

Wales - Transgender prostitute charged with spreading HIV to WA man refused bail again

Westerville, OH - Sheriff: Columbus man with HIV charged with assault for having sex with woman

Winnipag - Manitoba woman jailed for 2 years for giving partner HIV

Murder-for-Hire Plots

Albertville, AL - Woman arrested in Albertville in murder-for-hire plot

Allentown, PA - Allentown woman pleads to murder-for-hire plot tied to husband's homicide trial

Annapolis, MD - Annapolis woman pleads guilty in murder-for-hire case

Ashland County, OH - Woman arrested in Ashland County murder-for-hire scheme

Baltimore, MD - **Baltimore woman hired hitman for ex-boyfriend's wife, court records say**

Belpre, OH - Wife admits murder-for-hire role

Bethlehem, PA - Woman sentenced in Bethlehem murder for hire plot

Bloomfield, CT - A Murder-For-Hire Plot Foiled, Mother Still Has Custody Of Daughter

Boise, ID - **Woman pleads guilty to Facebook murder-for-hire scheme**

Charlotte, NC - Former nursing supervisor sentenced to 10 years in murder-for-hire plot

Claremont, N.H. - 83-year-old accused in murder-for-hire plot says in recording she wants son's ex dead

Cycleville, OH – **Ohio Model Convicted of Trying to Hire Assassin to Murder Her Husband's Ex-Wife**

Culpeper, VA - Culpeper woman charged in murder-for-hire plot

Denton, TX - Daughter defends mom accused in murder-for-hire plot

Eveleth, MN - Girl confesses to murder for hire

Gastonia, NC - Gastonia woman accused in murder-for-hire plot, bond set at $1 million

Grand Haven, MI - Police: Ex-wife's murder for hire plot foiled

Greenwood, IN - Woman gets life sentence in murder-for-hire case

Greenville, TN - Cocke Co. woman pleads guilty in murder-for-hire plot

Harrisonburg, VA - Grottoes Woman Arrested on Attempted Murder-for-Hire Charge

Hartford, CT - Tiffany Stevens Gets Probation In Murder-For-Hire Case

Hyderabad, India - Doctor attempts to inject senior doctor with HIV+ blood; bid foiled, doctor arrested

Independence, MO - **Grandmother charged in murder-for-hire plot to kill a parent of her grandchildren**

Keene, NH - Woman to face trial on murder-for-hire charge

Lakeland, FL - Woman sentenced in murder-for-hire plot against husband

Layland, WV - **State Police charge 2 women in alleged murder-for-hire case**

Lincoln, AR - Lincoln woman's murder for hire case reset

Moulton, Alabama - Town Creek woman gets 60 years in murder-for-hire scheme

Palm Beach, FL - **Florida Woman Claims She Was Just Acting in Police Undercover Murder-For-Hire Video**

Louisville, KY - Celebrity Baker Charged in Murder-for-Hire Plot to Kill Ex-Boyfriend

Lyndhurst, NJ – **Soccer mom who hired hit man to murder her ex's new lover speaks out**

Madill, OK - Marshall County woman convicted of murder for hire

Manitoba, Canada - Woman handed life sentence for role in murder-for-hire plan

Maryville, TN - Maryville Woman Sentenced in Murder-for-Hire Scheme

Mcallen, TX - **Mexican Woman Added to FBI's Most Wanted over Texas Murder For Hire**

Midvale, UT - West Jordan mom arrested in apparent murder-for-hire attempt

Milford, CT - Woman accused in murder-for-hire plot pleads guilty to assault conspiracy

Monett, MO - Monett woman busted in murder for hire sting

Nampa, IN - Nampa woman sentenced in murder-for-hire plot

Neillsville, WI - Woman get 7 years in murder for hire scheme

New Orleans, LA - Murder-for-hire plot alleged in slaying of husband

Phoenix, AZ - Bernadette Beanes update: Judge sentences PHX woman to 30 years in prison in murder-for-hire

Ponca City, OK - Oklahoma woman accused in meticulous murder-for-hire plot released from federal detention

Pontiac, MI - Two women headed to trial on charges they targeted Flint man in murder-for-hire plot

Port Orchard, WA - Port Orchard woman accused of killing husband after alleged murder-for-hire plot

Port Huron, MI - Woman involved in murder-for-hire scheme pleads guilty

Portland, OR - Oregon woman accused of murder-for-hire plot

Providence, UT - Woman arrested in murder-for-hire scheme in Providence

Riverside, CA - W**oman who allegedly tried to have 2 exes murdered gets out of jail, talks**

Rockford, IL - Rockford Woman Arrested in Murder for Hire Plan

Roanoke, VA - **Former Franklin County nurse involved in murder-for-hire plot seeks license reinstatement**

Russell County, AL - Russell Co. woman charged in murder-for-hire death to be sentenced Thursday

Selbyville, DE - Murder for Hire Plot Foiled, Selbyville Woman Arrested

Savannah, GA - **Wife of slain Fort Stewart soldier sentenced to life in federal prison**

Stone County, MO - Woman pleads guilty in husband's murder for hire killing

St. Charles, MO - Police: Woman tried to hire undercover officer in murder-for-hire plot

Tuscon, AZ - Jury finds Pamela Phillips guilty in murder-for-hire trial

Vista, CA - Carlsbad woman lured her husband into an ambush

Volusia County, FL - **Police: FL woman hired hitman to kill homeless man**

Waterford, MI - **Two young mothers sentenced in murder for hire plot**

White Township, PA - Joanie Pepperoni' investigation busts woman in alleged murder-for-hire plot with boyfriend

Also Available from TPC Books

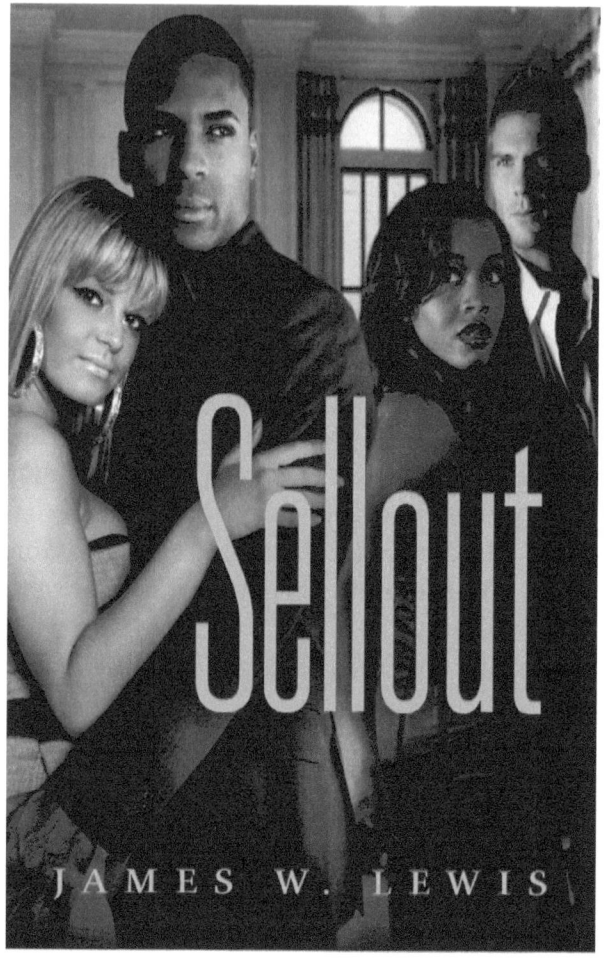

SELLOUT
by James W. Lewis

SELLOUT follows three individuals and the consequences of dating outside their race. In the quest to find what they think is missing in their lives, they encounter guilt, fear and mess they never anticipated… including murder.

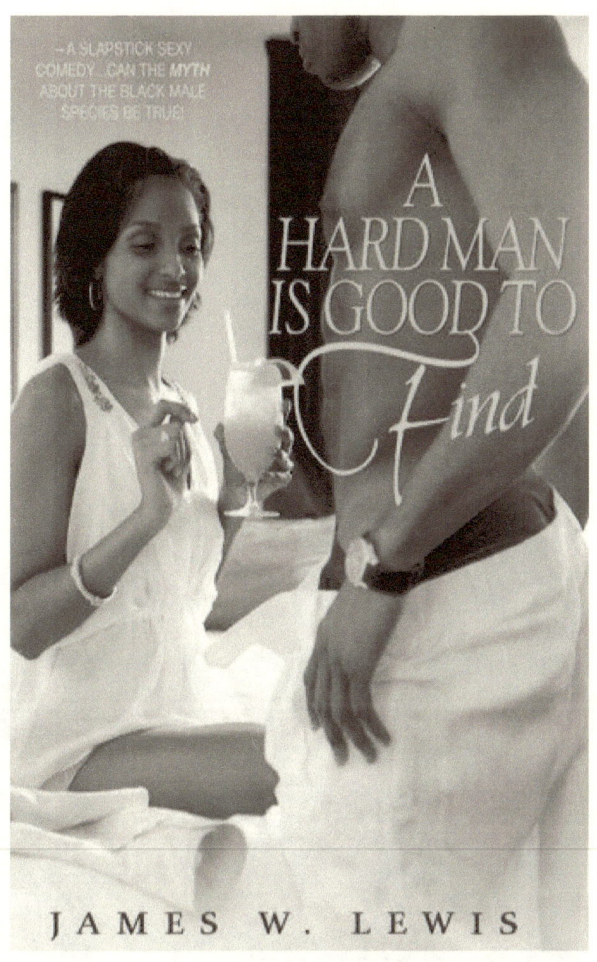

-A SLAPSTICK SEXY COMEDY...CAN THE *MYTH* ABOUT THE BLACK MALE SPECIES BE TRUE!

A HARD MAN IS GOOD TO Find

JAMES W. LEWIS

A Hard Man Is Good to Find
by James W. Lewis

An erotic romance about a woman who meets the man of her dreams with the exception of one major issue - his refusal to have sex with her!

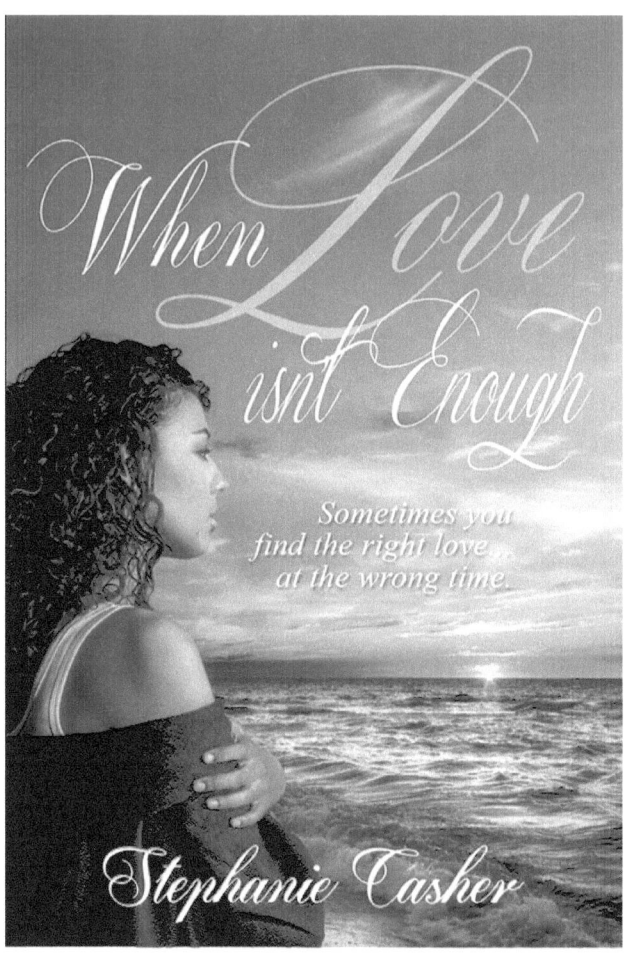

When Love Isn't Enough
by Stephanie Casher

A heartbreaking tale of true love, terrible timing, impossible choices, and how you find the strength to go on when you discover that sometimes, love just isn't enough...

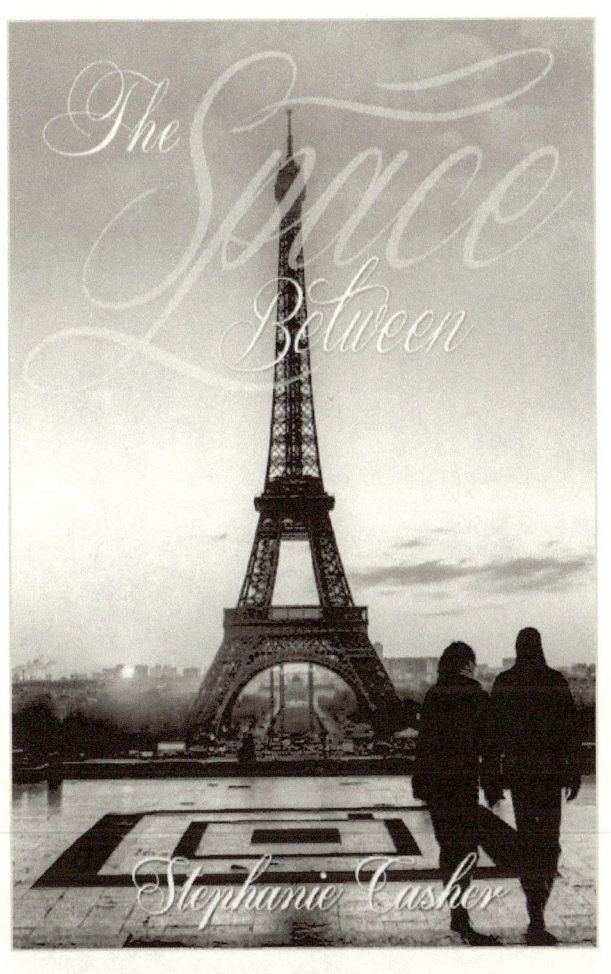

The Space Between
by Stephanie Casher

After finding (and losing) her soulmate in *When Love Isn't Enough*, Samantha Merrick is back and ready for the next chapter in her life. Can her broken heart learn to love again?

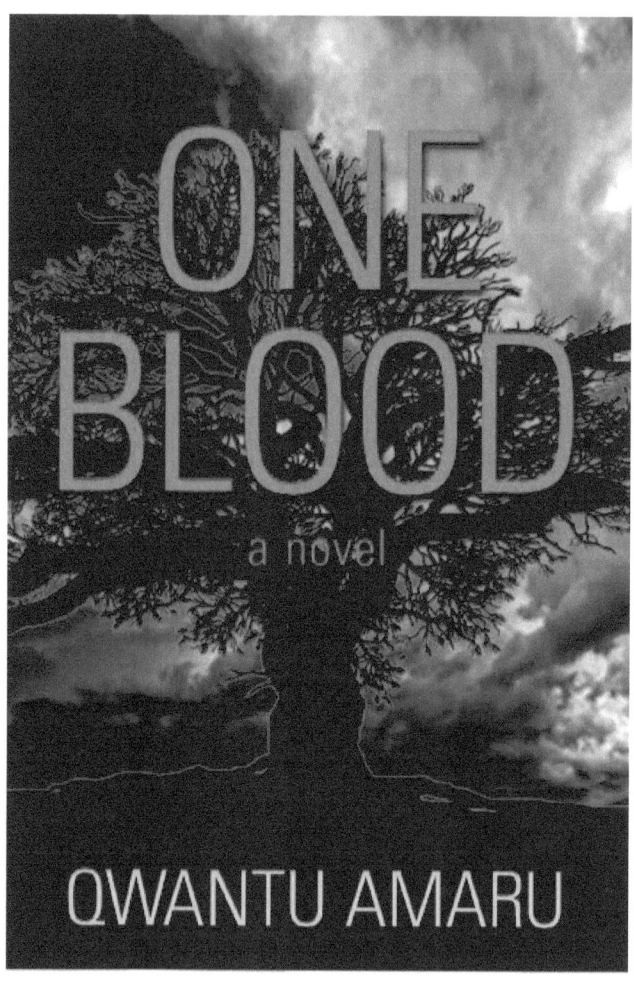

One Blood
by Qwantu Amaru

A supernatural curse terrorizes a group of
people unaware of their hidden connections.

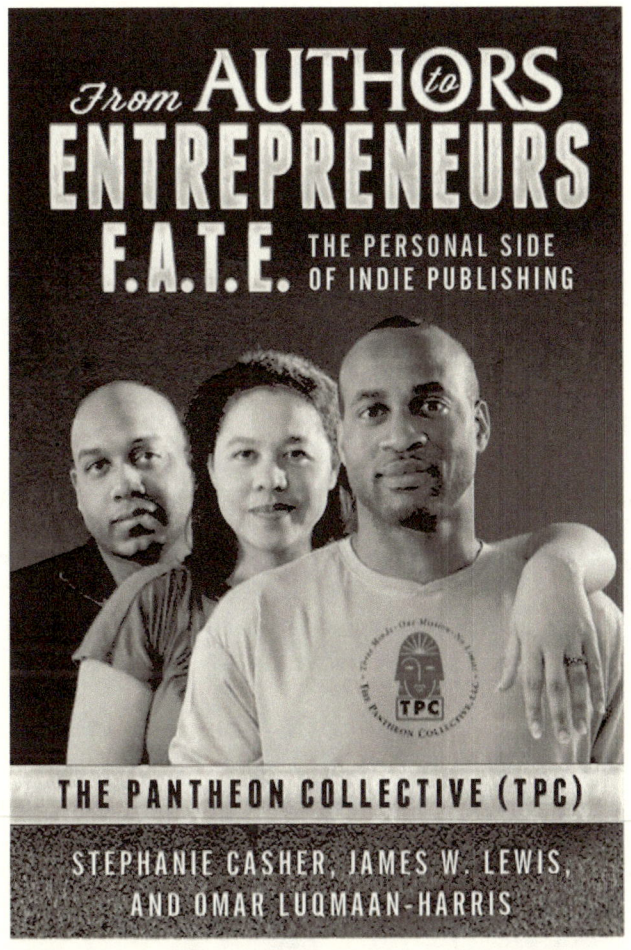

F.A.T.E: *From Authors to Entrepreneurs*
by Stephanie Casher, James W. Lewis & Omar Luqmaan-Harris

In November 2010, three authors stepped off the long, twisty
road toward traditional book publication, and charted a new
course under the umbrella of their own creation,
The Pantheon Collective (TPC).
Read how it all began...

For ordering information visit:
www.pantheoncollective.com